The Goldie Standard

A NOVEL

SIMI MONHEIT

AN IMPRINT OF ALL THINGS BOOK

Sibylline Press

Published in the United States by Sibylline Press,
an imprint of All Things Book LLC, California.
Sibylline Press is dedicated to publishing the brilliant work
of women authors ages 50 and older.
www.sibyllinepress.com

Distributed to the trade by Publishers Group West.
Sibylline Press
Paperback ISBN: 978-1-960573-97-1
eBook ISBN: 978-1-960573-09-4
Library of Congress Control Number: 2023947584

Book and Cover Design: Alicia Feltman

PRAISE FOR

The Goldie Standard

"Simi Monheit's genius is to slowly reveal the complexity behind a stereotype. In Goldie Mandell, we have a new Jewish heroine—acerbic without bitterness, tender without sentimentality. "Who knew what I had to say was so interesting?" says one of the most memorable characters in contemporary Jewish fiction. A book of pure delight."

—Yossi Klein Halevi, author of *Like Dreamers*, winner of the Jewish Book Council's Everett Book of the Year Award

• • •

"An aged Jewish woman kvetches her way toward love while solving everyone else's problems in Monheit's bittersweet comic novel. Goldie is a spellbinding protagonist, full of dudgeon and crabby insights into all things newfangled. Monheit's sparkling prose poetically and humorously conveys the collision of romantic dreams with crotchety reality. A hilarious saga of family renewal and last-chance romance that plucks the heartstrings.

—Kirkus Reviews (starred review)

• • •

"Monheit has the real deal knack of bringing her characters to life with the most surprising, charming, and readable voices. Goldie is a protagonist who will stay with me for a long time: a friend, a mentor, a pleasure."

—Josh Mohr, author of *Model Citizen* and *Damascus*

• • •

"This delightful, insightful debut novel crackles with the different ways to love and the many ways to harm. At its center, the flawed, fierce, and marvelous Goldie Mandell—a Jewish child wrenched from Nazi Germany; a young woman wildly in love; a mother and grandmother thick with love and regrets; and a hard-headed guardian of history, identity, tradition, and family. *The*

Goldie Standard is a tragicomic balm against a too-often inhumane world rife with incalculable suffering that ultimately sends up a rally cry for togetherness, for grace, for peace, for being fully, majestically alive."

—Ethel Rohan, author of *Sing, I*

• • •

"Simi Monheit has created a novel that is alternately hilarious and heartbreaking, a tour de force about the weight of generational trauma. Goldie is one of the most unforgettable characters I've encountered in years, and Monheit does an amazing job of capturing this elderly Holocaust survivor's voice as she reminisces about the past while scheming to find her granddaughter a nice doctor for a husband. The way that Monheit weaves between Goldie's life and that of her equally wonderful granddaughter's—and between past and present—is nothing short of masterful. We need this novel right now, to shine a light into the darkness and remind us that of the transcendent power of love."

—Malena Watrous, author of *You Follow Me;* Lead Instructor for Stanford Continuing Studies Novel Certificate

• • •

"Can you have an acerbic yet golden heart? Oh yes, you can, as Simi Monheit proves in her compassionate, compelling and comedic debut, *The Goldie Standard.* While this novel reads like a romantic caper, Monheit doesn't shy away from examining the most fraught of our human complexities. Much like her main character, Goldie, Monheit's magic lies in her ability to touch the tenderest of heart strings while tickling all the funny bones. Another bit of magic? No one can live up to *The Goldie Standard,* and then, somehow, everyone does."

—R. Cathey Daniels, Author of *Live Caught*

• • •

"How to describe *The Goldie Standard*? Wry, certainly, but also incisive, assertive, and deliciously uncompromising in the voice Monheit creates. But most importantly, necessary: this book is a beautiful reminder that it is never too late to come to ourselves, to allow love to expand the borders of who and what we think we are, and ultimately, to let go of our incessant need for control and let life happen. In Goldie's continual unfolding, and in her resistance to it, Monheit excavates an authentic expression of how the self can be reclaimed."

—Matt Muth, Editor-In-Chief, *Pacifica Literary Review*

• • •

"Great novels need great characters, and in Goldie Mandell, Simi Monheit has created someone so indelible and so alive that I half expected her to leap from the pages into the real world. A generational story, a romantic comedy of errors, and a wise examination of the human heart, *The Goldie Standard* succeeds on all levels—and is a debut novel that readers won't soon forget.

—Martin Wilson, author of *What They Always Tell Us*

• • •

"*The Goldie Standard* reads like a love letter to the generation of holocaust survivors mostly gone. Yet Monheit's affection for her characters never precludes portraying them as less than perfect—we get to know the mishpocha, warts and all. Goldie lets no one off the hook—she's got opinions about everyone but manages to keep it to herself. Lucky for us that we are privy to her thoughts and opinions—because they're brutal—and funny as hell. Goldie and her family are people we know—brought to life in a riveting story of love, loyalty, trust and taking chances. It's a story that weaves the joys and the trauma of the past with the challenges of today. Goldie, the consummate survivor, must learn to deal with the "new ways" of her children and granddaughter. Having been a stranger in a strange land herself, she is nonetheless confused—yet intrigued—by a "different" newcomer to the family circle. I loved watching the characters enfold and grow—and truly didn't want the book to end. Sequel?"

—Mindy Berkowitz; Retired CEO, Jewish Family Services of Silicon Valley

• • •

"Goldie is the Bubbie we all wish we had. Poignant and funny, Monheit captures the vagaries of aging and the folly of youth. A great inter-generational ride."

—Moshe Waldoks. co-editor of *The Big Book of Jewish Humor*

"Simi Monheit's *The Goldie Standard* captures life in all its facets. At its heart, it is a love story—love for family, friends, the world, and one's self. Monheit captures voices in such a way that the world fades away and the reader is there with Goldie and Maxine through times of sorrow, challenge, and joy. This multi-layered story keeps the reader engaged and waiting to see what will happen next."

—Jill Gerard, Editor, Chautauqua

• • •

"*The Goldie Standard* is a Shabbat banquet of Jewish love that Simi Monheit skillfully braids like a challah. From her assisted living home, Goldie Mandel is the every-bubbe who beams affection—and opinion—into her relationships with her daughters, granddaughter, beloved husband of blessed memory, and a new love. Her efforts to make a shidduch for granddaughter Maxie are soon foiled by a quirky newcomer. Monheit's charming and engaging story is a delight from start to finish."

—Pam Janis, Contributing Editor, *Moment Magazine*

• • •

"Warning—you're about to fall in love with a vivid cast of characters who will live in your head long after you've reached the last page. For me this was a story of the way family and their traumas can shape us, and the power of love to heal it all. Funny, poignant and thoughtful—I'm enamored of *The Goldie Standard.*"

—Samantha Dunn, journalist and author of
Not By Accident: Reconstructing a Careless Life

To my mother, Paula (z"l):
"I don't speak because I have the power to speak;
I speak because I don't have the power to remain silent."
— Rabbi A.Y. Kook

and my father, Freddy (z"l):
"Example isn't another way to teach, it's the only way to teach."
—Albert Einstein

And to Matty, Rifky and Naftali. Who shared them with me.

The Goldie Standard

A NOVEL

SIMI MONHEIT

CHAPTER ONE

Goldie

2017

THE DINING ROOM HERE: a whole social event—where to sit, who to sit with. The dribbler or the talker? Or the one who stares into space?

And there, on the wall. A picture of a happy sunrise helps anything? And why always a fish tank?

Used to be, get up, shower, get dressed. Make the coffee, pour the cereal, get the kids out the door, put the dishes in the sink. I didn't even exhale until I was sitting in the car, but even then, the shopping lists, the meals, the appointments. At work was when I could breathe. Now the big event? Counting minutes between pills.

This they call the Golden Years.

There's Bernice. Everyone rushes to sit with her. I don't need to rush. I'm not some *nebbish* who needs to be friends with the popular girls. Better I'll sit at a table by myself; they can come to me.

But the staff doesn't like you to sit alone. That's how you get stuck with these *schleppers*.

"Hello, hello." A man pushes over his walker. He has on a red vest with a bow tie. Fancy pants. And cufflinks. A regular Clark Gable. With glasses and without the hair. The ears, he has.

"You want to share the table?" He smiles a nice smile before he shrugs, then pulls out the seat and settles himself nicely. Already a good sign. He'll probably get the food all the way to his mouth.

"My name is Harry," he says. "My kids just moved me in. It's a nice place."

Making the best of the situation. I like this. "The food, it's not so much what I would make, but nothing to clean up. I'm Goldie, by the way."

The waiter brings us the soup of the day, a green liquid like a bowl of tea without honey or lemon. This is what they call here vegetable soup. Or lentil soup. Or pea soup. The name changes, never the flavor.

Harry dips his spoon into the soup and watches the thin liquid pour back into the bowl. Without looking up, he says, "Goldie, when you make a soup, what do you put in it?"

Not just water, is what I first want to answer. "When I made a soup, I put a piece of chicken or flanken in it. Then some carrots, celery, squash, an onion. And parsnips, such a flavor they give. And my secret? One sweet potato." I never told nobody about the sweet potato before. But so what? Like here it will make a difference?

Harry closes his eyes when he brings his tea-soup to his mouth. "Goldie, I'm going to pretend that this soup has all the things you just said." He swallows. "Delicious. Try some."

It's a *mishagas*, but I pretend like he says, and all the flavors I remember. It doesn't work. But at least I remember my kitchen, the kids running around, Mordy polishing his shoes while I prepare the food.

"This soup," I say. "It still tastes from nothing, but I thank you for trying."

"Goldie, I can ask you a question?"

"You just did. So what's your next question?"

"My children," he says, "they're coming to visit today. For Father's Day. This bowtie, is it too much?

An old man sitting at a table.

1947

POPPA—SITTING, WAITING I should bring him his lemon-*vasser*. I just told him all about Father's Day. He looked at me like I was from another world. It *was* another world. The war finally over. The boys were back. The air, like a promise, something, something, out there. Something for me. God Bless America!

But for Pa? He'd let me go on that boat ride? With everywhere still signs in the synagogues, on telephone poles, in the *Forverts*. Broadcasts all day long on WEVD. Clouds over the pushcarts on Belmont Ave.

"Auschwitz."

"Dachau."

"A detention camp in Sweden."

"Sweden?"

"Take a child? A *Yiddisha Kint*?"

I'm allowed to *live*, I want to shout at him. It's over. We came out alive.

2017

THIS IS ALIVE? A table with a washed-out tablecloth and plastic flowers, and across from me an old man in a bow tie and vest and fancy cufflinks. A clown.

"Harry." I remember his name. Also his question. His children are coming, it's Father's Day. "The bowtie is fine."

His eyes are soft blue behind his glasses and the skin around them folds into deep crinkles when he smiles. Like he must smile a lot. I'm glad I could put his mind at ease. Nobody here so friendly. Me, too, I don't rush to make friends in this place. Who knows how long they'll last, or if they'll remember you from one day to the next? But this man, he has a nice face.

"Father's Day, it's an important day. I met my husband on Father's Day."

"Goldie, let's go to the courtyard. It's nice outside."

Together, not together really, but at the same time, from opposite sides of the table, we push ourselves up leaning on our walkers. It's embarrassing, but this Harry acts like it's no big deal, and I like him for that. Feeling bad about it? Not going to make it better.

He motions I should go first. You can't walk out side by side without banging into something or somebody. Most of the dining room is empty, but Bernice's table is still sitting, watching. Always they watch.

Like something exciting is happening? I run my fingers through my hair and want to see if my lipstick is still on, but I can't stop to look for my pocketbook in the compartment of my walker. People stopping in the middle of everything is what causes accidents.

So I keep going until I push the big button with the picture of the wheelchair on it, and the heavy door, such heavy doors, swings open to the courtyard. It's nice out here, with chairs, and fireplaces even. Sometimes they make pizza, but the cheese—it sits in the stomach.

Harry and I get situated on a love-seat near the fireplace. A few leaves blow across the ground, and the air, it smells good.

1947

THAT LONG TIME AGO MORNING from the boat ride, the air still-early sharp, only a little hint of warm starting to sneak in on the soft breeze blowing through my small bedroom window. Almost close enough to taste, promising the soon to come color and light.

My life can't wait no more for what Poppa says. I quick get dressed, climb out the window and jump from the fire escape.

A little later, standing on the docks, Shirley sees him first. Shirley—the Army could've learned from her how radar works.

He's tall, but not too tall. He's wearing a baseball cap like all the modern boys wear instead of a *yalmulka*. There are all these little black curls falling out of it, creeping toward his eyes, which I can see all the way here are green. And his shoulders, so wide, his pressed shirt just falls away from them, tucked into his pants, also neatly pressed. His sleeves are rolled up to his elbows, and I can see how his arms are strong, and his hands, holding a stack of little booklets or something, are wide, his fingers thick.

"Hi, girls." I think he smiles longest at me. I hope so anyway. In Naomi's borrowed dungarees and the Maiden Form Hold-Tite Dual-Control Brassiere that cost a week of Sundays doing Hymowitz's books, under the yellow sweater I knit special for this occasion, today I'm no *Greena* from off the boat.

"Hi there." Of course, Shirley answers. And her voice—now she's got laryngitis?

"I'm selling raffle tickets. Would you like to buy any?" *Vood*, he says, not *would*, with a rich deep voice. His teeth are straight, and his jaw is square and those eyes, I thought they were green? Like the first spring grass after the snow melts, when you can smell the green without even looking.

Shirley the show-off buys five raffles—and then my turn. I look straight at him, my heart pumping so hard I can't hear nothing else around me. My life. My chance. But no money to spend on raffle tickets.

"I'm not gonna buy," I say. His eyes go wide, his big smile starts to fall. My chin goes up. "I'll help you sell."

Those words, still I hear them. His smile so close and warm like the sun in this patio. I reach out my hands. Stay. Please. Just a little while stay.

2017

THESE HANDS. SUCH HANDS, spots, wrinkles, veins.

That funny little man—Harry? He catches my hand and gives it back to me. "We're still here, Goldie." He looks deep at my face. "I got you."

Smooth operator. "You were in sales, Harry?"

"I was an accountant. Back and forth on the train every day for forty-five years, then I got this watch." He waves his wrist where I see a gold watch. "Then my kids gave me the cufflinks to match."

The cufflinks I already noticed. Very fancy, with jewels. Not my taste.

"But in my dreams, Goldie, in my dreams—"

And before I know what he's doing, he pulls himself up, then stands with one hand on his walker, and in middle of everything, in the courtyard, he starts like he's Nat King Cole, crooning how I'm unforgettable.

What's to forget? He doesn't know me from Adam. Where is the staff when you need them?

Finally he finishes with the whole song, and bends and kisses my hand! *Chutzpah.* I gave him permission? But he can carry a tune, I'll give him that.

"Very nice, very nice," I say, putting away my hand.

This lunatic, he gets a look in his eyes. "Goldie," he says and bows. "Dance with me."

Ganz meshuga! A complete nutjob. "Harry, with our walkers we'll dance?"

"Goldie, you can dance. Come, come."

"There's no music."

"I'll make music," and he starts to sing again, and like the song says, *incredible*. He's holding my hand, pulling me up, and I have my other hand on the walker, and he takes his walker, too, slowly, slowly we let go of the walkers and he holds my hand, and I hold his, and I admit, I'm not so comfortable, and he says to me, "Relax, breathe, just breathe," and then he hums "Unforgettable."

And my feet, if I stand with them just a little bit apart, and I hold both his hands, I can move forward and back, then maybe a little bit I make circles with my hips and my waist, like they make me do in physical therapy, and Harry, he's doing the same thing. I don't know if we're dancing or holding each other up, but he's singing, so nicely he sings, and I'm looking into his eyes, and then I laugh. Again and again. I laugh and throw back my head and give even a bigger *shuckle* with my breasts and shoulders, maybe a little bit my *tuchus,* too, and suddenly there's clapping.

"You go, girl," someone's saying.

Now the staff comes. A bunch of them watching us. For how long? And behind them, their mouths already going, Bernice and her gang. Finally, something to see around here.

"Harry, enough." I reach behind me for the chair, but—no, no. Not this. Not now. My foot starts to slide. Dark spots float in my eyes—I can't stop this once it starts. If I can reach the walker, maybe—but the spots getting darker, the walker, too far. It's too far.

Everyone around me. What am I doing on the floor? How'd I get down here?

Dancing? I was dancing.

CHAPTER TWO

Maxie

MAXIE WASN'T SURE OF A LOT THESE DAYS, but some things she knew. Every morning for the last two weeks—two weeks, four days today, if she was counting—she'd fallen asleep and woken up listing them.

MAXINE JACOBSON:

- Was in a great program at a fabulous school.
- Had guaranteed research funding for the next three years.
- Had a role in that prestigious community leadership program.
- Had manageable student loan debt.
- Lived in a decent apartment—not in Brooklyn, but in Washington Heights, which in her case was a plus since she could walk to work.
- Had good, no, *great* hair.
- And, depending on the brand, was almost always a size six.

What wasn't on the list, which hadn't even been a list two weeks and five days ago—if she was counting—was a badass straight razor in the medicine chest, matching electric toothbrush chargers on the bathroom sink, boxer shorts in the hamper, European size 48 trail shoes within tripping distance of the bed. What wasn't on her list—*who* wasn't on her list—was Daniel Wolinsky.

Not that he was the love of her life. Not that they'd ever considered the long-term, having-children, going-forward thing. Starter

Relationship—understood. She just hadn't expected the expiration date to come so soon. Or that he would be the one to call it. Or that she would miss him this much.

But Maxie was great. Beyond great. She had—she was *earning* a doctorate degree from a fabulous school. Fabulous funding. A decent apartment—*yeah, yeah.* Was it time to worry when you started to recite that list more than twice a day? Before noon?

She ignored her phone ringing in the pocket of her sweats. Who but her mother would call her on a Sunday morning? Everyone she knew would still be sleeping off their Saturday nights. Or—wait. No. Now it was Sunday morning, post-yoga, post-jog, baby-backpacks-on-big-Daddy-man-shoulders, family-time-coffee. Babyccinos for the toddlers, please.

The gritty gray New York City morning wasn't helping. That story she used to tell, how growing up in Berkeley—so close to Oakland—gave her street cred? Street cred? Streets? How about just a hint of blue sky and brown hills? One redwood, even a eucalyptus would do. What about flipflops and sweatshirts in the dead of winter. Winter? Those few and far between drizzles that were Storm-Alert Traffic-Advisory headline news in Northern California? Maxie'd never even owned a pair of pantyhose before college, never mind a winter jacket not designed for skiing. She stomped in her fleece-lined boots, the ones that had been bought for their cool factor, not their now much appreciated warmth. She eyed the kids schlepping their plastic sleds up and down the graying pebble-pocked mound they thought was a sledding hill.

Maxie Jacobson closed her eyes, conjuring an image of bright blue skies, snow-capped mountains, golden hills, roaring surf.

No.

She was great. *Really* great. She had, she had—*yeah, yeah.* Three times an hour?

Her phone buzzed again. She could always go into the lab, her safe place, lose herself in her research.

This was a real call ringtone. Somebody really wanted her—Daniel? Daniel! Skin tingling, she yanked out her phone with traitorous fumbling fingers. *ESTI* glowed on the incoming call ID. Esti? Maxie's heart, ready to slam through its narrow enclosure, retreated to its cave. Her Aunt Esti? This couldn't be good. Before she could even say hello, her aunt's breathless download was already running.

"She was dancing?! What kind of place—anyway, she's conscious. Didn't hit her head, fell on her hand. The EMTs checked her out. Doesn't seem like anything's broken. Thank God. But what was she thinking? What were they thinking? No doctor yet. Can you get here? She hates hospitals. You're the only one she trusts when it comes to medicine."

If Esti said it wasn't serious—her aunt wasn't one to minimize catastrophes. Maxie exhaled. Inhaled. Exhaled. Safta, her grandma, would be fine. Safta was like the NYC air, brash and gritty. She was probably already bullying her aunt, along with the entire ER staff. Still. Any fall at her age was serious.

Maxie felt herself flushing, her guilt tell. Not because she wasn't attentive enough to her grandmother, who despite Maxie's infrequent visits, still *kvelled* over her little lamb, her Sheyfe, almost with the PhD.

No, Maxie was suffering from her shameful relief at having somewhere to be.

CHAPTER THREE

Goldie

I HEAR VOICES. But not yet I'm seeing anything. The seeing always takes the longest. I need to sit up.

"I'm fine," I say. "I'm fine." I try to lift my head. Things around me, I'm starting to make them out. Harry's face. Shocked. Bernice, her mouth still open.

A hand on my shoulder. "Stay still," a woman says "We're calling an ambulance."

Harry's face, all scared, looking down at me. "Goldie, Goldie, I'm sorry."

From the corner of my eye, Bernice. The crowd getting bigger. Like I'm the entertainment. Everyone to see me this way.

I make again to get up. "I'm all right," I say in my loudest voice.

Nobody listens. Only that girl from the staff, the one with the perky breasts still pushing me down.

"Please," I push against her. My head starts to spin. "I'm fine. I'm fine." Not the hospital. You can't let them put you in the hospital. You go in with a sneeze, a nothing, you come out with *whoknowswhat*, nothing good.

If you come out at all.

Big men in blue shirts and bulging muscles putting me on a stretcher. Asking me questions. Five question they said. Stupid questions: Who I am? Where I am? What happened?

I fell. Not the first time this happened. Why I'm in this Assisted Living in the first place. Never I was a burden to my children. Never I will be.

But to end up here? Residents, they call us. Everywhere wheelchairs, walkers, canes. The whole room so overheated. Smells clean, at least—like from chemicals, but so hot—nobody knows to open a window? For such living you need assistance?

That first day. My know-it-all daughters—the skinny-one-now-fat, the fat-one-now-skinny—I should be happy they care? They came? The skinny-one-now-fat all the way from California. The fat-one-now-skinny from just down the street. Where she keeps such a tidy house, runs such a tight ship. A *balabusta.* Always nervous, that one. Live with them? Never.

Look, Ma, look at this, they kept saying. Activities, they said, showing me a piece of paper like it was I don't know what. Art classes? Activity walk? What, nobody here looks like they can even see, never mind do. Finally, we go to another room. At least out of that hallway of *tsoros,* with the walkers and the wheelchairs, the sunrises and the fancy-colored fish.

Sit, sit, they said. An 'intake-interview' they tell me.

Excuse me, I know a test when I'm taking it.

Asking if I take my medicine myself? Who else should take it for me? Weight loss, weight gain, they want a stool sample maybe? A *bissel* privacy I'm entitled to?

Ah. Another question, and again the girls look at each other. So what, I was distracted. So much to take in.

That pert girl with the perky breasts—her smile so forced it has to hurt. Breasts. Headlights, Mordy used to call them. His hands, so big, strong. A gentle giant. We knew from privacy. These girls, letting everything show, so many straps? And the getups, especially my daughter from California, like she's wearing something from out of the desert, flowing and layers and straps. No taste. The other one, from here, she dresses sensibly. Tasteful.

Oy—I missed the question again. And the girls, the look they give each other. I'm sitting right here, I could see. Nothing wrong with my eyes. Not too much, anyway. Big question, do I need help bathing or dressing? For this I had to pay attention?

"No," I tell her. "Do you?" I smile, too. I have nice teeth.

Everything I say, she writes down on her, what do they call it, a *tablet*—that used to mean a pill. Now it's a device. Again with that *fakokta* smile she asks if I can walk for her. I should walk for her? Put on a runway show, maybe?

Deep breath, one hand on my walker, good I remembered to apply the brake before sitting in this chair. Such a deep chair. They did that on purpose? They'll say she needs help getting out of chairs, another hundred dollars. A hundred here, a hundred there, like it grows on trees?

My daughters, they say they don't care I'll be spending their entire *yerusha*. *It's yours, Ma.* That's what they keep saying. Like I don't know that. Like they don't let me know they don't need it. Of course, they don't. I raised them to be independent. To marry well.

Where am I? Beds like cars in a parking lot. Everywhere people moaning and groaning, coughing their lungs out, a couple fighting in the corner, she's yelling that he promised, he promised, no more, never again, she's telling his mother. Always the mother's fault? He has already gray hair. A little late for that argument? How she's hollering, and his head is rolling around like his neck is one of those slinky toys. Now they're kissing? And again, when she comes up for air, hollering?

An ER in NYC. Faster attention you get at the DMV.

Esti so busy watching the couple, too, for a few minutes she forgets about me. Of course, the place called Esti. Now I have to calm her down, too, always so nervous.

"It's nothing, nothing." I keep saying. "I fell, just I landed on my hand. Everything is all right." I hold up my wrist. True, it's a little swollen. "A doctor didn't even come yet to look at it. If it was a real emergency, you think they'd make me wait like this?"

To tell the truth, everyone here looks terrible, so this argument maybe doesn't make sense. With the moaning and groaning, the smells, the noises, like a waiting room for hell. Or the subway. Nowhere a doctor in sight.

"Safta?"

Maxie is here, too? My Sheyfe, so pretty, with her long curls. Really a little lamb. "Sheyfe, it's nothing, nothing," I say. "Why are you here? Everyone making such a fuss."

"I work here, Safta, remember? Aunt Esti called, told me to come."

Esti turns to Maxie. "Do you have any pull? Can we see a doctor? How can they treat her like this? She's old. *Old.* And they make her wait. Not right, an old woman." She points around the room, showing Maxie what a disaster the whole place is. She expected crisp sheets and pink flowers? Maxie goes off to speak to someone, and sure enough, that girl, so sweet, everyone listens to her, she comes back with a nurse, a big strong woman with a loud voice who puts me in a wheelchair and tells me they're gonna do X-rays. "You have my paperwork?" I say. "Don't I need to register?" "Ma," Esti says. "We took care of all that when we got here. I did it while you were sleeping." What sleeping? When was I asleep? Meanwhile, I hate X-rays, but with all this commotion, and Esti standing over me, they do whatever they want. They put on me that heavy blanket, and sure, they run away, and leave me there exposed to that X-ray machine. Finally, they're finished, every which way they turned my arm, if it wasn't broken before, now it will be. "Now what?" I say to the big nurse. She shoves at me a pill and water. "The doctor will read them and come in to talk to you." Sure, sure, in a year from now, maybe? Who knows what I'll have caught by the time he gets here? Then, then, everything changes. The doctor who comes in, *this* is a doctor. So tall, the white coat hangs off his big shoulders. He smiles, teeth like a television commercial for toothpaste.

"Mrs. Mandell? You took a tumble. What were you doing?"

Esti says, "Dancing. They told me she was dancing."

I feel my face going hot. My business, like this, to everyone. They told, she tells. No dignity once you sign off your life to that assistance.

The doctor smiles another TV commercial. "All right, but maybe not hip-hop? Still, you're a very strong woman." He turns to Esti. "Remarkable. For a woman her age, only a sprain. No fracture."

I turn to Esti. "See? Nothing."

I turn back to Dr. Gorgeous. "I can leave?"

He smiles again. He should bottle it, better than medicine. "We just need to wrap your wrist up. But I recommend a follow-up with your regular physician. Blood work, and an EKG." Me, Esti, and Maxie, we're hanging onto his every word, like pearls are dripping from his mouth.

"Sure, doctor, sure." I give him my arm for the bandage. "You're the doctor, you know best."

So gentle he takes my arm, I don't feel any pain. Sure, they gave me that pill after they pushed me around so much for the X-ray, but it's his touch, I can tell, not some pill that feels so good. I watch his hands wrapping the bandage around my wrist. Nice hands. Nice fingers. No ring.

Strong hands. Man hands. Mordy hands. I try to read the name on the doctor's jacket.

"Doctor," I say, "I don't have my glasses to read what it says on your coat."

"I'm Frank," he says.

Frank? A first or last name? Makes a big difference. For a first name, *trouble.* For a last name, *perfect.*

"Frank D'Angelo." Such a smile. *Feh.* Oh well, Maxie has that boyfriend anyway. Only for sure, she deserves better than that *schlemiel.* A doctor like this, that smile, now that's a catch. Only he needs to be kosher.

CHAPTER FOUR

Goldie

1947

MORDY'S SMILE WASN'T LIKE A PICTURE TO SEE; it was an experience to feel. With those straight teeth and his square jaw, he laughed with his whole self, his shoulders and neck going all loose, his whole face opening like from the inside a light bulb turning on.

Some guys don't like when a girl speaks up. This one says, "You wanna sell? Sure. Let's go." Like I should show him what I got.

I hold out my hand for the raffle books. Up and down the boat we go, me asking all the boys, him asking the girls. I like how he does all the numbers in his head, quick making the right change. I like his hands—fast folding, tearing. Handling. Whether we sell all those raffle tickets or not, who knows? Then the horn blows, the boat thumps to a stop. He has to find the guy who gave him the raffle tickets to sell; my friends call for me to come and he goes his way and I go mine.

But I keep my eyes open to find him again. There's a baseball game. He's standing—in his nice clothes—like a golem in the outfield.

"Over here," I call out. Surprised, like it fell from the sky, he catches the ball I throw to him. Then he sees me. Again that smile.

Right away he tosses the ball back to me. I throw it to him, back and forth we go, the whole time walking closer to each other and farther away from his game. Finally, I can smell his soapy clean smell and can see his separate curls and we stop with the ball and just keep walking.

"Baseball?" I say. "A real Yankee-Doodle."

"They called me the ninth, like they were counting for a *minyan.*"

He grabs my hand and starts running away from the field. When we finally stop, we can't catch our breath and I hope he doesn't see my nose running. We collapse against a fallen log and finally I'm breathing slow enough to hear all the noise the woods make.

"You know how to run." He says to me, but looking away at the trees.

"So do you," I tell him back.

I don't know when we slip into German, then Yiddish, then back to English. Mordy and me, we speak the same languages. A familiar story: He came on the Kindertransport, got to America, got drafted into the army, even found his mother. His father, not yet.

When finally he stands up and says, "Gotta find Arnie," this time he holds out his hand to me.

Why he needs to find his friend in middle of everything? Because Arnie has a car. And he owes Mordy a favor for selling the raffles. And he's no *fa'shluffana.* No boat ride back to the city. Instead, alone in Arnie's car, Mordy drives me all the way home to Brooklyn. On the way, he stops in the Bronx to tell his mother he'll be late. I should worry he's a Mama's Boy? No. He just got her back, he's not gonna make her worry. Every minute I like him more.

At a red light he kisses me. Not fresh. Nice. We kiss at the next light, too. Then every red light after that. Soon we're making all the red lights.

But too soon we're at my house.

Before he says anything, I go, "The candy store has a phone. President 1–7991. I'm home by seven o'clock every night. You ask for Goldie Fischel. They'll call for me. Don't leave a message; the whole neighborhood doesn't need to know my business. You'll remember the number?"

His lips are right by my ear and when he wraps my hair around his finger places in me wake up that I never knew were asleep. With the eyes, the teeth, and the jaw, he smiles.

"President 1-7991. I'll remember."

Already I bought a Hershey Bar, a pack of gum, and a nickel's worth of jellybeans at Joe's candy store. Just to be there. Just in case. Finally, Joe smiles from behind the counter, one eyebrow making a question mark while he points at the phone which finally rang.

I smile back but keep quiet. My personal business I don't tell to the entire world.

"Goldie." All the way from the Bronx, like chocolate fudge, his voice. Just like, better, than how I've been playing it in my head all day, over and over, again and again. I pull the cord tight so I can be private-like behind the Superman comic display. Already my knees going soft. "I was waiting all day to make this call."

Vas vaiting.

So was I, I don't say. Waiting my whole life.

CHAPTER FIVE

Goldie

THAT PHONE! BEEPING, BEEPING, all the time with its commotion. Even it dances and buzzes, can scare the daylights out of you. Then it calms down before you can find it. Like right now, quiet. Still. Where is it? I smack the pocket of my skirt, then look inside my purse, always hanging from the walker. Next, I dig through all the pockets and pouches of my walker, so much Velcro, and so hard I need to pull. But it's a good day. There it is, right on the couch. The feeling—like when you wake up all nervous for the day and outside, beautiful white snow like a soft blanket telling you, shh, relax. Just relax.

Now it says it's locked. *Feh,* the whole secret password situation. A phone? A time machine is what I need.

Where was I? The pill. With the whole to-do yesterday, enough I'm alive, never mind the pills. Makes a difference? The yellow one, the green one, the capsules, the white one—the big white one, the shiny one. They say to take it with food. What food? The fridge here fits nothing. Maybe I can flush it down the toilet. Any minute she'll be here, counting. Since they moved me here, her nose is all in my business. I see her—counting—and then she lectures. Me, *her mother*, who changed her diaper, she lectures.

Too late. Already the door is opening with the key she took for herself.

"Ma, how are you today?" Esti looks at me like something she's studying. "How does your arm feel?"

"Fine, fine." I nod, giving her the full body response, waving my arm, still in the bandage, to show her. A pretty girl, only she shouldn't be so nervous. It makes her have lines already. Still, she makes her face nice, and her clothes, always neat. All the ladies here admire her, I see how they pay attention when she comes. Alone? Forget it. Like I'm invisible. After that show I put on yesterday? Better to stay invisible.

"Good. I can't stay long today. I need to go into the city." Already, she's making order with my things while she's talking.

"Maybe I'd like to go to the city with you?" I can't hide in this room forever, but in another day or two, I'll be old news. Some other tragedy will have happened to somebody else.

"Did you say something?" Esti turns with all my newspapers in her hands.

"Nothing. Nothing." Just she shouldn't get started on my pills.

"You went downstairs today? For breakfast?"

I should be happy she comes. Some of the other people here, I never see any company for them.

That stupid phone starts again with its song and dance. Right away I grab it, but not fast enough.

Esti's standing over me. "What are you doing with your phone?"

"I don't know." Sounds stupid, but it's the truth. "All day, this thing. It makes these noises, it beeps, then flashes, then nothing. Making me crazy."

Esti takes it from my hand. "It says you have six missed Facetime calls."

"I don't even know what that is."

She runs her finger over the screen. "Ma," she's giving me her voice. "Did you give somebody your information?"

She thinks I'm an idiot? "Of course not, I never give nothing. But this—it just started."

Now Esti's fingers tap dance all over the phone screen. "Yeah, a bunch of incoming calls. The same number each time, I can block it."

"But what if, I don't know, what if I'm missing something? It could be important?" The way Esti looks at me, like what could I have important? "What? It could be, I don't know? Maybe my retirement fund?

Or my insurance? I need to know these things." I get an idea. "Did they leave messages?"

"No, I checked. It's probably a marketing thing but, listen, here's what we can do." Like she's doing me a favor, which I guess she is. "I'll call the number, and if it's real, fine. We'll find out what they want. Otherwise, I'll block it."

"Fine."

She holds the phone out from her face, looking into it.

"What are you doing?"

"Facetime."

"What's Facetime?"

"I'll show you." She sits down next to me, still holding the phone in front of her, like she's going to talk to it, instead of into it. She does talk to it. And on the screen, *vey iz mir,* it's that guy. Harry. From yesterday. What? I'm not embarrassed enough already? Even I'm ashamed to go out from my room.

"Hello," Esti says.

"Hello, hello." Harry says back, in the phone face. "Who is this? Never mind, who cares. How ya doin', whoever you are?"

Esti shakes her head. "You've been calling this number. What do you want?"

"You called me. Not that I'm complaining. I'll take it, a call from a pretty girl, now that's not something that happens every day."

"Hang up. Hang up now," I tell Esti.

"Goldie, Goldie, is that you?"

"Ma?" Esti says, pointing the phone at me.

"Goldie! I've been trying to reach you. It's me, Harry. From yesterday."

"I know who you are." I yell at the phone. Such a thing, nothing works anymore like how it used to. What does he want? Why is he calling? Already I'm feeling all over clammy and hot. I don't need to make from myself an advertisement for shame.

Esti takes one look at me and pulls the phone away. "Sir, stop harassing my mother. How did you even get this number?"

"She gave it to me, swear to God."

"God has nothing to do with this." I tell Esti. "He's *gantz meshuga.*" I gave him my number? When did I give him my number?

"Goldie, c'mon. I just wanted, please." He says to Esti, "Please give your mother the phone."

The last thing I want to do, but I take the phone from Esti's hand. Better to get this over with. Not like I can hide in my room forever. Anyway, look, he's calling me. After that calamity, I thought for sure he'd look the other way when we passed each other in the hallway.

"Goldie," he says. On the phone he's in one box, I'm in another. That's what I look like? Where's my neck? And my face, so much extra skin? I reach my hand to my cheek, and *oy vey,* he can see everything I'm doing. This is what the kids are doing all day long? Looking at themselves non-stop? Not healthy.

"I wanted to thank you for your company yesterday. And to apologize. These walkers, they're supposed to help, but it got in your way. I saw it happening, and I didn't get there fast enough. I just saw it happen and I couldn't—anyway. I wanted to let you know how sorry I am, and how I enjoyed meeting you. I wanted to see how you're feeling."

His fault? He...he takes responsibility? Blames himself?

"So," he says. "Maybe I'll still see you around?"

That voice. It pulls at your *kishkes*—like those television commercials to make you cry over nothing. Here I was ready already to walk past him with my nose in the air. And he's telling me he's sorry?

"Like I'm going somewhere?" I say. Esti is making at me all kinds of faces, pointing at her watch. I wave to her *good-bye, go, go* I nod, *it's okay, I understand*. She's standing like she's not sure. I again wave goodbye, smile, and point to the door. *Oy*, I forgot Harry can see all of this.

"One minute," I say to the phone. "My daughter she's leaving, she's just saying goodbye." I watch the door close behind her.

"So," I say back to Harry's face in the phone, remembering yesterday, before it all went so bad. "Your kids. You were waiting for them. Did they come?"

Now he looks down. "No," he says, still not looking at the phone. "There was some, I don't know, trouble or something with the car. One of the kids—" His voice trails off. "No matter. There's next Sunday."

"Sure, sure," I say, in a loud voice, crazy to see and hear yourself like this. "These kids, all the time telling what to do, what to eat. They forget we raised them? Then when their schedule gets in the way, off they go. My daughter, already she's here this morning bossing me around. My other daughter in California? Her, who knows when next I'll see her."

Of course I keep track when she comes, or promises to come. Like watching the Oscars, it's a major activity here keeping score of each other's company: When they come, who they visit, what they wear. How long they stay.

"But she comes? All the way from California?" Harry sounds, I don't know the word. Like hope and sadness mixed together.

"She and I, well, long story. Anyway, it's better now, but still she lives far. Her daughter though, she makes the effort and comes. She works nearby at Columbia University, getting even a PhD. Girls today, something." I don't like to brag, but with Maxie, it's not bragging. It's the truth. "Anyway, so your kids are coming next week?"

Look at this, we're having a conversation and not about the fall.

"Yeah, something like that." He waves his arm, but this happy dancing guy? His voice, the sound of hope not there anymore. Just the quiet of his disappointment hangs on the phone line.

"Harry, tell me something," I say. "How did you do this, this thing where we're talking into the phone with the pictures? You can show me?"

"Sure thing," he says, smiling.

It's nice, his smile.

Chat Group: Mom's Status

Members: Esti, Tamar

ESTI

Dancing? Whole day in the ER. Then she throws me out of her room—FT'ing—with him! Dancing? FTing?

Seriously? After I spent all weekend sorting her pills in those container things, even wrote a whole chart. Norm helped, btw.

TAMAR

The place will do her meds.

You/Norm not the assistants—they are!

FTing? ??

ESTI

They charge for that. She can't even have aspirins.

TAMAR

??

ESTI

???

TAMAR

W/is FT? What $$$? Aspirins? Her heart?

ESTI

Her heart! She has a heart issue? Nobody said anything

to me a/heart! She doesn't tell me anything.

TAMAR

NO HEART ISSUE! WHAT IS FT? Why no aspirins? WHAT CHARGE?

ESTI

FT = FACETIME! On the med plan, she can't....

NM, I'm calling. Too much to type.

TAMAR

NO! @work!! Can't talk!!

Chat Group: Safta

Members: Tamar, Maxie

TAMAR

On phone w/Esti > hour. please PLEASE visit Safta?

MAXIE

Bad timing

TAMAR

Who are you!!??

MAXIE

Sorry sorry Work

And

TAMAR

Daniel? Again? Why do you

MAXIE

Stop ... ... We broke up

TAMAR

mazal tov?

MAXIE

You didn't say that – He traded me in. Like I'm a car. A Prius for a ...

TAMAR

Stop. You're a TESLA. Self driving. Beautiful, smart.

TAMAR

Never good enough for you. Little putz.

Sorry. Sorry. How are you? I wish I could hug you.

You're beautiful, smart, so strong. Good at your job.

At everything. And kind. You know that, right?

MAXIE

Sometimes Thx Wassup w/Safta?

TAMAR

Can you find out? PLEASE?? Esti losing it. worried a/that guy?

Her pills? Her heart? Facetime? Maybe she'll talk to you.

MAXIE

Kk I'll go on Sunday I like Safta She's funny

TAMAR

Not touching that one.

MAXIE

LOL

CHAPTER SIX

Goldie

I WANT TO LOOK NICE FOR MAXIE, so nice how she comes to visit. Even I go for my nails and hair, and I tell the salon-lady my granddaughter is coming. I look so good, I get the idea to call Tamar, Maxie's mother. I know now how to do the Facetime because Harry's been giving me classes on the phone, and I write down the instructions. Then I practice.

"Hi Ma." Tamar already sounds like she's doing me a big favor. As expected, she looks terrible. A little lipstick would hurt? And that hair? She tells me "It's natural." It's a mess, is what it is.

"Tamar, you see, I'm doing the Facetime."

She forgets I can see her rolling her eyes?

"So listen, Maxie is coming today, so I'm all dressed up. I even did my hair. You see?" I hold the phone over my head, and then all around, so she can see the front and back views.

"Ma, what are you doing? All I see are ceiling tiles. And the wall behind you. Now I see the floor."

I hear her laughing. Such a sweet laugh she always had. When you heard it.

"They call it a bob. You see, the little curl in the front." I hold the phone to my cheek.

"Not really. I see skin. Like every pore."

"No, you see, she colored it. I'm not so sure about it though. I think it's a little too orange-y." I press the phone against my hair.

"Ma, just look into the phone and I'll see your face. Stop waving it all around. Seriously, I can't see anything."

"No, pay attention, I'm showing you the color. You see?"

I hear her exhaling. "Yeah, all right. It is kind of orange-y. But it looks nice." She says like it's a big concession.

"I know it's nice, that's why I'm showing you. You have good hair—if you ever ran a brush through it. You should make an appointment, show them my picture, tell them this is the style you want. I think it will look nice on you. A lot of the ladies here have it."

"You want me to look like the ladies at Assisted Living?"

"No, of course, you can keep it longer. Just you know, a curl, some waves. Maybe a clip. And some color. Enough with that messy hippie look. Maybe some highlights like all the girls have now. Something to fix yourself up. You're too young to give up."

"What makes you think I'm giving up just because I don't want to look like I'm in an old—I mean, just because I prefer a different style?"

"What style? You have no style. That's what I'm telling you. Here, take another look." Again I move the phone all around my head.

"Great Ma, it's great. Let me hang up so I can make an appointment."

"You mean it?"

"No!" She hangs up.

Hanging up. Banging doors. Tamar—like a kite she flies. Always me on the ground, pulling on the string to keep her safe. Flying through the door, bringing the whole beach inside with her. Her whole *tuchus* you can see in those *shmatas*—all strings—that she calls *shorts*. On top, a nothing with straps. And that hair—I used to brush it, so beautiful.? *Feh,* all the way down her back, full of sand and salt and who knows what else.

"Come here." I point to the sewing box at my feet, like I'm going to ask her help to thread the needle. A big favor and if she walked any slower time would stop altogether. My fingers are getting angrier with every step she takes. Finally she's right in front of my face and I quick snip the scissors and *schoen* the shorts—what there was of them—disintegrate in a pile around her dirty sandy feet. I'm still shaking—but even so, I look back up, and like a statue she stands—like she came out from the shreds around her ankles. Her legs, so long, strong from riding her bicycle everywhere, her stomach shiny tan from the sun and hard with muscles. But her face, not so proud. Her lip is trembling like when she was a baby.

"Get dressed like a normal person." I pretend like I'm sewing.

Then the running, the door banging. Full-time theater. Full-time heartburn. A teenage daughter, better they should be butterflies, wrap them up safe for a few years, then let them come out finished with all the craziness.

CHAPTER SEVEN

Maxie

MAXIE STANDS IN THE LOBBY of Safta's assisted living. Three weeks and four days. If anyone was counting. She studies a heartbreaking display: a wall of resident photos: WWII fighter pilots, bobbysoxers, Frankie and Deano Ratpack wannabees. How to reconcile these glamor shots with the diminished people left here to do—well, whatever it was they did here.

But a promise is a promise. Besides, Solitary Sundays were the worst. Walking here, walking back, an hour or two with Safta, that would bring her to late afternoon. Not too early for a glass of wine, and binge-watching something, anything, hopefully something good. Not stalking Instagram for Daniel updates. Not, definitely not, checking her phone beside her on the coffee table. Maybe she'd be radical and leave it in the other room. Yeah. Right.

She took out her earbuds, and texted. "I'm here, Mom." Paused, fingers hovering. Added the Smiley face. Smiled to herself.

Maxie Jacobson knew how to be nice. She was good at it. Maxie was good at a lot of things. Just right now, she wanted a break from being good. Everyone deserves a break, and Maxie, doing the right thing, all the time, had earned hers. Maxie Jacobson knew a lot of things, but she didn't know how not to be good.

Apparently, pathetically, she also didn't know how to be elegant. Not that she was gonna go back there, no. Unbidden—or more accurately, the constant she was perpetually, unsuccessfully suppressing—it rose, the hot red flush of that last Sunday.

She'd tried. Spent time on her makeup, her hair, her shoes. But when she'd come out of the room, instead of basking in the warmth of Daniel's appreciative smile, he'd cocked his head to the side and suggested, in his new way, "Babe?"

Babe? That was the pig in that movie. Not (almost) Dr. Maxie Jacobson.

Who was this stranger judging her and where was her formerly adorably nerdy physicist/mathematician boyfriend? The one who would have rolled his eyes at the thought of getting all dressed up like Old People on a Sunday to eat and drink. Not when there were papers to read, social issues to acknowledge, workout challenges to conquer, and research questions to ponder.

When was the last time she'd seen him engaged in something that mattered? Something real? It had been months since that day when his face had turned red when she asked what he was working on. He'd explained, embarrassed, that he was writing a paper for a Big Boy Wall Street interview.

Wall Street?

A friend, he said, suggested it. There were huge opportunities for quants.

Quants?

He'd fussed with his only jacket, a not quite threadbare tweed and found an old pair of wool pants. Both of them laughing when they were challenged by the tie knot. That night, his eyes behind his glasses were large and feverish: the windows, the offices, *the money, the money, THE money.*

"We could do so much. In just a year I'd make more than in four years in a lab, no publish or perish, no chasing tenure. Just think, Maxie, I'd do it for a short while, then we can do whatever we want. Return to academia. We could travel." He spread his arms wide. "Africa. Syria." He named all the hot spots, at least the ones he could think of in the moment, where they'd give back, be real.

But in less than six months, for the new improved, Lasiked-eyed and Pelotoned-muscled Daniel Wolinsky, *real* didn't include Maxie Jacobson and her suddenly too-fat ass in her all-wrong jeans.

Enough. Safta. Today was about Safta.

Maxie scanned the sweltering room. What went on here anyway? What did Safta do here all day? In the corner, Maxie saw her grandmother's papaya colored hair cresting the top of an oversized floral-fabric chair. Her walker off to the side, as was her head.

Her head was off to the side? Maxie ran across the room, upsetting the library quiet. A few heads lifted, a few eyes followed. One dapper man in the corner smiled, raising two fingers to his forehead in a jaunty salute before swinging away with his walker.

"Safta?" Maxie leaned in, noting the polished nails, the puffed hair with roller dents delineated. She exhaled, her grandmother's hands were cradled around her phone, she appeared to be talking. But the phone was off. Nobody was within earshot. Maxie felt a tug at her gut. For the first time in three weeks and three days (if anyone was counting) Maxie was entirely focused on someone besides herself.

"Safta?" Maxie patted, then shook her grandmother's shoulder. "Safta, it's me. Maxie."

CHAPTER EIGHT

Goldie

"TAMAR?" NO, NOT TAMAR. Maxie. Tamar's daughter. So *ts'mished.* All the time lately. "Shayfe, come, let me get a look at you."

Something not right. Her face so pale, her hair up in a messy bun, her shoulders down like all the *alte kackers* here. And what's she wearing? Looks like pajamas. A beautiful young girl to walk around like this?

"What's wrong?" I ask.

She looks surprised, like I should notice something altogether. "No, no, nothing." She stares at the wall. Some nothing.

"You want something to eat, a bagel, lox?" I bought special for her visit. I told Harry maybe I would call him; I like to show her off. Now I'm thinking not. Just the two of us is better.

"No, Safta, not hungry." She reaches for her phone. Then stuffs it back in her pocket like I shouldn't see.

"What, what? So busy on that phone. What are you looking for?"

Her face turns red and her eyes fill. My beautiful Shayfe. She's not a crybaby. Never. Like she had to be the grownup with Tamar for her mother. My Sheyfe crying? That boyfriend. Not worth the toilet she *pishes* in.

"Come, come, Sheyfe," I tell her. I pull her close, like a baby; she's shaking all over. "He's an idiot. You're better off without him." I say all the things, but I see she can't hear me. "Who needs him. You're too good for him, way too good."

"It was never the same, after—" Suddenly she looks afraid like her mouth was ahead of her brain.

After? After what? No. Not what I'm thinking. The oldest story. But what else could it be? These kids, living together.

No *chupa*, no *shtupa*, I told her. They think an old lady doesn't know? We know. They think they invented sex? Ha.

1948

I THOUGHT I KNEW EVERYTHING.

Sure, the cooking, the cleaning, the shopping, the doing that I did all the years for Pa? That's the same. But it's all different now. Because, after the counter is wiped, the dishes are put away, and the floor is swept, then, then Mordy comes to me and those places in me—that he has the secret key that they only open up when he turns it. All day long I can't wait for him to touch me. And, to tell the truth, I'm surprised, I like to touch him, too. How excited he gets, his whole body so happy just when I sit down next to him.

It's normal to want like this? All the time, thinking about it, waiting, waiting, for the day to end and the night to start. Even while I'm doing the books, I'm remembering. All the time remembering. Then quick, pressing down my skirt, fixing my hair, studying the numbers in front of me. A minute later, the same thing again. It feels like all the time I'm nowhere in space, just wanting, until he comes to me, and then, I'm finally exactly where I want to be. Like jumping into the ocean, the water with no end, tickling me, licking me, all over, everywhere, filling me up, until, until. I'm tossed and turned and flooded and I don't know, like I'm riding the fastest, strongest, wave, riding it, riding it, and then, safe on the shore and I can't catch my breath.

Like he knows what I'm thinking, always thinking, I hear it now. Our special signal whistle coming through the window. I run to the window and see around him all the kids from the block jumping up and down, big excitement like when the ice cream truck comes, or when the rough kids, the ones afraid of nothing, open the hydrants on the hot days. That's when they all play together, everyone with their different accents and colors. The whole melting pot they're always talking about, finally it really melts. Even the old-timers from the different countries and places forget for a minute to hate each other and manage to smile together. A little relief from the heat and everybody's friends. Until the police come to shut the whole thing down.

Mordy looks up, excited like the rest of them. Only bigger. He quick waves me to come downstairs. I'm all out of breath when I get there, and Mordy pulls me to the car. I see, next to it, two shiny brand-new fancy black bicycles.

"What? How?"

And Mordy, he's like a little boy, his curls all falling into his eyes, and his eyes like green marbles with the shiny spot in the middle, and he says, "Goldie, English Racers. Three-speed English Racers. Look." He shows me how one has a bar between the seat and the handlebar, and the other one doesn't. In big silver letters I read RALEIGH against the black frame. "A boy and a girl bike. For us!"

"For us?"

"I was driving home, on Eastern Parkway. And I saw, the beautiful day, and people were bicycling, and the grass was coming up green, and the flowers blooming along the curbs, and I thought, me and Goldie. This is how to live."

And my heart goes faster, and I rub my hand over the shiny girl's bicycle handlebars.

"Were they very expensive?" I have to ask.

"So what? We live once, Goldie."

Which is what we say on Saturday night, when we skip breakfast on Sunday to go to the movies. How many breakfasts will this cost?

"I had some extra money this week, from a special delivery Rosenfeld threw my way. Goldie, this is what it's for."

Vat itz for.

And those green marble eyes are sparkling, and his strong arms and long legs are twitching, how they need to be running, jumping, doing, and for this I love him even more. I take the girl bicycle and with all the kids all around us, he gets on his, and I stand up on the pedals and call over my shoulder, "Race you to the parkway."

And before I know it, he's riding in circles around me and I'm laughing and crying together, so happy. But I'll have to tell him that I won't be able to ride so much soon, because all our delicious nights together? Inside me, where Mordy planted it, our baby is growing.

CHAPTER NINE

Goldie

2017

THAT.

That's what Maxie should be feeling. This is the time in her life to be laughing, crying, stupid crazy in love. Instead, she sits there, so sad. If I could take from her the pain, in a minute I would. But that I can't do.

My hand is up by my neck and I feel the gold chain with the heart that's always there, never I take it off. But now? It's too big. It looks silly on my chest. It's for a young girl. Like I was when he gave it to me, that first anniversary.

"Sheyfe, take it. Take it. You should have this. One day, you should have everything not just the necklace, the man to go with it. One who deserves you. Not one who—who—"

What did he do to her? What happened?

The whole afternoon she doesn't look at me. I don't ask, I don't need to. Just she slips the heart around her neck and keeps saying, "I'm all right, Safta. I'm all right."

No. Not what I'm thinking. The happiest thing can also be the saddest. Life, it likes to laugh at you, the one time you don't pay attention. The oldest story.

1970

WE THOUGHT WE WERE DONE. Over forty years old—I thought I knew everything in that department. So many years with nothing happening, you relax. Sure, it's sad to think that part of your life is over, but to be wrong?

"How can I be now pregnant." I say to Mordy, "I'm too old."

Mordy, he says, "It's what He is giving us. A present." He couldn't maybe give it to us fifteen years ago?

"Mordy, everyone says, even the doctor told me that it can be dangerous to have a baby so late in life. It can be *nisht mit aleyman*. You know, mongoloid? And the *parnassa*? To start all over, where will the money come from? And Esti, we're making her wedding. It's an embarrassment."

I asked for this? Sure I did—fifteen years ago. Now He gets to my request? Some sense of humor, He must be laughing up there. "Mordy. It's not a sin when it's a danger to bring a baby into the world."

Mordy's handsome face falls, his eyes, soft, look a little wet. But with his big hand he holds my cheek, he looks into my eyes and he says, "Goldie, we have to do what's right. Just let me read a little."

His Holy Books. Always he finds his answers in them.

"But don't ask," I beg him. "I don't want no *Rebbe* deciding this for me."

Mordy straightens. We always talk, sure, but sometimes he doesn't like how I say what I think, especially about the rabbis. But so many people, they ask everything, should I buy a house, should I buy a car, should I have an—*abortion*. There. I said it. And then, the rabbi speaks and it becomes holy. No, he's just a man. I respect Mordy's decision; it's his baby, too. But the *Rebbe*, no, he doesn't poke his nose into this.

"Goldie, this is between us. But I need to find my answer."

Of course. Besides, with all those books, his *seforim*, if you look hard enough, you can always find the answer you're really looking for anyway.

Sure enough, in the morning, Mordy, his eyes all tired, says, "Goldie, we do whatever you feel is best."

So now I have my permission and what happens? I call the doctor, I make the appointment, we're already on the way in the car and I say to Mordy, "Turn around. If He gave it to us, we don't give it back. We managed with Esti and Tamar. We'll manage with this one, too."

And Mordy doesn't say a word. With his chin strong, his eyes straight, his hands on the steering wheel, he makes a U-turn and we go back to the house. It's like we both start breathing for the first time in a long while.

They cut me open, a Cesarean. Ten pounds, a big boy. Again, the answers from the books. We don't need to sit shiva because he never breathed. But still he needs to be buried and we have to give him a name. Finally, a name for Mordy's father.

Chat Group: Safta

Members: Tamar, Maxie

TAMAR

Esti called/texted 10K times!! Talk to me!

MAXIE

… …

TAMAR

!!! Now!

MAXIE

Kk! Sorry! Thinking Sad, It was intense S kept getting lost in space She gave me her necklace. That big gold heart.

TAMAR

Her necklace? Wow.

MAXIE

Talked a lot about Saba. Did they have a stillborn?

More like talking to herself. Like she thought she was me? Or you? When I came she thought I was you? I told her about D More like she guessed Seemed real upset. Kept going back to Saba Bicycles? Babies?

TAMAR

She NEVER talks about the baby she lost. It was a boy. Is she losing it? You think it's the place?

MAXIE

Dunno. Seems nice. It's clean She's still sharp just ... distracted. Almost didn't register when I left her wheels were spinning–

just definitely distracted.

TAMAR

Physically, how was she?

MAXIE

All right. Seems to have friends -frenemies? Bernice? Beatrice? Safta loves to hate her. Definitely still sharp. Even pulled out no chupa - no shtupa Classic! Kk Pretty late here. Going to sleep. She really is fun. Just old maybe sad?

TAMAR

Don't know what to tell Esti. Ok. Thx for this.

MAXIE

It was nice to hear about Saba, I never knew him, really.

TAMAR

She misses him everyday. Me/Esti too.

MAXIE

☹ G'nite xx

CHAPTER TEN

Goldie

SHE SHOULDN'T THINK I'M IN HER BUSINESS. But a granddaughter, she *is* my business. Something I have to do. But what? And from here? *Feh.* From here, or there, who cares. There has to be a way. Whatever happened, finished. What's gonna be, that's the important question. Maybe I can't predict or control, but at least I can steer a little bit in the right direction? What can it hurt?

If only I wasn't stuck in this place. Impossible to collect your thoughts here, everywhere everyone looking already half-dead. Even me with this stupid bandage. How am I supposed to come up with an idea when all I see all day is broken people surrounded by healthcare uniforms—aides, nurses, doctors.

Doctors! The solution staring right at me. That emergency room doctor was the only one? For sure where he came from, there are others. Only with the right names. And background. And family. Time to go downstairs.

"Harry, I need you. I have an idea for us."

His eyes light up. "Hello to you, too, Goldie."

"Good. Good. We have to move fast."

"I couldn't agree more. Let's go." He reaches out a hand like to lead me somewhere. He leans on the arm of the loveseat where we like to sit. "It's not like we have time to waste, Goldie. What do the kids say? We have to fast-track this." He smiles, making like he's getting up. "I'll go on Facebook and say so."

What is he thinking that I'm talking about him and me? All day long the two of us to look at each other? We'll count our wrinkles with our bad eyesight? A blessing not to see. And then what? Romance he wants? To go steady? One bed? All that fumbling, with my flabby stomach and loose legs, the folds in my back, the blotchy skin. And my breasts. They're not such knockers anymore, I can tell you. And who knows even if all his equipment works. And this I'd have to know, too?

"Harry, what are you talking? Calm down. Not us, I'm talking about Maxie my granddaughter. You and me? We're not young like that. We're at a different stage."

He's shaking his head, "Goldie, Goldie, we're at any stage we want to be. Take a chance, why not?" Then he smiles, like he's giving in. "So what's the big idea?" he asks.

At least he stopped pushing.

"Maxie. She needs a man to hold her at night, to keep her warm, to let her know that the roof is not going to cave in and that she's not alone. I can't do it without you." I say, like a diplomat. He should know I like him, just he has to relax.

"I want we should look up all the doctors in the Facebook. They tell everything, right? Where they work, what they do, their reputations. But also, *everything*. You can find out if they're married, what their hobbies are, even what they do on weekends. So, easy. I find all the doctors who are single, Jewish, already we know they're smart or they wouldn't be doctors. Even we can find their financials, if they were sued for malpractice, right? We read their reviews. We see if they have pictures from bar mitzvahs, or better, a party for their parents. When we find the right doctor, I'll make like I have the right disease. Maxie already works in the hospital—she takes me to the appointment, and 1-2-3, a love story."

"Goldie, I'm not sure this is a good idea." I never saw Harry look like this, always he wants to do anything. "You're going to pretend you're sick so Maxie will meet doctors?"

"I'm her grandmother," I say.

From: Esther Abramson <Estia@gmail.com>

To: maxj; TamarJ

Subject: Advocacy - Mom

I appreciate that Maxie is willing to be Mom's medical advocate. I agree that it's appropriate for the younger generation to assume adult responsibilities, and Maxie's work in the lab does make it easier for her to accommodate Mom's medical appointments. I just want to be clear that this was Mom's decision—apparently there was some workshop she attended where she was told that she needs an Advocate, and that it was best to restrict that role to one family member! Mom's made it perfectly clear that she has selected Maxie, based on her belief that Maxie is most qualified because of her biology degree. She's also convinced that after that dancing fiasco, Maxie's intervention at the ER was the only reason she left the hospital alive. I'm not resisting any of this. It's just that in your email you implied that Maxie taking on this role would be a relief to me. Maybe so, but I want to make sure that everyone knows this was Mom's idea, and I'm not foisting responsibility onto Maxie, who's young and has a fulltime intense work commitment. If it proves to be too much, I'll step (back) in. We all want what's best for Mom.

--E

From: Max Jacobson <maxj@gmail.com>
To: Estia; TamarJ
Subject: RE: Advocacy- Mom

Esti: Thanks for sending this!

Yep, Safta was clear. I'm happy to help out, it's no big deal, I work right there, and there is some truth to medical staff paying closer attention to elderly—any—patients when they're accompanied by somebody with knowledge of the medical/healthcare profession. Too bad I'm not going for the MD! Which Safta pointed out (again!). "Why just a PhD? All those years studying, why you're not becoming a real doctor with an MD? Still, very nice. Better even, for when you have children."

Anyway "advocate" is her new favorite word! After "husband"... I'll keep you posted.

—M

From: Tamar Jacobson <TamarJ@gmail.com>
To: maxj; Estia
Subject: RE: RE: Advocacy - Mom

Ladies!

Thank you both. Of course, I always feel like I'm shirking off, being so far away. Esti: you know how much I appreciate you being there for her. I'm glad Maxie can step in, but only if we're all on board with it. Let me know when it all becomes too much (Esti: you've been a rock!), and I'll fly out to help.

Maxie: Must be generational. I'd be so pissed when she'd say that stuff to me! Glad you can laugh it off.

From: Esther Abramson <Estia@gmail.com>
To: director@riverdaleseniorliving
Subject: Appropriate Messaging for Seniors? Medical Advocate Selection

Dear Helen,

It has come to my attention that you held a lecture advising/encouraging residents to seek medical advocates. Though in principle this is sound advice, I would like to suggest that in your capacity as Director, your lectures have a huge impact on your residents. My mother is fortunate to have a granddaughter in the medical sciences who can assuage her discomfort over doctor visits; however, were this not the case your lecture would have introduced unnecessary insecurity and distress for her. Please assure your patients that any concerned family member (or vetted friend), can serve as an "advocate." Our elderly parents are already vulnerable, they must be secure regarding their ongoing care. They absolutely don't need additional stress regarding the quality of care their family can ensure them.

I hope you will consider your significant influence when planning future events.

Thank you for all you do for our loved ones.

Sincerely,

Esther Abramson

Primary Caregiver/Daughter

Mrs. Goldie Mandell, Rm 907

From: Riverdale Senior Living

Helen Factor, MSW, MA, Director

To: missmt

RE: Forwarded Message: Medical Advocacy Lecture?

I see no reference to this lecture in our agenda? Was it a last-minute sub for something else?

From: Riverdale Senior Living

Millicent Taylor, Social Activities Coordinator

To: helenf

RE: RE: Forwarded Message Medical Advocacy Lecture?

No such lecture, workshop offered. Chatter among the residents?

RM 907: Mandell, Goldie, RM 512: Silver, Harry, RM 608: Rosen, Bernice: newly formed clique. Popular: Highly functioning, engaged residents.

CHAPTER ELEVEN

Goldie

I TOLD ESTI NOT TO COME, how Maxie wanted to be my "advocate." A little lie. Still, I asked Maxie and she agreed. So, also a little truth. Not important which came first. Anyhow, so now—Big Shot—I'm waiting in the cold by myself. If you're not outside, they say you missed your ride. And still charge the three dollars. But not too bad, soon I see a white car with big red letters, Access-A-Ride. I wave my hand, *yoo-hooing* at the same time. Inside a crazy beanie hat all colors moves up and down. What, he's nodding to let me know he saw me? Good. At least he's paying attention.

The car pulls up nice and slow. Also good. A lady here, Harriet, told us how her neighbor knew somebody who got hit by one of these guys. A bunch of ex-cons, she said they were.

What's he doing, getting out of the car? They take advantage when a lady is alone. But he's not going to get away with anything right here, in front of the building. Just because we have walkers, they think we're weak? Even if it's true, you can't act it. That's just common sense.

What I'm seeing—a walking mop—under the beanie, shiny black curls out all crazy around his face. A grown man, if that is what he is, in *shorts*? Like he outgrew his pants and cut them off halfway. Why a hat and shorts? It's either hot or cold. He can't figure it out? An undershirt? Not even a real shirt, like he forgot that he had to finish getting dressed? All covered in splotches like the arts and crafts projects the kids made from old *shmatas* at summer camp. *Vey is mir*, on his arms—pictures. A tattoo. Also one on his hairy leg. This I have to see? And his feet? Sandals? With socks? There's no dress code for these drivers? His mother, she didn't teach him anything?

What? He's holding out his arm for me to take? I quick press tight my pocketbook, which I know to put across my shoulder under my sweater. He nods like to tell me to relax, his eyes very dark, such thick eyelashes every girl would cry to have. On him, wasted. Bushy eyebrows, too, and that hair, such thick curls, more of a waste.

And he smells. Not like from body odor, like from oil? Or paint? Something. But so gently he helps me into the car. But what's he doing? Why's he tugging so hard the seatbelt? Who knows what he's up to. I hold up my hands in front of my face, but he just points to the latch and closes the door. I lock the belt, easy, so nice. Nobody thinks how hard it is to reach the belt all the way to the latch. Maybe they give these drivers lessons? About time. Wait, he's walking away? He's going somewhere? I turn first to one side, then the other, but he locked me into this seat. I twist my head so I can see out the back window, and there he is, nice folding my walker into the trunk. So why he couldn't tell me where he was going?

He settles into his seat and while he locks his own seatbelt he says, "All right, my lady?"

"I'm not your lady."

He smiles. I'm surprised, he has such white teeth. "Where are we going?" He asks to the mirror.

"Columbia Presbyterian. By 168th Street."

He pulls out from the driveway.

"You have to pick up other people? We're gonna go around in circles now for an hour? You need I should tell you the address? Columbia Presbyterian?"

"You're my only passenger. And I know the way." Again, in the mirror his big eyes with the heavy eyelashes and eyebrows look at me, very happy.

"You take a lot of people there?"

"I drive there quite often." Like with some kind of an accent, how he says *quite.*

"But you're not from here."

"I'm from—" He stops like he has to think about this? "Canada."

"Canada? It's cold there, no? That's why you're wearing shorts? You think it's hot here?"

Always everyone talking about how hot or cold it is. Meanwhile, the house on the beach sits empty now. Esti's husband Norm says that with the global warming a house by the beach—not a good idea. But to walk out your door and smell the ocean, to hear it? To feel the sand between your toes? And the sun, who knew it was poison?

I look for the paper where I wrote down all the information I found for the doctor. Dermatologist. Sure, from all that sun I can always use a skin exam. He's highly recommended, lots of stars. Not so handsome in the picture, but not bad. One look at Maxie is all he'll need.

"Ma'am," Mr. Canada says. "We're here."

So fast? I need to let Maxie know, but my phone is *shtupped* in my sweater under the seatbelt. What's he doing? Getting out of the car again. He brings my walker to the door.

"Is anyone meeting you?" he asks.

"It's none of your business." I tell him. "It's your service, never they give an exact time. Impossible to let people know when to expect you." *Feh,* all of sudden, my stomach hurts, my hands shake. "My granddaughter works here. Five minutes, she'll be in the lobby."

He holds out his arm. "Where I'm from it would be rude to leave an old gran." He stops, like he's searching for the right word "A woman alone."

"Yeah, yeah," I pull myself together. I let him take me to my walker. The shaking stops, a little. Not from his help, from me telling myself to make it stop. "I read how in your country—Canadians—always polite. Very nice. Very nice. But tell me, do all the men go around in short pants?"

"That's just me," he says, walking slowly. "I like to feel the elements."

"Elements you need to feel? What elements? And then why you have on a hat? The breeze in your hair makes sense. But what, you need your legs to have ventilation?"

He's laughing as we reach the automatic front doors of the hospital. "You're meeting your granddaughter here?"

"Any minute she'll be here."

His eyebrows go up and down like he's not believing me and while I'm busy with the phone calling Maxie, all the time his eyes are watching.

"You don't have other people you need to drive somewhere?"

"None of your business."

Chutzpah!

Thank God I see Maxie finally. Now I can say thank you, you can leave, to this *Budinski* driver.

Maxie looks between me and the driver. "Do I know you?" she says to him. "You look so familiar—from campus?" She puts out her hand to him, looking at him like she's confused. "Why are you here with my grandmother? Is everything all right?"

He says back to her, with a big surprised smile. "*Your* grandmother? I drive for Access-A-Ride. She was my ride."

She looks at this lanyard he wears around his neck, which I see is a badge of some kind.

He sees where she's looking. "Yeah, I'm an adjunct," he shrugs. "Not really a livable wage. This helps." He holds up his hands, like to catch something in the air. "It's flexible. Leaves me time for my art."

Maxie so polite. "I'm sorry, I didn't get your name."

His name? Who cares? All this conversation, now he'll expect a tip.

"T-Jam. T-Jam Bin Naumann," this driver says.

Newman? Such a normal name. The rest of it, whatever he said, that fits, makes more sense. Not that any of anything is making sense. Especially how Maxie is looking at his eyes and lashes and eyebrows.

"Maxine Jacobson. Maxie. I'm, uh—in the bio department here."

"Cool." he smiles—now he flashes her the white shiny teeth. "Biology, that's important. It's all important."

I make like a cough. Neither of them notice. I cough again.

"Well, thanks for taking care of my grandmother."

She thanks him? For taking care from me? I asked for his help? I even needed it? It's his job. It's that California thing, everyone like in some fairyland with pretend please and thank yous.

Maxie turns to me. Finally. "Which doctor are you seeing?" She points toward the directory sign in front of the elevators.

"Maxine—Doctor Jacobson?"

Still he's here? No wonder nobody ever gets anywhere on time with this service. "There's this art exhibit, week after next, on Saturday? On campus—showcasing emerging artists? I've got a few pieces—and there'll be an introductory presentation about the art department. Wanna come?"

Max stops, her hand on my walker. She's smiling. "I'm not a doctor. Not yet anyway. And I'm not studying medicine, I'm in research." From this answer she gives him, I can tell she likes that he called her doctor. Sure enough now she says, "Next weekend?" She shrugs, but her body is happy. "Yeah, sure, why not?"

Why not? A hundred good reasons I can give her. He's reason number one.

"Good," he says, smiling. "I'll see you there. Then he says to me, "And you take care, Mrs. Maxine Jacobson's grandma."

What? What did he just call me? With his snow white teeth and those hot desert eyes.

She's watching him walk away.

"Come on," I tell her. "We'll be late already."

CHAPTER TWELVE

Goldie

THIS IS A DOCTOR'S OFFICE? It's more like a beauty parlor. The walls all papered in some soft color, and everywhere brochures of models with beautiful skin. Even a TV screen going non-stop, showing before and after pictures, everybody getting treatments. Some pictures, not even of the skin, but something to cut away fat from the belly. I thought I was seeing a real doctor. And the office is full of teenage girls.

Why are they all here, I ask Maxie. She tells me it's for acne. What *acne*, one girl is more beautiful than the next, a few pimples, so what. You outgrow it is all. They sit with their phones, chewing gum, in their cute school uniforms, and their mothers—these are *mothers*? They look like teenagers themselves. I look again at all the pictures. What's wrong with everybody—they can't just be?

There are a few older people like myself. Most of them with big bandages on parts of their bodies. *Vey is Mir*. And behind a glass partition I see a whole store selling ointments, and I hear the receptionist where you check in asking if anyone wants this or that cream. What kind of doctor's office sells beauty creams?

"For this you go to medical school?" I ask Maxie.

Maxie turns the pages of a magazine. "It's a grind, Safta. After so many all-nighters and intense rotations, a lot of people get burned out. Maybe they see dermatology as an easier way to go. I don't think you get called in for emergency life and death surgeries for skin conditions."

She looks up and her eyes take in the whole waiting room. She lowers her voice. "But it's real, these guys probably had some cancers removed. It's a serious procedure. But all the cosmetic stuff, that's probably where the real money comes from."

The nurse calls my name, and I see that her skin, too, is smooth like glass. She must get a discount for all the procedures. I don't think this is the right guy for Maxie.

When we get up I see what Maxie is wearing. What with that driver and the excitement of the office, I didn't pay attention until now. This is what she wears to work? For this she also went to school all those years, and so expensive, too? She looks still like a college student. Even then, I didn't like it, but she was in school. Now she's a professional, almost a PhD and she wears the dungarees and sneakers? Good this doctor isn't for her. I'll make sure she's fixed up nice for the next one.

"Maxie," I ask. "This is how you dress for work?"

"It's a lab, Safta. I wear a lab coat all day. It's not like working in an office."

I think about this. "Still, how do they know you from the students? You're like in charge, right?"

"No. Not at all. Besides, we dress the way we want. And this is how I want to dress."

Now, if this was Tamar, I'd tell her off. But this is Maxie. Still I'm the grandmother. "Maxie," I say. "I think you should dress a little nicer, it's the best way to get noticed."

"Not for the right reasons," she says, laughing.

At least the examination room looks like it should. After that waiting room, I was already expecting a chair like in a salon, but there's the table with the paper on the top, with the scale in the corner, the counters with the cotton balls in a jar and the gloves in a box, the sink in the middle. So I'm at last relaxed that it's a real doctor's office and I'm not just wasting time.

And he acts like a real doctor, too, making us wait such a long time before he can see us. Why bother making me get *ganz nakadik* to sit waiting in the cold room? The nurse came in and asked me questions, and then nothing. They didn't even weigh me or take my temperature. Just she gave me one of those gowns that never close and told me to get all undressed.

"You can keep on your underwear." She told me. Good I wore new bloomers. I always do when I go to a doctor.

At last, a gentle knock on the door, and even though I already made up my mind, I tell Maxie to fix her hair. She looks at me like I'm crazy, but she runs her hands through her long curls as I tell him to come in.

He's better than the picture, but something's not right. It's his face. Maybe from studying all the brochures from all the time we've been waiting; I can see that he has no lines. Not a single crease around his brows or mouth. And his forehead, too. He does the beauty treatments on himself? I think maybe he even tweezes his eyebrows. *Feh.* But on his finger I see, while he's putting on a pair of gloves, a wedding ring. This didn't show up in my Facebook research. *Feh,* who cares?

He's professional, I'm not saying not. He looks very closely at all my spots with these big glasses with special lenses, explaining this and that to me and Maxie. He stops at one for a long time and says they need to do a biopsy. A biopsy?

"Nothing too serious," he says. "Not life threatening, but we want to check it out and take care of it."

"I'm going to look like those people out there with the bandages?" I ask.

The spot he's looking at so much is right on my nose, a little scab I noticed a while ago. "We'll see. For now, we need to make a small cut and look at it under the microscope."

He brings back the nurse who takes pictures of my face, and I think maybe this is a trick to put me on the wall, with all the other before and after shots. "I'm going to be on the wall?" I point, and the nurse and doctor look at each other.

"No, Safta." Maxie says, patting my hand. Normally I get the willies when people touch me, all the hugging and kissing, not for me, but from Maxie it feels nice. "That's for the cosmetic stuff they do." She shrugs at the doctor, like she's saying she's sorry. "This is a real skin problem."

"I have a real problem?"

"No, Safta, nothing that we didn't catch in time. This is good, it was smart of you to come here."

Now the doctor is telling me he'll call me with the results, and we'll see what happens next. If there was gonna be a next visit, this wasn't the way it was supposed to happen. It was supposed to be for Maxie. That wedding ring, probably another guy.

Nowadays, anything goes.

CHAPTER THIRTEEN

Goldie

MAXIE'S BUSY WITH HER PHONE the whole time we're eating lunch, looking all happy, laughing to herself, pushing her finger every which way. I ask her, like innocent, the driver, what a character, no? The way he dressed, like out of the Goodwill bin. And those socks and sandals? At least we didn't have to see his dirty feet. And so pushy? The way he came inside and waited, then talked to you.

She says, "Look, I just looked him up—that exhibit he was talking about. I knew I recognized him—he does these—here, look. He's good."

She shows me some screen that I would need a magnifying glass to see it. All I can tell is that she's excited.

"Amazing, how everyone nowadays can do everything. Even go to fancy schools to make drawings. I thought in college you learned to make a living, have a profession. Studying to draw, for this you need a degree?"

"Really, Safta? You can't ever consider art," She stuffs the phone into her bag. Such a nice big bag, sitting here in this restaurant, so comfortable in her life. "Oh, forget it. Just forget I said anything."

Forget. My granddaughter whose life is a fairy tale tells me to forget?

Never.

Wismar, Germany. 1938

I WATCHED FROM BEHIND THE CURTAIN.

At first, they stopped when they walked past my building. Gretchen's long ponytail swinging and Dorli's short curls spilling out from the barrettes she thinks can control them. I start to lift my arm, to wave, but something, like a string pulling from inside, forces me to keep my arm at my side. I step back from the window instead, so I'm behind the wall but still able to see out the curtain.

We locked our pinkies, we kissed our hands. The three of us, until forever. In forever, I'm erased. But we locked pinkies. We made a promise.

I sneak down to the street. I yank the yellow star from my coat, and let it fall from my hand. The wind picks it up and just like that, it's gone. Only me, not the nothing with the yellow star—me. I'm here. Dorli's face turns up, watching the yellow star fly in the wind. I step toward her. Smile. Another step. My smile is so hard it feels like my face is splitting in half.

"Dorli?" My voice a whisper, strange. "*Eins zwei drei.*" The words hang empty in the gray street. The quiet stretching out while I wait.

Her arm goes up.

And I exhale, I let my body go soft while I pull my arm out, too, to meet hers. Her arm continues to go up. Her eyes like blue ice.

Her arm stands straight up and out. My hand closes into a fist while hers is open and flat, pointing forward. I look straight into her eyes, daring her to say the name that goes with this filthy salute. She looks away first. She doesn't have the guts—not to my face. Gretchen standing next to her, watching from me to her, finally her ponytail still. Dorli drops her arm from that terrible salute to grab Gretchen and turns away. Gretchen almost running to keep up with Dorli's march. In another life, before this forever, it would even be funny.

Dorli's voice, now when she's away from me it's loud and strong. "*Eins, zwei.*" One, two. No *drei*. No three. No me.

The street all quiet. Not a sound. Who knows, maybe someone somewhere like me, watching from behind a curtain. A few meters away, pressed into a corner where the brick wall meets the sidewalk, something small and yellow flickers. I go, my feet heavy and slow. I lift the star from the pavement and brush the dirt from it. I fold it and put it in my pocket. I'll sew it back on, with Mama. Back inside our house.

CHAPTER FOURTEEN

Goldie

2017

All Maxie's big ideas, equality, this life matters, that life matters. Her life matters, that's all. I blame her mother for this. Also I blame California. Me, I live in the real world.

1970

From a small spark can start a five-alarm fire. Afterwards, no matter how much you clean and paint, always you can smell the ruins. Our house with the mezuzahs all over the doors, and That Boy, with the big cross around his neck, walks—what walks—how he moves his hips and those shoulders, more like he dances—right past them. A boy with so much beautiful hair, with steamy eyes and a black ponytail, a Samson. What I want? Scissors.

Like puppies they sniff and jump around each other. Tamar says she wants to go away for a semester—to do good. Oh, the carrying on, she's going to save the world, the children, the planet. Such drama. For sure he's telling his mother the same thing. They think we were born yesterday?

I play along. "Collect oranges on a kibbutz, if you want to do good." I tell her like it's a great idea. "Feed the poor children in Israel that we're always giving money for." Those Israeli soldiers? So gorgeous—from our ashes they bloom in the desert. A miracle what we're making there. "He'll be here when you get back."

Ha. No way. Italian men, I know from the fruit store man. Always he stares when I pick the tomatoes, he comes and cuts me a piece of melon, watching while I put it in my mouth. A whole opera just to buy a salad, but his produce—much better than Waldbaums. Anyway, for sure the boy will be gone in an hour, maybe even sooner, after Tamar with her *tuchus* isn't anymore a distraction.

A few days later, all yelling, another scene.

"You don't know anything," she's carrying on like the end of the world. "You—his parents. He goes to Sicily; I go to Israel. It's all Romeo and Juliet."

So he also has a smart mother.

Immediately when she comes back from Israel, they go back together. I go to her room, and there's letters and letters he wrote her. A boy who writes letters? Of course, I read them. And the passion—from eighteen-year-old *pishers*.

It's beautiful, what he writes her. He tells her she's special. Even I blush to read some of it. And so much of it. A poet, he is. I let myself get carried away, happy that somebody loves my girl so much. But nothing good can come from this. Nothing.

How did they meet? From different worlds? Then, I read, on the bus! Every day, he and her, in their private schools, they take the city bus, she gets off at the Jewish school, and he goes to the Catholic one. And somewhere between the stops, romance?

All those sexy Italian and Irish girls in their uniforms with the plaid skirts and knee socks, and on the other side of the bus, the Jewish girls and boys, not even supposed to look at each other, never mind the Goyim. Our girls don't have uniforms, only that their skirts have to cover their knees. Elevator skirts we called them, how they'd go up and down. And the boys, with their yarmulkes, so cute. So strict, they're even supposed to start school at different times so they should be on different schedules. But the kids—they go late, they go early, nature doesn't follow school rules.

So much effort to pay for that school, to keep her safe from the outside world of public school, just she should stay with her own kind—and my Tamar, she finds this Anthony, or Salvatore, *feh*, maybe even a Christopher, on the city bus. I'm sure the Italian girls didn't like her butting in. He's a handsome boy. And her friends, they didn't warn her?

Now that I think of it, I haven't seen her with her friends so much. No Chani and Henni calling her every night. She gave up everything for this *West Side Story* in my own house?

Where was I when all this was going on right under my nose? Pregnant, that's where. I couldn't see nothing but that big belly. And the tragedy afterwards, I took my eye off the children I already had. Never you can relax. The second you get distracted, something happens. Never something good.

Always a sweet girl, bringing home cats and if we would have let her, a dog. But this she brings home, too? A Goyisha boy? No. To sit shiva? One baby I already lost, this one I'm going to throw away?

2017

My Maxie, sitting, watching me.

What do they say? Never again? Tamar all over again.

We didn't survive the Nazis for this.

From: Max Jacobson <maxj@gmail.com>
To: estia; tanij
Subject: Goldie Mandell – Dermatology debrief

Dear Mom and Esti,

I've attached copies of the biopsy report that Safta received about the spot on her nose. As the doctor suspected, it's a Basal Cell Carcinoma, but there is NOTHING TO WORRY ABOUT. These are fairly common for anyone who has fair skin and excessive sun exposure, and all those years that Safta lived on the beach are catching up with her. The good news is that it's highly treatable with a topical cream that she needs to apply twice daily for the next four weeks. She took the news very well. It was impressive, though heartbreaking in a way, watching her put daily reminders into the calendar app on her phone. She refused to let me do it for her. (I did check though, when she wasn't looking, that the reminders were actually there. They were!). She was also very careful about which of her many walker-compartments in which to store the cream, you could see her taking mental notes the whole time.

My overall impression is that she's mentally alert, but physically compromised, which we already knew. She had a lot to say (as always), about the doctor, and dermatology in general. The only surprising thing was her reaction when the doctor indicated that there was any cause for concern. Didn't her regular internist give her any indication before he referred her to dermatology? She definitely has absolutely no hypochondriac tendencies. If anything, the opposite!

Again, overall, she's pretty impressive. She got herself to the hospital with access-a-ride, which she made out to be the ordeal of the decade.

Esti: It's easy for me to just walk over to accompany her. Growing up in Cal, this is like making up for lost time. It's nice getting a chance to know her.

I think that covers it. Send me any questions you have!

Xoxoxo, M!

CHAPTER FIFTEEN

Goldie

THIS TIME I'LL GET IT RIGHT. Just I have to get Maxie in front of the right doctor. But what Maxie wore to that doctor visit. Dungarees? A nice skirt, a pair of stockings, a shoe with a little heel. She has what to show off, this girl.

When I call her I make like I need her help. I tell her, ask her, to go with me shopping, that I need new clothes. I say something or other, about all the activities at this place, how I need to dress up, how I have nothing to wear.

"Great idea," she says. "I'll pick you up and we'll take the train into the city."

The train? I wish. But not for me, not anymore, even with Maxie. She should see how slow I am, how difficult the steps? How nervous I get from all the people pushing, the doors closing so fast. "Sheyfe, let's meet there, no reason for you to come all the way here. I'll call Access-A-Ride."

The Access-A-Ride bus that pulls up crowded already like rush hour. Back and forth, in circles, an inch at a time closer to where I have to be. Finally, more than an hour, what should take a half hour—my stop, right in front of Lord and Taylor.

Maxie tells me it's closing. The city without Lord and Taylor? No more their Christmas window, so elegant? Never I shopped there, but always we went to the city, a trip with the girls, to see all the lights, the windows, the tree at Rockefeller Center.

It's a funny feeling, to miss a city, not like the city is going anywhere. Just everything in it changing.

Maxie helps me off the bus, setting up my walker. She waves at me a bunch of shopping bags. "Great sales! I picked up a few things while I was waiting."

Already this bus trip worthwhile "What did you get?"

All excited, she shows me another blue shirt, another pair of jeans. A pair of boots like she's in the army.

Worse even than I thought. "Maxie, my treat. I wanna buy you something pretty. More girly."

Her eyes light up. "Like you used to send to California? I loved when you sent those dresses— opening the boxes."

Sure she did. Poor girl, Tamar dressing her all the time like a little communist.

"Make me happy. Let me dress you like a little doll again."

So much fun to go through the racks, pulling out one thing after another. At these prices, more like stealing than buying. Maxie pulling things out, too. "Look at this, Safta! This would look so good on you."

A cream-colored wool pantsuit? I'm Jackie Kennedy? Katherine Hepburn? But, what can I say? It looks good. Would Harry like it? Bernice—wow, her eyes would pop from out of her face, with all that makeup. *Feh.* I need to get my head on straight. "Enough with me, your turn," I tell Maxie.

Right away she goes for the Berkeley no-style flow-y dresses like her mother wears. *Vey is mir.*

Definitely an emergency situation.

"Maybe you want a little black dress?" I ask her. "Every girl needs a little black dress. So, you know," the word comes to me, I don't know from where. "Versatile!"

"Versatile?" Maxie laughs.

"Yeah, sure. Like, Audrey Hepburn." Already I can see her, her long curly hair on top of her head, some eye-makeup, lipstick. She has on Mordy's mama's pearls, the ones I never wear. Where did Mama even come to them? Never mind, not the time to think about that. Maxie is looking interested finally in getting something nice.

"Never you go wrong with a little black dress."

Sure enough, she comes out of the dressing room—not the dress I would have picked. It's short. It's tight. It's sleeveless. It's plain. She wears it with her army boots, and over her shoulder, a bag like she's going to climb mountains. But it shows her figure. Her beautiful face.

We got the bait, just we need to hook the fish.

CHAPTER SIXTEEN

Maxie

Maxie surveyed the eyeliner over her left eye, sucked on a cotton swab, and smeared the black smudge into a wider mess. Though accidental, it looked kind of sexy. Smokey. Her green eyes peered back at her. She tried to duplicate the effect on her other eye. She pulled her hair up into a sloppy half ponytail, letting curly tendrils fall here and there. She applied lipstick, darker than any red she'd ever tried before. She finished by putting on her large silver hoop earrings.

She barely had to squeeze into that tight black dress. Damn but those five pounds had just melted off with Daniel's departure. She wrapped a scarf around her neck, the way she'd studied in a YouTube video, letting it hang over the clingy sleeveless top of the dress. It didn't look quite the way it had on the model, but standing tall in front of her mirror, Maxie had the shoulders to pull it off.

So there, Daniel Wolinsky. How good do I look now?

She fastened her belt, slung low on her hips, slipped into her boots, and grabbed her bag.

The large hall was less than half full. Well, an art exhibit showcasing different mediums depicting the journey through life—whatever that meant—versus frat parties during the doldrums of mid-semester? Maxie slid into a middle row aisle seat, tugging at her raised hemline. Back in her apartment, it looked female-warrior chic, but in this bleak space she feels like an undergrad freshman during those heady early weeks of her first fall semester. All unsettled and highly nettled. That was Maxie these days. A little black dress—bought by her grandmother, no less—to an art lecture/exhibit.

Her mother would laugh out loud. "You know your father and I met at a teach-in?"

Of course, they had. Berkeley in its heyday. Her mom probably wore a long flowing skirt and flowers in her hair. She still did. Probably why Maxie was in a little black dress.

Somebody sat in the seat next to hers. "Hi! You're Maxine Jacobson, aren't you?"

Maxie turned to a tall redheaded girl she maybe recognized, seen running around with her hair flying, her lab coat trailing behind her. With her freckled face and too big mouth, she had a Pippi Longstocking vibe, but with Harry Potter glasses. Maxie held out her hand.

"Yes. Hi. Maxie. Maxie Jacobson."

"I know! I read your work on—" She took Maxie's hand into her own, shaking vigorously. "Jessica Schwartz. Jessie, please. There's me, Jessie, and there's Jessica and JessQ—her last name's Quinn; you have to tell the Jessicas apart." She turned bright red. She looked suddenly shy—then horrified, her hand went to her mouth. It was like watching one of those video face morphs.

"I'm babbling. I'm a grad student. First year. I, you, I can't believe I'm working in the same space as you." She turned redder. "I just mean, nothing creepy. Just, when I was applying, you were like, I read *everything* you wrote, and here you are. I'm like, wow. Thanks. I mean," her voice trailed off, her face as bright as her hair. And her red framed Harry Potter glasses.

Maxie didn't know if she wanted to hug this girl or strangle her. It's not like she was a senior citizen, except, well. Except. That qualifying exam loomed so large; Maxie remembered being on the other side of it. Oh, well.

"C'mon, Jessie. Tell me, what are you working on? Grad school, it's a rush, right? Intense?"

"T-Jam is so inspirational." Jessie answered, apropos of nothing, her mouth slightly open, her voice breathy.

Maxie was starting to wonder if this girl was quite right in the head when Jessie pointed at the stage. It was the driver, up at the podium. Maxie knew he'd be here, known it when she chose this dress, but didn't expect—he sat behind a little placard with his name and his department on it.

"This is incredibly important to him," Jessie offered with much authority. "Wait 'til you hear him; he's so passionate. He's the main reason I joined the interdepartmental committee for arts and sciences."

Were they together? This uber-earnest girl and the intriguing oddly appealing artist/driver with the deep dimples and complicated name.

Jessie leaned in, becoming conspiratorial. "It's tough for him. He's, you know, committed to his work? He has a following, but he can be—well, some people think he's sanctimonious. Not that I think that. No. I really don't know what his story is." Clearly she'd spent a fair bit of time trying to figure it out. "He's got some horrific backstory that he never talks about. He does all these odd jobs, too. For the money, but also for his art? He's like—I don't know. But he's brilliant. Just, wait, you'll see."

Maxie did see. And hear. She listened to every word he said, rising with everyone else in a standing ovation when he was done. She walked around the room, searching for his work on the walls. Looking around, she'd never felt so old and so conventional. And so overdressed.

The room was thinning out, with a small circle still gathered around the illustrious T-Jam Bin Naumann. Maxie slipped out the side exit. At least there was still time to get to the lab and do something worthwhile.

CHAPTER SEVENTEEN

Goldie

1971

It was to save her.

I quick go through the whole pile again. Finally, one, at the very start, one of the envelopes has a printed return label. The name, Romano. What else? The address—I need to find a map, I don't know the Italian neighborhoods. Could be Bensonhurst, or near the Verrazano Bridge, Bay Ridge. For this, I cross lines. This one I can take care of. This one I'm keeping.

One quick call to 411 and I have a phone number.

I get there a half hour early but wait outside because—I don't know why. Just I'm not ready yet to walk in. Not five minutes later, but also early for our appointment, a lady marches right into the coffee shop where we agreed to meet, like she owns the place. She's wearing pants with high heels and a fancy leather jacket. Her hair looks like she just came from the beauty parlor. Too much. I'm glad I decided to put on a nice dress, nothing fancy, but good enough. My shoes are old, so is my coat, but what? I don't have to get so dressed up to go to a coffee shop on Avenue U in middle of a weekday afternoon.

I remind myself to be nice, to remember that she and I have to be partners. She's not the enemy. She's a mother, like me. I smooth down my coat and cross the street.

"Mrs. Romano?" I go straight to her table and ask. She's a very pretty woman, in the Italian style of pretty. Sophia Loren-like. But not gorgeous. And too much makeup.

"Toni," She tells me. "And you're Mrs. Mandell?"

"Goldie," I tell her. Really, I want to tell her she can call me Mrs. Mandell. With her I'm not looking for a friendship.

She waves her hand for the waitress, like she's the big *macher* here. "Just a cup of coffee for me." Then she looks at me all of sudden concerned. "Is that all right? Did you want to order lunch?"

"No, no, that's perfect. Two coffees." I say to the waitress. Really, I like a piece of cake, a Danish with my coffee, a toasted bagel and butter. No wonder this Toni is so skinny. Probably all day she starves herself, then at night drinks wine with her husband. They do that, the Italians.

"So," I say to her.

"Yes," she says to me. Her nails are very long and red. Obviously she doesn't spend a lot of time in the kitchen.

"Thank you for meeting me. I think we have what to discuss." I smile at her, I hope it's a smile, but how I'm feeling, who knows?

"That's for sure," she says, and she gives me a big smile. She's happy about this thing with her boy and my Tamar?

"Listen," she says. "I'll cut to the chase. I don't mean to get out of line, and I'm speaking from my heart." At this she passes her long nails across her chest. "Your daughter is a lovely girl. Lovely. They're good kids. Gorgeous kids." She smiles at me like she's telling me something I don't know. "But who are we kidding here? Culturally, they're miles apart. Miles apart." She waves her hands wide, like to show how far apart they can go.

"You're absolutely right." I tell her, glad we're not going to pretend to each other. "It can never happen."

"Never."

I get the feeling this is a reasonable person with whom I can talk frankly. "So you have a plan?"

"We tried with Sicily already." She gives me a look that I feel is respectful. "And I know you sent yours to Israel." She makes the sign of the cross–*vey is mir!*–"The holy land."

"A lot of good it did us."

She nods.

"So what's gonna be?" I ask her.

"Look," she says to me. "My Junior—" That's his name, Junior? No wonder I couldn't remember it. It's a rank, not a name. Anyway, she goes on. "He's a great kid. Not really much of a student though. Never had to be, he was always going to go into the Business."

I know better than to ask what business. This is when I'd be making the sign of the cross if we had one.

"That's another reason we sent him to Sicily, to get a feel for his heritage. We're in wines."

"Very nice," I say. I don't know one wine from the next, only the Kiddush wine on Shabbas. I like a nice Cherry Heering once in a while, for a *l'chaim*, which for sure this isn't. "But," I say, "what does any of this have to do with our situation?"

"So it's not for me to say, but your girl, your people, they're good students. Education, right? It's a big deal."

It's how you get ahead in this world. Everyone knows that. At least it is if you don't have a "business" to rely on. And our business? No reliable goldmine there.

"So," she continues. "Tamar was at our house one night."

She was at their house? What can Tamar possibly have to say to them, eating spaghetti at a red and white-checkered tablecloth?

"And the way she talks and thinks. So insightful." Tamar is insightful? I never heard this word. "She could be anything, girls today."

"Thank you," I say to her. "We never had—Junior to eat by us, but I'm sure he's also very special."

She waves her hand at me like I'm missing the point.

"What I'm getting at," she says, "is why should she go to Brooklyn College? She could apply to a better school, get the best education she deserves."

Nothing wrong with Brooklyn College, all the kids in the neighborhood go there, they do just fine. Tamar asked to go away to college, not like we could afford it, but also, not safe. Who goes away to college? I asked her. The Goyim? The fancy people on the Upper West Side? Besides, a girl. She doesn't need so much that education, it's not like she'll be a doctor or lawyer. How she carried on. Look, I told her, if you want to be a doctor or lawyer, lots of them started in Brooklyn College, too.

"We should send our daughter from home to keep her away from your son?"

She holds up her hands like to show me she's not fighting. Even she reaches across the table to put her hand on top of mine, like we're best friends. *Feh*. I slide my hand out to drink my coffee. Even I don't taste it I can tell, it's terrible coffee. "Look, Junior isn't college material. Your girl is. What other options do we have? Do you have any ideas? I'll listen."

What am I gonna say? If I had ideas, I wouldn't be here. If she had the girl, she could send her to a convent. We don't have such a *mishegas,* locking our girls up. And really, I don't want to lock Tamar up, I want she should be happy, with the right kind of boy. I keep hoping I'll wake up from this nightmare, but it keeps going.

Going to school, it's not such a terrible idea, a better class of people she'd meet. But impossible. Who are we to even think about it? But Tamar always she had the good grades and the curiosity, asking all the time questions. Even her school contacted us to tell us her scores were "exceptional."

"It wouldn't have to be far away," Toni is still talking. "Once she's in that environment, with all those smart kids? My Jewish friends—" She looks me straight in the eye now. "I have a few. They have nice lives, married to professionals they met in college. Believe me, your daughter and my son will fall apart."

"It's true, she has the grades to do anything. But it's not for you to tell me where my daughter should go."

I'm embarrassed to tell her that we could never even consider it. Esti, so musical, should have had piano lessons. I'm sure this Toni never had to choose between a movie on Saturday night and breakfast on Sunday morning. Still, we did good by our girls. Brooklyn College is still college. Better than anything Mordy and me ever had.

"Our daughter always had everything she needed." I need to take this conversation back. This lady is like a runaway train.

"Look, Goldie. We don't want to fight with them. We have to let them think it's their idea. Wouldn't Tamar love a chance at a great school?"

"Look, Toni," I imitate her. "We come from different worlds. Going to a fancy school is not—is not—it's not something we could ever consider."

"Why not?" she says. "I'm sure there are programs, scholarships. Just think about it."

How I fought with Poppa to even take a few classes at night, and my girl should go to a hoity-toity sleep-away college? Impossible.

"Listen, honey, it's a win-win. You have to think creatively. Overcome the obstacles. It can be arranged."

Honey? Again with her hand over mine.

"We can make this happen." She gives me a deep look. "We really can." The hand on top of mine, the diamond on it reaches all the way to her knuckle.

Overcome, arranged, make it happen. The business.

"Toni," I say. "My husband is a very religious man, pious even. Never he accepts things, never he makes promises he can't keep. He's his own person. And he's very proud."

Toni smiles. "I see where Tamar gets her smarts from, Goldie. This can be our secret, right?" Those long red nails, and the eyes with all the makeup. Like a spider, she's spinning her web.

"I'm not agreeing to anything, Toni. It's an interesting suggestion, sure. But secrets. And lies. I'm not comfortable with any of this."

"Who gets hurt? Your daughter gets the education she deserves, maybe even the man of your dreams." Again that stare from her deep-set eyes. "Why should some people have so much more than others?"

CHAPTER EIGHTEEN

Maxie

From: T-Jam Bin Naumann <BinNaumanntj@columbia.edu>
To: jacobsonm@columbia.edu
Subject: Work proposal

Dr. J,

Saw you at the gig on Saturday night but you vanished before we could connect. I'd appreciate your biologist perspective on the life-cycle art. And, there's another – more immediate idea I'd like to run by you.

Coffee, lunch?
Looking forward to it,
TJ

Maxie's fingers hovered over the keyboard. What insights could she offer about his art? She wasn't even clear what—where—the intersection was—other than that she studied the human body. A small piece of it. Any data she'd provide she'll have gotten from the Internet, which he could do as well. What did he really want? Cool guys like him didn't need to make excuses. And he was cool. Too cool for her. Walking chill. Way, way out of her, anyone's league. A league of his own.

She looked around, the coast was clear. She typed his name into the browser search bar. Again. Studied his face in the photograph.

Reread the interview. Didn't learn anything new this time around. Was Jam short for Jamal? Bin Naumann. Maxie looked that up. *Son of a new man? Bin, Arabic. Naumann – German spelling. New man.*

She shut down the page. Took a loop around the lab. Checked out snacks in the coffee area, stopped to look over her samples. Which was pointless. The tests would still run for another hour. A bathroom break.

"Dr. Jacobson? Dr. J?" A male voice reverberated down the long corridor, its cadence the slightest bit off, musical almost. Maxie smiled. Dr. J. He'd already elevated her cool quotient. She turned around.

Today his pants reached the tops of his ankles. Almost. They were paint smeared, as was his shirt. And he still had on socks and sandals. Birkenstocks. It had been a long time since Maxie and her friends tossed Frisbees on the Berkeley campus trying to pass as underclassmen. The look was familiar and timeless. Just out of time—and place—here. Still, something about his studied dishabille stirred something warm in her. She couldn't put her finger on it. It felt—soothing. Affected, sure. But—her mother. Fuck. He reminded her of her mother.

Except. Damn, he was cute.

Maxie ran her hand to her head, doing a quick mental inventory. Her hair, the sloppy bun, her face, blotches on full display, her lab coat, pens in her chest pocket. Good. All good. This was how she should appear.

"I just got your email." She said when they were within speaking distance. "I guess this is as good a time as any? What did you want to talk about?"

Nice Maxie. Taking control but also making it easy for him, as if his being in her building wasn't indication enough that he'd come looking for her.

He bounced on the balls of his feet, lifted his hand to massage his neck, turning his head right and left, releasing little hints of paint and oil with every move. Maxie's reaction was surprising and immediate, charged, her skin releasing reciprocal—what? Wafts of Oil of Olay body wash?

They pushed out into the sunlight, T-Jam—she so wanted to ask what the T was all about— matching his long-legged stride to her shorter one. He lifted his face, inhaling deeply, running his hands through his unruly hair, expanding it so it looked like some deranged fishing net. His eyes were large and expressive when he started to speak.

"Your grandmother. She's perfect."

"What?" Maxie stopped in her tracks.

"Her face. Her hands. Her posture. Her fucking attitude. She's great."

"Thank you?"

"Seriously. She's—listen. I want to draw her. Would she sit for me?" He shook his head. "Never mind. Of course she won't. But she's so rich. I'm working on this installation. Big." He spread his arms. "To be displayed throughout the campus. Depicting time. The ravages of time. Different mediums. Clay, oil. On the planet, the environment—us—as a species. I've been trying to find an older woman, the right one. And your grandmother, there's so much integrity in her face. And compassion."

Maybe he was a stoner? "This is Goldie Mandell you're talking about?"

"Absolutely. She's the best candidate I've seen. I've love to do her nude—but yeah, that won't happen. Still, even clothed—the way she wraps herself. That's good too. Maybe better. Yeah. Definitely." He looked off into some distant location. Did he even register that Maxie was still there?

"Hey, T-Jam?" She really did have to wrap her head, then her tongue around that moniker. Seriously. "You just met her for a half hour. But she's not exactly—what in the world are you talking about?"

"Look. I get what you're trying to say, but if she got to know me, trust me, you know, maybe she'd sit for me?"

"Trust me. She won't."

"You don't know. I can be pretty persuasive."

Maxie took in the tats on his—admittedly well-defined—arms. Might work for her, but on Safta? Not a chance. She shook her head, feeling him watch her as she studied him from head to toe. He was definitely a piece of art—or work. She liked what she was seeing. Her grandmother though?

"Listen. I have a way to make this work." His eyes, you couldn't not look at him when he spoke.

"Keep talking. I'm listening." Maxie shook her head to break his hold. "But it's never gonna happen."

"She needs a driver, right? She uses that crap service, Access-A-Ride."

"Don't you work for them?"

"Yeah, that's how I know they're crap. Anyway—obviously she wants to go places on her own, right? What if, how about, I become her regular driver. Instead of calling schlep-a-ride, she can call me."

Did he just say *schlep*? With that unidentifiable accent?

"My schedule is pretty flexible, I'll get her where she needs to go. I can give you my references, my driving record? You wanna run a background check?"

"You really want this so badly?"

"Absolutely. Would you run it by her? Think about it?"

Maxie couldn't believe she was even considering this. Getting her grandmother mired into a portrait sitting? But really, what would it hurt—to quote the lady herself. It would be amazing to have a painting of her grandmother. And he was an "emerging artist." It could even be worth something someday. Safta in a museum? Well, a gallery? And then there was Access-A-Ride. It was truly awful. And the sheer entertainment value of this whole undertaking. Safta needed some stimulation in that place. Even if she was only gonna say no to it, she'd talk about it forever.

No. The mere idea was beyond ludicrous. Besides, no way Safta would ever get past the hair, never mind the tats.

But those dimples.

"All right." Maxie made a point of sighing audibly. "I'll think about it." She would? "But, if, and it's a big if, I don't want this to be weird. So I'd pay you for driving. Like a real job. Otherwise, there's all this obligation and expectation, and I'm fairly—no, absolutely—certain that you're never gonna get her to sit for you."

"Great. That's great. Perfect. Any advice on how to win her over?"

Hadn't he heard what she just—and already regretted—saying? But those dimples. The openness in his eyes. This guy wore it all on the outside. Under all the—"Yeah. Clean up. Smooth down your hair. Wear a long-sleeved shirt." Maxie pointed. "She won't appreciate your skin art. Put on long pants." She shrugged. "She has her opinions."

Did he already look like he was regretting his offer? He should.

"Sleep on it?" Maxie offered. "It's really a long shot."

Nope, she'd misread him. He lit up like a pinball machine. "Great. Got it. I dress like a Republican. No need to think about it. We're square?" He reached out his hand to shake hers. "Figure $25 a ride one way to or from the city. And tolls separate."

That came out fast. And was hella more than Access-A-Ride.

"Make it $25 round trip. Tolls included."

"Deal." The hand shot out again. This time Maxie took it. It was big. Warm and calloused. Rough. His fingernails were trimmed into neat lines, but his stained fingertips betrayed him.

"No promises," Maxie promised.

CHAPTER NINETEEN

Goldie

Time to go downstairs and have not-hot-enough coffee with the others. Read the newspaper. See what activities, what lectures they're having today. Anyway, there, the blue sweater with the black slacks, that looks nice. The shoes with the Velcro straps that Esti bought for me. Where's that other thing she bought me, that contraption for putting on socks? Amazing, the things they make now. I just need to put the sock over the tube thing, stick my foot in the other side, pull the pole. One, two. Again. One, two, three, bend, reach, pull. One more time. There. I'm all *fa'shvitzed* and still I have the next foot to do. Wait. *Feh.* The sock is hanging out over my toes, all limp and loose like, like those birth control things. Oy! How Mordy hated those things, all slimy, so embarrassing. But after that last pregnancy, that disaster, no taking chances.

Just putting on a sock comes to this?

Now the cream for my nose. Everyday Esti calls to remind me. I tell her, I know, it's in my phone. She listens? At this rate, breakfast downstairs will be lunch.

Finally, I'm in the elevator. Only one other person, a miracle. Or that's how late I am. This other lady, she has strange red hair. Like really red. Like Christmas card red. Nail polish red.

It takes all kinds.

And there's Harry, waving me over. And there's Bernice, watching. There's an excitement, like a buzzing around all the tables—never a good sign. Usually means an ambulance, but I quick look around and don't see any paramedics or anything.

"What's going on, all the excitement?" I ask Harry.

"They just announced, a trip."

"So what?" Always they arrange trips to the shopping mall, sometimes a museum. But not like the big museums in the city, only small ones, nearby.

"Atlantic City!" Harry sounds all excited. "They hired a bus. First come, first serve. Goldie, you weren't here, but I put your name down. It's a two-and-a-half hour bus ride, not so bad, but you have to be ready early."

He looks at me when he says this, and I know he's thinking how I'm always late every morning. It's the socks, the pills, the cream, I want to tell him. Not me. Atlantic City, for this I can set my alarm. Maybe if I shower at night, I'll sleep with my socks on, save time in the morning. The pills I'll still need to take in the right order, but other arrangements I can make. But two hours on a bus?

"A luxury bus." Harry is still talking. "Plush seats, legroom. *Bathrooms.*" This, the most important detail. "Where they put the suitcases, they said they can fit our walkers. That's why the space is limited." He looks at me, his face creased with worry. "That's why I signed you up Goldie; I didn't want you to miss it."

"Thanks, Harry. Really, I mean it. Thanks for thinking of me."

His face lightens up. "And get this, vouchers too. For lunch *and* the slot machines." He looks like he's ten, no twenty years younger. Even his voice sounds more alive.

"The tables, Goldie. Blackjack. I love the tables." Then he looks down. Fast. "Just for fun. A little fun."

GET THIS. EVERY NIGHT NOW, instead of the movie, it's Harry, Joe, Arnie and Sam, and can you believe—Bernice, Charlotte, and me, playing cards. Like we're practicing for Atlantic City. I have to give it to her; Bernice isn't half bad. Charlotte you can read like a book, and in middle of everything she gets confused, asks questions. I think they're gonna kick her out of the game, but Sam, all of a sudden, he's sitting next to her, laughing, explaining. Soon they're walking around all day, every day, holding hands. Ridiculous.

But, all this excitement, this practice? At first, it was great. Fun. Something to look forward to. But Harry takes it too seriously. He focuses. He pays attention. He has experience. When he's winning big, well, *for us* big, but the most we play is five dollars, he's the funny, laughing guy. But when he doesn't have good cards, when Charlotte says stupid things, then he looks like he could bite her head off. The first time, I thought he was joking, making like he was Jimmy Cagney or Edward G. Robinson—but then when he didn't smile and give a punch line before becoming himself again, this makes me pull my sweater on close, like all of a sudden the room is too cold.

So what? Just a game. Some fun. Socializing, like they say we should do. Still, I tell everyone I'm feeling tired, going up to bed. They can still play without me. Harry hardly even looks up, quick, maybe one second, less, then back to his precious cards. Five dollars and I'm a nothing?

With Mordy, I was a queen.

CHAPTER TWENTY

Goldie

TODAY'S FAKE TROUBLE, MY EARS. A runny nose. Sinus trouble. For Maxie, only the best.

Now I just need to make arrangements to get there. That Access-A-Ride nightmare bus last time? For that fake doctor—the one who wanted to operate on my feet. And that eye doctor, also not a real doctor, for sure something going on with him and that receptionist. On the way back, somebody's walker wouldn't open, another hour we were waiting. Everyone on the bus complaining. Then somebody needed a toilet. A total disaster.

Bottom line, I need a ride. He's a driver. Settled. Some *bubbameiser* that he's a big shot artist and he likes my face? Feh. Never even when I looked good did I look that good. But if he's happy to drive me privately to talk about it, what do I care what he says? He can *plaplen* all he wants, as long as he gets me where I need to go. Maxie, such a good girl, even she did all the paperwork to tell me he's safe. But that's enough. She doesn't need to make these arrangements for me. He may be safe but he's still a man what doesn't have to be so much in contact with her. I can call him myself.

Good I get his answering machine, better not to have to talk to him directly.

"Hello, hello?" I talk slow and loud after the beep, which I know to wait for. I want he should understand what I'm saying. Always the messages on my phone, I can never figure out what anyone says.

"This is Goldie Mandell. I made up my mind, it's okay that you can drive me. You remember you picked me up from the Riverdale Adult Community Residence, on the Henry Hudson Parkway, near 238th street. And you remember also, I have a walker that has to fit in the car." Stupid, I should say that. Everyone has walkers. But it's too late; you can't erase what already came from your mouth. "You took me to Columbia Presbyterian, and you waited with me inside until my granddaughter came. I never asked you to wait, it was your idea." I don't really want to even bring this up, but this is what I'm sure he'll remember.

"Anyway, this idea that you can drive direct for me, then I won't get stuck on a bus that schleps me all around the city first, I'm willing to try it. Doesn't mean I'm agreeing to any picture. So forget about that. Just I need a ride at ten o'clock for Thursday the nineteenth. I'm giving you lots of notice." It's only Monday the second. "My appointment is for eleven o'clock. But I need you to confirm for me that you received this message, because otherwise I'll need to leave earlier if I have to call that Access-A-Ride instead. So you call me back, soon, because they make you schedule these rides with two days in advance notice. See, I'm giving you two weeks. You should call me back, at this number, 917-355-8765. Again. 917-355-8765." I really stretch this out, he should get it right. "You have to let me know. Okay, that's all I have to say. Thank you. Good-bye. Goldie Mandell. Don't forget you need to call me back. Goldie Mandell. 917-355-8765. Thank you. Goodbye. Goldie. Mandell."

And now I need to lie down.

But the elevator, going up and down, people rolling their walkers through the hallway. And now the phone. Better I should remove my hearing aids before I try to take a nap.

Something in his voice, the funny way he speaks? No, not that. Something else, something I recognize, but what can I recognize from his voice? "Mrs. Goldie Mandell, this is T-Jam Bin Naumann returning your call as requested. It will be my great pleasure to fetch you at ten o'clock on Thursday the nineteenth, to drive you to your appointment at Columbia Presbyterian. Regards, T-Jam Bin Naumann."

Again, I listen to his message and then I hear it. *Feh,* this driver. His voice is smiling.

Chapter Twenty-one

Maxie

Maxie slipped in the side door. She wasn't late, Maxie was never late. But when she'd strode directly into the main sanctuary, she'd been directed by a prayer-shawled man, not discourteously, but with some firmness, toward this side alcove. Oh, of course. The women's section. The segregation of women and men in synagogues. They still did that? Apparently. They did a lot of things on the East Coast that Maxie had never seen back home. The room had a good crowd, for a weekday morning. That was another thing. The law stated it had to be exactly eight days after the baby was born. Who was counting? Did it really have to be done—all the way in Long Island no less—on a workday morning?

This whole thing—so strange. The breathy phone call with Gina. "You get a little nuts, you know. It's all about him. I'd do anything, give up anything, I have given up everything, for now anyway. I mean, I'm sure I'll get my life back. But there'll always be a part of me now that's living outside of me. Like I have this external limb, hosted by a new being." And there'd been a pause. "I'm so glad you called. Could you, would you, I know this is barbaric but, I, I'm even embarrassed to admit this. We're having a bris for him."

A bris?

"All along we said we weren't going to do it. Oh, we'd have him circumcised in the hospital, sure. But none of that religious hocus-pocus. No way were we going to subject him to any barbaric ancient religious ritual. We weren't. My mother-in-law was absolutely green when we told her we weren't gonna do it. I was almost afraid she'd take a knife to him herself." Maxie's friend, her colleague, rushed on. "And then he was born—We, Jeremey and I, it was like, a switch flipped. We just—Jeremey's parents are arranging it all, and we let them. We let them. All the ceremony, men in their prayer shawls, my baby entering into some holy patriarchal covenant." Another pause. "We wanted, needed him to—you know? Belong? Be a part of something?"

So here Maxie was: Congregation Ahavat Shalom, sunlight filtering in through stained-glass windows, shul dust—a combination of musty books, fresh flowers and fried eggs wafting through the ventilation system from the adjacent reception room. Maxie found Gina, her former colleague, roommate and sister-in-science, behind the curtain separating the weaker sex from the exalted men. She sat in the center of the front row, surrounded by beaming matrons. The teeny orb, curved and fuzzy, pressed against her breast hardly seemed human. A white trickle slid down his puffy face, into the creases that compiled his whole. With no distinction between neck, shoulders, chest, he was all unformed round squishiness, soft and baby-smell intoxicating. Absolute power fueled by total dependency.

Maxie watched a woman who she assumed was Gina's mother-in-law take the infant away, making a big show of strapping him to some sort of satin covered cutting board. Gina sat at the edge of her seat, wan and postpartum swollen, wringing her empty hands, watching and averting her gaze simultaneously.

The room went silent, ancient murmuring, mumbling coming from behind the curtain. Gina looking terrified, straining to hear the wail of her newborn when his foreskin would be lovingly, precisely, and ruthlessly sliced off his tender tiny penis. The matrons in the room pressing handkerchiefs and tissues to moist eyes, red made-up lips and cheeks glowing, fussy dresses shimmering with anticipation. They smiled, nodding encouragement at Maxie. This, this, is what you are here to do. But Maxie wasn't on this trajectory. She lowered her hands, unaware that she had raised them to her inflamed cheeks. She stared at those previously unacknowledged but always reliable appendages as if they provided fascinating evidence that she'd chosen to overlook until this moment. Her unusually long fingers, and her somewhat curved pinky finger. They were her mother's hands. Her grandmother's mottled liver-spotted hands.

She didn't exist in a vacuum.

A blood curdling yell, so tinny yet incensed, so young, so young, filled the air. Shouts, smiles, *mazal tov*. Maxie peeked over the separating divider; the new dad slumped in a chair, his face sickly pale. The baby was rushed back to his mother's breast.

Maxie's legs and arms quivered. She reached for her jacket, a blanket to wrap around her exposed nerves. She fell back onto the hard seat and kissed the prayer book she'd been holding. Once on the left side, once on the right, then softly, closing the book and pressing her lips to the leathery front cover, noticing the gold Hebrew lettering inscribed into its tough, black surface. How did she know to do this? She squeezed her eyes shut. The smell, the taste of honey on her fingers growing stronger. She was five? Six years old? Saba Mordy holding her on his knee. Before them, an open book. Enormous with a thick black cover with gold squiggles pressed into it.

"*Bet*," Saba said, pointing to the top of the open page. Silly Saba. He was reading the wrong way. "*Bereshet*." Funny word. The pages were yellow, with the same squiggles that were on the cover, only these were heavy and black, not the blocky A B Cs Maxie already read with ease. Saba took her finger, Mr. Pointer, and held it to the top thingy covered in some goo. *Oh, goo in a book.* Not allowed. But Saba didn't care, he stuck her finger right in it, then led it to her mouth. She sucked her finger, eyes still on Saba. Her mouth filled with sweetness. Magic. Saba smiled with his eyes.

"The words of the Torah, always when you read them, so sweet. Each letter a little bit of honey. Always remember how sweet." He kissed the top of her head, then pulled out the small piece of paper where the honey had sat next to the big black letter. Sneaky!

"Watch, *Sheyfaleh*, this is how we end our study." He kissed the big book. Saba kissed a book. Once, twice, one side, then the other, then he closed it, and kissed the cover.

Exactly what Maxie had done with her organic chemistry textbook. A spontaneous reaction, but one she'd been taught by her grandfather long ago. This, this is how you close a beautiful book. With gratitude. And awe.

There's a tap, more like a poke, on her shoulder. She's led into the reception room. Balloons festoon the ceilings, bright blue centerpieces of papier-mâché rocket ships and football helmets, tables laden with bagels, lox, whitefish salad, humus, pita, and bean salads, an omelet and waffle station, and a dessert table covered with every kind of Danish, muffin, brownie, cupcake with blue icing, cheesecake and coffee crumble cake. In the center of it all an enormous challah, over which the new father, with some rabbinical assist, recites the traditional *bracha.* Tears flowing down his cheeks.

"Maxie, Maxie Jacobson. Let me get a look at you! How long since I've seen you!" Gina's mother peers at her, multiple chins bobbing. "You girls, can you believe, Gina married. With a baby? I worried about the two of you, all your convictions about the climate, and population control. Here, have a piece of challah. They say, my mother always said, the challah from a bris, it's blessed. Ha, listen to me, saying it now myself, God willing, your turn soon."

"God willing." Maxie repeats, always fond of Gina's religious family, taking the challah and kissing her cheek.

"Come, come. I want you to meet someone." With a firm grasp around Maxie's wrist, she pulls her toward an overweight woman whom Maxie had the distinct impression had been studying her. "This is my sister, Mildred."

Mildred balances a full plate in one hand and waves her other, thick, multi-braceleted arm her way. "So you're the Maxie Rachel has been telling me about. Maxie. Maxie Jacobson. So nice to finally meet you. I've heard so much about you."

Gina's mom—Rachel—cut in. "See, I told you."

"Who's this?" Another woman, older, more a human safety pin, all rounded edges covering sharp pricks inserts herself between Mildred and Mom.

"My mom," Rachel lets her in.

She peers at Maxie from too close-set eyes. "For Itzy? I don't know what you're thinking. He's a bum. She looks like a nice girl. Better for Howie, he should stop running around with those *shiksas.* Ever since he opened his own practice. Estate law. Very successful. Your Itzy? A bum." She turns back to Maxie. "Howie, he's a catch. But you, I don't even know who you are, who your family is?"

Maxie starts to sweat. She has her list. Follow the list, do the work. Achieve, succeed, progress. That was her imperative. Not this, this obligatory edict, this passing of the baton. She never signed up for this—this weighted sack her—their—even this new baby's—forebears carried for forty years in the never-ending desert, the one they all still carried. Nobody ever signed up for it though; you were born into the glorious discomfort of this shared heritage. There are no secret passwords required for belonging; nobody from the outside ever wants to join in any case. But once inherited, you spend your life proving yourself worthy of it. And responsible for safeguarding it. Against all odds. And obstacles. And ensuring its tenuous, always threatened, always cherished, perch.

And, and—always passing it along to the next generation.

Through the loud party room, the guest of honor let out a howl, a full-throated panic-sounding indignant cry, from zero to sixty in no time at all.

Oh, baby, Maxie thought. *You and me both.*

CHAPTER TWENTY-TWO

Goldie

SEVEN-THIRTY A.M., AND HERE WE ARE, the whole gang, ready. Harry's dressed up for the occasion even. Not in a suit or anything, but he took care with his appearance, a nice shirt fresh from the laundry, ironed and starched, of course the cufflinks and the watch. A silk scarf, fancy, I never saw it before. And with the pants and shirt, a black leather jacket, like some tough guy.

"Goldie, come, sit next to me. You'll be my lucky charm."

Bernice catches my eye. She rolls her eyes at Harry, and even though maybe I'm doing the same thing, at her I get angry.

Once we're all settled, Miss Perky Breasts—never I can remember her name—and never I can read the label on her sweater, so tiny the print and I don't want to stare at her chest, anyway, she hands out the vouchers, ten dollars for lunch, and twenty-five dollars for the slot machines.

Good thing there's bathrooms on the bus, everyone getting up and down the whole time. Just when you're about to fall asleep somebody bangs your shoulder. Harry is also awake, and my mind, always, before falling asleep, it rolls where it wants to go. Lately, it's very busy with Tamar.

"Harry, in your lifetime, ever you did something you wish you could take back?"

"You don't get to be our age without making some mistakes." Already, just talking to somebody, I feel calmer. Also, I like how he says our age, never asking me how old I am. When you're young, every hour has a name. Infant, toddler, preschooler, pre-K, K, youngster, tween, a whole dictionary for just the first ten years. Then, the first gray hair, the last period, and that's it, on the slow train to the last stop. They save the dessert to the end of the meal, the best part. This is what they call sweet?

"I decided a long time ago what good does it do if I sit all day feeling sorry for what already happened. Sure, I'm sorry, but life goes on, right?" Harry looks down at his cufflinks. Those cufflinks his kids gave him. Those kids who still I never saw.

"You never think about it?"

"What's there to think about? Brooding about the past doesn't solve anything." Harry's eyebrows go up and he makes a face like Groucho Marx. "What did you do Goldie? Leave breadcrumbs out on Passover?"

He's right. Spending time in the past—a waste of time. And living here in this place, it's like a reminder every day is precious. Why make it worse by—what did he call it? Brooding?

I smile at Harry. "Yeah, once I cooked a whole meat meal in the dairy pot."

As soon at the bus pulls up, Harry gets that face again, the gangster one, and heads right into the big casino, not even stopping by any of the machines.

Also, sure enough, as soon as I sit down I start to lose at the slot machines. It's like a fever, one more, one more. Every so often, just so I don't give up, the machine spits out at me a few coins. Still, I'm behind from where I started. Enough. They're not gonna get me.

I walk through the casino, pushing my walker between all the aisles of slot machines, until I get to the tables. Crazy, how they make it nighttime inside here. Everything black, red, and gold. And green. The carpeting all swirls, the seats so high. A whole adventure just climbing up there, and then what? You're stuck trying to figure out how to get back down. Such a tumult, every second the clang-clang from the machines. Like sucking you in, the darkness, the smells from the drinks, and all the perfumes and body smells even you can smell them in the freezing air conditioning.

And everything hits your eyes, shiny, glitter from the outfits the waitresses wear—more glitter than material—but the real lights so dim, so everyone is also in shadows, all funny colors from the strange lights. And how everyone walks like with purpose, talking fast, eyes moving every which way inside heads turning this way and that. Then there are the people sitting at the tables behind towers of chips all different colors, nobody looks happy. Everyone's mouths pinched into tight little lines, their eyes squinting, their hands waving, their legs jiggling under the table tops.

So many tables, with signs, two dollars, ten dollars. I see also twenty-five and fifty-dollar tables. How high does it go? There's a crowd around one table, so I can't see the sign, but I know that's where I'll find Harry, and that whatever the number is, it's high. Maybe the highest. He's sitting with a few other guys, all of them *alte kackers*, the early-bird-special crowd. These guys, including Harry, look hard, their faces all lined, their mouths pressed tight. A few ladies, too, with too much blue eye shadow and black eyeliner clumping up around their eyes. Also their lips dark red, almost black, and all pulled down by the wrinkles on either side of their mouths. Their hair all styled and stiff, and with their long fingernails tapping on the cards on the table, telling the dealer to hit them, bust, surrender, a whole language they have with gestures and eye signals, and just a few words.

There Harry is—right in there with them. His fancy jacket is hanging from the back of his chair, his shirtsleeves are rolled up, his glasses are all the way down his nose. His whole face is shiny from sweating, even with all the air conditioning. The little bit of hair he has is standing up, and he always takes such care to look nice. On the table in front of him, his pile of chips, also a half empty glass. Drinking? In middle of the day? But here there is no day.

He doesn't see me, and I don't want that he should. I stand with my walker to where I can watch their game. Everyone is tense, even I start to sweat, and I don't even know what the stakes are, only I can tell they're high.

Then, a big sigh, and one of the ladies collects all the chips, and Harry's pile is gone. He looks up and his eyes, I don't recognize them. He turns this way, then that, and I see in his hands he's holding his cufflinks. What? He's thinking to sell them? But no, he puts them in his pocket, just he rolled up his shirt sleeves.

"Harry," I call to him. "Harry."

He doesn't answer. I see his hands shaking, he pulls out his wallet, he motions to one of the glittery practically naked girls standing nearby, says something to her, hands her some money like he does this all the time; she comes back with a tray of chips.

I SHOVE MYSELF AT THE TABLE. I slam all my chips onto the green felt. "Is that enough?"

Harry pushes over at me a big pile of chips. "Use these," he says, Mr. Bigshot. Only his eyes are saying something else. "My luck has been crap."

I don't know how much he gave me. Lots of different colored coins. But such a way to speak?

The dealer nods and gives me the cards. The top one is a nine. The one under is an ace. Showing on the table I see one queen, one jack, and some other lower numbers. When it's my turn, I have to decide, another card, or stop at twenty. But an ace is also a one. So I have ten, or twenty. What are my chances of going over twenty-one? My head is hurting, but, but twenty is good, it's excellent. I have to be crazy to go on. I should go over twenty-one, though, just so he sees. He gave me the chips. I can do what I want. I don't care how angry he'll be.

I point at the cards, and say to the dealer, "Gimme one."

Everyone at the table makes a face, like I'm too stupid to know what to say. I get a two. So now I have twenty-two. Or, twelve. Again, I tell the dealer. This time a five. But I was better with the twenty. "Another." I tell the dealer.

Everyone is looking at me like I'm crazy. I have seventeen. But around me I see all high cards are out. I saw more high cards than low cards the whole time I was watching. I didn't know I was watching, but, now that I think of it, I was.

I peek at the card I got. I quick turn it down.

When everyone else agrees to no more cards, I turn over my first card: A nine, an ace. I can hear Harry breathing. Then the two, the five and the final card, the four of diamonds. Bells go off, people clap, and they push at me all the chips. *Five to one*, around me everyone is saying.

"Harry," I say, while I shove the chips into the shopping bag I always have in the compartment of my walker. "Enough, yeah? Let's get lunch. You still have that voucher?"

"Goldie, c'mon, you can't leave now. You're hot!"

"Hot? In this air-conditioning?" I see he doesn't appreciate my joke. I admit, it wasn't funny. "I got lucky is all. You leave a winner. I'm going. You can come with me, or not."

"Those were my chips. It's my money."

"I won the game."

We have a staring contest.

"Goldie, Goldie." What, he's gonna try singing to me? "When you're on a winning streak, you can't leave. Not even the dealer, never mind the table."

"What, you stick around until you lose? That makes sense? You do what you want. I'm getting lunch, and then I'm going outside. This place," I wave my hand to show him, but he's only looking at my walker like it's a treasure chest, which, now, I guess it is. "Forget that. I'm going to the boardwalk. You want money, here, take my lunch voucher." I start to rummage for it in my pocketbook, pulling out all kinds of tissues, and mints, eyeglass cases, lists, receipts, until finally I find it and push it at him. "I'm going to get French fries and cotton candy."

There, that's what you do on a sunny day at the beach. Staying inside like permanent night? *Feh.*

There's sweat all around his upper lip and even in the creases around his eyes. His nice pants are crumpled from sitting for so long, and his shirt is sticking to him under that stupid jacket.

"French fries?" He runs his hand through the few hairs that are still on his head, and that were already standing up. "Do you have any idea how much—Goldie, c'mon, one more game, we'll play only half the chips. We'll still be winners. Then we'll have steak, champagne, anything you want."

"I want French fries." I turn toward where I think outside is, but who knows, I'm all turned around in this darkness. "No winners here."

"Just a few chips," he calls from behind me.

I keep going, making like I didn't hear. This is a test. If he follows me, then maybe he's okay. But then I remember I have all the chips. Of course, he'll follow me. Some test.

"Goldie, wait, wait. I'm coming."

Sure he is. Okay, new test. If he asks for the chips, then he fails. I slow down, but don't stop entirely. He can catch up, if he wants. He puts his hand out and lands it on the handlebar of the walker.

"What, you're gonna pull out the bag?" I ask him, not even trying to make it sound like a joke.

Immediately he puts both his hands up in the air, like to surrender. He looks like I slapped him. Right in front of my eyes he crumples, his leather jacket like a silly costume for a kid on Halloween.

"Goldie."

How hard he's not looking at my walker, the compartment where the chips are. He's looking everywhere else, up, down and sideways, until finally he's able to look at me.

"Please, Goldie, I only wanted to catch up to you. I'd never—" He shakes his head, like that will erase anything? "It wasn't to, I only meant—I wanted to ask, please—can I join you for lunch?" He's getting smaller by the minute, only his eyes getting bigger.

I shrug. But when I start walking, he's next to me, and our walkers are side by side, going at the same time. Together we find the door, and the sunlight and the hot air hit so strong I have to stop and catch myself, like losing balance how fast the change is. We're both holding onto our walkers, blinking, until finally we can see what's what.

"Come," I say, leading like I know where I'm going. All you have to do is follow the noises and look where everyone else is going. Also you can follow your nose, but here, the smells are coming from everywhere. Lots and lots of food stalls, and Harry buys me those French fries I wanted. When we pass the cotton candy machine he stops again, but I just shake my head. He thinks I meant it? That stuff will kill your teeth. But when we see the ice cream vendor, I point. This time, I buy.

We find an empty bench, and Harry only looks once, but very hard, at my walker. Some Mr. Tough Guy. I make a big deal of parking my walker right in front of me, even though it blocks my view of the sea.

"So," I say, one hand on the handlebar, the other holding my cone, while I lick all around to make a smaller and smaller tower of the chocolate swirl so it won't melt down the sides.

"You're good at that," Harry says, slurping fast to catch the drips running down his cone.

"I have experience," I say. "With ice cream." I say, to get him started. But I'm not going to ask. Harry licks again at his cone, he really is bad at this. He's got a bunch of napkins squished up in his other hand, to catch the mess he's making. Amateur. He wraps the napkins around the bottom of the cone, terrible idea, he'll end up having to throw the whole thing out. He stares again at the storage compartment of my walker. "Experience." He finally says, like the word is a rock, he's carrying such weight. "I thought I could handle it. I really did." I keep licking my getting-smaller tower, almost ready to bite into the rim of the cone. I don't look up from what I'm doing. "I figured, coming with this group. I'm sorry, Goldie. I'm really sorry." He looks down at his hands, shaking his head. His face, all pale and sweaty. I go back to licking. I may as well be swallowing sand. "This, this, gambling, it ended my marriage. My kids, the college savings, I screwed up. I kept thinking I'd win it back, double it, triple it, make it right." His ice cream is a mess, he looks around, sees the garbage pail and tosses it. "Even when I won, especially when I won, I lost."

The ice cream misses the pail and lands on the boardwalk planks. I think he'll go clean it up, but right away a bunch of sea gulls come squawking and eat the whole mess.

What am I doing here? Gambling? Playing cards? Casinos?

"I'm going back to the bus." I pull myself up with the walker. Harry makes to get up, too. "No." I tell him. "I want to be by myself."

He falls back down on the bench, all of him crumpling up. "I'll see you later." He looks up, his face like a little boy's.

It's cold from the beach, but I won't take my sweater from the walker. Not with what's in it. Just I need to keep going. Keep going. One foot, one foot.

CHAPTER TWENTY-THREE

Goldie

1938

POPPA STUFFING A PAPER SACK with something from the bottom compartment of the clock. I go closer and can't believe what I see. Money. So much money. Stacks and stacks of it, like what's in the bank, not in the bottom of an old clock—in our house.

"Goldie," Poppa shows me the stuffed bag. "This is all we have in the world. Everything. You understand?"

No. But I nod anyway.

"Give me your things." He takes the nightgown and toothbrush I'm holding, the ones he just told —*ordered* me to get, and stuffs them into the sack on top of all the precious bills.

Mama finally wakes up, her face back from wherever it was. "Goldie, get a doll. Your most, the one you love the most."

It's not like I have all that many to choose from even if I still maybe play with them, secretly. It's not like they ever let me know we were so rich. I look at my shelves. There's the beautiful girl with the blond braids and glass blue eyes, stiff in her starched dress. But then I see Hount-Hount, the gray dog that *Zaidy* made for me out of his old flannel shirt. Hount-Hount's fuzzy yellowish stuffing spills out from big crooked stitches, and when I stick my nose in him, it tickles and a little

I can still smell *Zaidy.*

I grab him.

"*Gut,*" Poppa says, sticking Hount-Hount on top of the sack, where he looks out with his lopsided eyes. "Here, hold it. You understand."

Mama interrupts. "Goldie, *Leibchen.*"

Leibchen?

"They're coming. Maybe tonight." Her voice cracks, tears are in her eyes, her hands are shaking, running up and down her apron. "I'm sorry."

"Goldie, you'll hold the bag, and we'll tell them, we'll ask them, to let you leave." Poppa's voice trails off and he and Mama stare at each other. His big shoulders fall like he's a turtle who can't carry his shell anymore, and he goes back downstairs to the shop.

First a knock, gruff voices, Poppa's voice so low and whiney like if I'm seeing him with no clothes on. I grab the sack tight against my chest. Boots stomp up the steps then a wind fills the room when they throw open the door. I'm sure the bag is jumping up and down, so hard my heart is pumping. I count to myself to try to make it stop.

Next to them Poppa looks like a little box. Their faces are stone. Their hands are in fists at their sides, their boots are shiny and stiff, reaching all the way to their knees, and the creases in their uniform—they look like they would stand up even with nobody inside them.

Poppa says to the taller one and his voice is again terrible to hear, all soft and awful, like the kid in the class you don't want on your team. "My daughter, she's only nine years old. Let her go."

They'll know he's lying. I'm tall for my age. Everyone says so.

"Please, the child is so young. *Bitta.*"

I scrunch down and try to look sad and young. I stick my nose into Hount-Hount all lopsided on top of my pink nightgown sticking out from the bag, holding him tight like I'm a baby. But I peek through my eyelashes. The taller soldier moves his shoulders a little. The shorter one looks straight ahead like he didn't hear anything. The tall one looks me up and down, and I clutch the bag tighter. I begin singing to Hount-Hount, a lullaby. Not the Yiddish one Mama used to sing. A

German one. I use a baby voice.

Just then the clock chimes. It dings off the hours: three, four, five. Like every other day. I count along in my head, even while I'm singing.

"Go." It's a bark, but for sure that's what he said.

Mama rushes forward, and with a look at the soldier like she's begging permission, she turns to him her back and drapes her cape tightly across my chest. From her face her eyes shout at me all kinds of things I wish I wasn't seeing.

Outside, I never look at the shop, or up at the lace curtains covering our living room window.

Just I walk and walk and walk, then I walk some more. Past the school, the library, the shops. It's dark and cold and I keep on walking. My ears sting and my nose runs, and I keep on walking. My throat hurts and my stomach growls, and I keep on walking. Past the post office, the town hall, the big park. My fingers burn and my knees ache and I keep on walking.

2017

"HEY, LADY? YOU LOST?"

Around me, the ocean. In front of me, miles of boardwalk. That's right, Atlantic City. But what happened to all the shops, the buildings?

This man. Where did he come from? What does he want? So skinny, with a funny knit hat and baggy pants. So terrible a smell—coming from him, and closer, he's coming closer.

"Hey, lady, you okay? You lost?"

My feet start to shake. I start to feel nauseous. I'm seeing black dots.

"Lady, lady, you okay? You got somebody for me to call for you?"

Take it. Take it. My pocketbook. The stupid heavy bag. Anything. Everything. I don't want it. Any of it. The money. The soldiers. Take it. *Take it.*

CHAPTER TWENTY-FOUR

Goldie

"SHE'S WITH ME." An old man with a thick black jacket, fancy cufflinks and a glittering watch. And a walker. Harry the hero.

I'm very happy he's here. He holds my arm tight, and looks at the man, who shrugs his shoulders and backs away. Now I really look at him, he's all bent over himself. A lost person. From this I was afraid?

"Harry, where, how?"

"I've been behind you all along." He looks down. "The way you took off."

"You worry about me? I—I'm fine."

"Sure, of course. I know. But still—" He waves his hand like to show how big the beach is, how small we are.

I don't say nothing, but my whole body relaxes.

"Let's sit down for a minute, you don't look so good. Then we'll get you something to eat." Harry says, his face is all mushy, his eyes soft.

"Sure, sure. We still have the vouchers, right? They shouldn't go to waste."

Harry looks at me across the table. How I walked right past the casino? So easy, how he brought me back to the restaurant, sat us down, ordered us lunch.

"I still want to explain," he says.

No. No. No explanations. Just—just. No. That was different.

1971

In the mail came a big envelope, in the corner a fancy logo, GIRLS it says. I'm about to open it when I see it's addressed to Tamar Mandell. Maybe a coincidence that it comes in the mail now? It looks so official. That Toni woman did this? How? I start to boil water to make steam. For sure I should just open it, always I would. Now I stop to think about it? Maybe I'll put it aside so Tamar should see it right away. If it's something, I'll think about it then.

Such a bad thing? An education. It's like a loan, better. Like winning the lottery.

Even Mordy's Torah would allow it. To save a life. Not just a daughter's life. Mordy's life, too. A child marries a Goy, she's dead. You sit shiva. A piece of you dies, too. A hole that for the rest of your life can never be filled.

This I could never let happen. It's nothing to think about. So why I don't discuss this with Mordy?

Because to tell that I'm taking, considering to take, something from strangers, it's a slap in his face. In my face, too, but I can take it. To let him know that we have to put our hand out, and worse, because our own daughter doesn't know right from wrong? How she's willing to overlook all our personal suffering? This is adding insult to injury.

No. Not telling him, it's not because it's the wrong thing to do, it's because I need to protect him. And Tamar, too.

Meanwhile, there's nothing to tell. For sure I'm worrying from nothing. I don't know how long I'm standing still holding the envelope when Tamar walks in.

"Here," I give it to her. "This came for you."

The look she gives me, like I'm a monster. Then she grabs it and runs upstairs. What? I'm not supposed to go through my own mail? She comes back into the kitchen a few minutes later, still holding it, but quiet. Her face, I can't tell what she's thinking. When can I speak? When did I have to become an actor in my own house?

"Tamar, come help me with supper, if you're just hanging around. Make the salad." I reach into the refrigerator for the vegetables she should wash, this way she can't see my face.

She sighs like the weight of the world is on her shoulders.

"What are you making such noises for? Something happened in school? You have tests?" When she was little while I washed the dishes I would put her schoolbooks on the windowsill behind the sink and test her with questions. It was a nice time, like we were learning together.

"Nothing, just, you know—"

"What? What do I know?"

"It's just, you know—"

Again, this mystery talk? If I knew, I wouldn't be asking.

"Just, do you ever think, there's a whole world out there, of possibilities and opportunities. And we're in such a tiny part of it." I peek and see she's holding the paper, and again she breathes out like it's the end of the world. "Never mind, I'm not making sense."

"No, what, what? That paper you have in your hand, it says something?"

"It's nothing, never mind."

"So much nothing, then why you can't peel a cucumber without making noises like you're climbing *Har Sinai*?"

"It's nothing, I just wish they wouldn't send things like this. Here, look. A fairy-tale." She hands me the paper, and her face is like how I remember when she handed me her report cards, so full of hope, and a little afraid.

I wipe my hands before I take it.

Very fancy, with the same logo from the envelope across the top of the page. An announcement, a call for applications it says. For a select group of female students chosen from the Tri-State Area. A full scholarship to a school I never heard of, from the picture it looks like the big cathedral in the city. Very hoity-toity. All girls with plaid skirts and sweaters, carrying books and laughing across a lawn as big as Central Park. Bryn Mawr, it says. In Pennsylvania.

This Toni, she did her homework. Pennsylvania, not so far, but far enough. But so Goyish? And so fancy. This will never fly.

Tamar sighs again and leaves the paper on the table.

After supper it's only fair I call Toni. She should know what's going on here. I pull the phone cord all the way to the closet, and whisper to her that we need to meet again. *Feh.* Soon they'll give us a regular table at that diner.

"Nice letter," I tell her, pulling my gloves off when I reach our booth. "But too much."

"Nyah, Goldie. It's just right. I consulted with a family friend, a lawyer, all confidential," she tells me like it's all decided.

"You even made the stationary?"

"It's easy," she says. "Did you see, a post-office box. This is not amateur hour here, I'm working with a professional."

I'm all over-sweating, doing business with this lady. But I have to say my piece. "Tamar, she's not interested in that school. It's too much a different world for her, nothing she knows. She acts all brave and strong on the outside, but she's not ready to jump into that society."

Toni nods, thinking. "I see your point, Goldie. I for one, would also be uncomfortable. You're right, I didn't think of my market. You need to know your market, that's what my husband always says." Her fancy hairdo never moves no matter how much her head and hands do while she talks. Then she really surprises me. "Do you have any suggestions?" With her big eyes, with all the black eye makeup making big circles around them, and the blue powder on her eyelids, she blinks at me and I'm caught like in a trap.

I'm feeling a little sick. This woman is dangerous. This is me, making a deal. Sure, she says it's all a present she's giving me, us. As much for herself as for me, for Tamar. But she's not letting me just take it. This is what happens, you start something, you get in so deep.

Still, Tamar doesn't have to accept. It's only an offer. But where does this money come from? This I want to pretend I don't know.

But if it fell into the street from the sky, I wouldn't think twice and grab it with everyone else?

One of the ladies in synagogue, always bragging about her son, a big shot lawyer in the city. Never a service could go by without us hearing how smart he was, how he went to that fancy college, how he was going places.

"You ever heard of Brandeis?" I say to Toni.

2017

NOT TONI. HARRY. Harry wants to talk, to tell. No. Too much.

"Enough. I don't need to know. It's your business. We all have our stories. You need to deal with yours, that's all," I say.

"Please, I want to tell you. It's how, why, I'm there, in the place. My kids, I told them I was sorry. I wanted to make amends, that's what they say you need to do. Make amends."

He waits, every Sunday, He gets all dressed up. He never gives up.

Never they come.

"I sold all my assets, put it in trust for them. I left out only enough to live on, to pay for the place. It's better that way."

To turn a father into a *shmata,* who waits and waits? He leaves himself with nothing? They allow this? I shiver, there's a breeze from the fan, the air cold on my neck.

Harry reaches for his fancy scarf, silk to go with his expensive cufflinks and watch, and that jacket. He holds it out to me, an offering. His eyes ask such a question, will I accept it from him?

He made mistakes, sure. Who hasn't? I reach for his scarf and wrap it around my neck. He smiles, like with relief. Such a small gesture—so easy to make another person happy.

I look right into his face. "But then how come today you had so much money to throw around?"

The smile goes away. "I guess I couldn't just give it all up. I still have one stash, you know, like insurance." He looks at me so straight now that I'm the one who looks away first. "You're the only one who knows." And with that voice, the one with hope and life, he says. "I can beat this thing. One slip-up. Please, Goldie, would you give me another chance? I'd like, I like your company." He holds up his hands. "Nothing more. No pressure."

"I don't know," I say slowly. "I admit, you're good company. And in that place, that's no small thing. Maybe. At least there what difference does it make, not like you can go up to your room and gamble with yourself, so how much trouble can you get into? Only maybe we stop with the nightly poker games now?"

The look he gives me? He starts to laugh, not funny though. "Ah Goldie, you have no idea. All right," he says, rubbing his hands together, his eyes shining behind his glasses, his hair in those frizzy wisps over his head. On his shirt there's a spot from where the ice cream dripped like I knew it would. "Let's go back to the casino, all right? We gotta cash out the chips." Right away he adds, "We'll get a cashier's check. And tomorrow, straight to the bank. Deposit it. Or whatever you want. That's that."

That's that? That's a lot. All of this is a lot.

His scarf starts to slide off my neck. His eyes ask if it's okay, and slowly I answer back, also with no words, that it is. He reaches out and rearranges the silk, making a knot in the front so it won't fall again.

At the casino again, right away I get the shivers. So much darkness, it reminds me of the spook house in Coney Island, how you spin through those tunnels and all those creepy faces, skeletons, those horrible clowns come flying in your face. "Harry, I don't like it here." My voice, to myself, even it sounds very strange.

"Just a little more, Goldie. We're almost there." He leads me with such authority, to a booth way in the back that I didn't see before. I follow, head down. He says a few words to one of the guys, shows them something from his wallet. He's bribing them? No, only he showed them something, and they lead him, and he makes I should follow, into an office. Here there are windows and light, clean desks. I start to feel better.

"Goldie," Harry says. "The chips, in your bag?"

Good. I want to get rid of them. When I start to hand them to Harry, he points I should just put the bag on the counter, behind which a man is standing. Harry's not even touching it.

The man takes the bag, pours out everything from it, and I see his eyes go big. "Just a minute," he says, and shoves the chips into a metal box, locks it, and leaves the room.

"Harry," I say, "This is going to take long? I'm going to sit down."

The guy comes back, they talk, they change chip colors, they use the computer, something I hear about taxes? From gambling? Finally Harry comes back with a check in his hand. "Here you go, Goldie." His face, very serious.

A piece of paper, a check, no big deal. Then I see the amount. I was walking around on the boardwalk, la-de-da—with that much in my walker the whole time?

"Told you, Goldie," He said, half laughing, half serious. "It's hard to walk away from when you know what it is, right?"

"I can't hold onto all of this."

"You better not give it back to me." He says, putting his hands up in the air like in TV shows when somebody is facing a gun.

I already had it in my walker half the day, what's another few hours? But for sure I'm not gonna sleep on that bus the whole way back.

The next day together we go to the bank, just I want to get this whole dirty chapter over with. At the bank, everyone so polite, so cordial, they all seem to know Harry. They make with him jokes, they ask how he is. How they treat him, never before I was invited to sit down, offered a cup of coffee at the branch manager's desk. Like royalty, how he's regarded. He explains how I'm there to make a deposit, the whole time he says she.

Then he says, "I'd also like to add this woman's name to my account."

In front of the manager I don't want to say anything, but this, this is too much.

"What are you doing, Harry?" I whisper to him, when the manager types at his computer.

"Goldie, c'mon. I promise, I just want your name on my account. Please. A favor. This way, if I'm tempted, I'll know that you'll be notified. Nothing more. It's a way for me to keep in line. And if I step out of line, you'll know that too, and that will be that. Then you can walk away from me because I couldn't keep my promise. That's it. No strings attached. Just your name while we're here. Please, a deal?"

My head is swimming. My name is everything. Who I am. What am I signing up for here? More money than I ever had in any account at any time. But it's not mine, not really. Yeah, I won the game, but with his chips.

"Maybe." I answer, "But no strings. I'm not taking anything from you, and I'm not keeping anything from you, either. And if my name goes on that account, then this money goes in it, too. You gave me those chips, so like I don't even know who this money belongs to."

Better. I don't take from anyone anything. And this way, it's even. I'm just helping him out. Keeping him safe. Always, it seems that's my job, keeping everything, everyone safe.

"Thank you, Goldie. That means a lot. But, of course, if *we* want to do anything, that's all right?" Now he gets that twinkle. "You know, we could, I could at least take you to a nice dinner sometime? Maybe a show, on Broadway?" Then he quick adds, "You'll be in charge of the withdrawals when we do that."

"Maybe, yes. I think that would be fine. Good to get out once in a while."

CHAPTER TWENTY-FIVE

Maxie

Dr. Lev's face hovered over Maxie's, his nose looming ever larger until their mouths connected. Otolaryngologist indeed. She shouldn't be thinking of that, but how could she not when at that very moment ear, nose and throat doctor Lev Itzkowitz was lunging his tongue into the former location of her long-ago discarded tonsils?

She still wasn't convinced it was even ethical to date her grandmother's doctor. One-time doctor. One-visit-only doctor. Dating? Was that what she and Dr. Lev Itzkowitz were about to do?

Dr. Lev Itzkowitz.

Was it his name that was distracting her? 'Lev,' which she knew translated to *heart*. All those old-world *shtetl* names, what happened to them? All replaced by Jareds, Harrisons, Justins, and yes, Daniels.

Daniel? Seriously? She was gonna go there, while her own Dr. Lev, Dr. Heart, was here. Right now. This was it. The Third Date. They'd filled out each other's questionnaires. Completed the cursory preliminary exams. Taken personal histories. If Maxie had a checklist, he'd tick off every box.

Of course, Maxie had a checklist. That's why she was in bed with Dr. Lev this very moment. Lev, not heart, not doctor, Lev, Level, Level-headed, Dr. Correct, Dr. Perfect.

His hands were on her breasts. Wait. His hands. Those were his hands? They were tiny. Little boy hands, baby hands groping at her breasts. How had she not noticed his hands? Did this mean what she thought it would? What she was about to find out? She reached for him. Mercifully, it was only his hands that were stunted. He probably needed small hands, for all those tiny surgeries on ears and noses. They were cute, really, weren't they?

None of this was cute.

She should never have let it get this far. She needed better dating guidelines. She'd write a list.

Dr. Lev rolled over.

"This isn't working, is it?" he said.

Maxie felt a physical letting go throughout her entire body. "No, it isn't."

"On paper, you and me, we should be great." Dr. Lev said.

"I know," Maxie sounded truly remorseful.

The silence hung in the room, over their discarded clothes, over the shadows creeping in through the window slats.

"Well, uhm," Lev started.

"Sure, yeah." Maxie replied.

"Take two pills and call me in the morning?" Dr. Lev suggested. He really was all heart.

They hugged, got dressed. The tension that had been so weighty evaporated instantly. They promised they'd keep in touch, knowing they wouldn't. But if they ran into each other, they'd smile. Maybe have a coffee. Probably not. And yet, he checked off all her boxes.

Maxie closed the door behind him, feeling airborne as the lock clicked into place. She took stock of her space, opening windows, straightening her bed. Maxie Jacobson was just fine being alone. She had this. She could do this. She was doing it.

Her phone beeped. Lev? Was it not going to be so easy after all?

One new message:

Esther Abramson <estia@gmail.com>
To: maxj; tamarJ
Subject: RE: Goldie Mandell – Gastro appointment

Thanks Maxie!

You're doing a great job with Safta. As you know, I've been following up on Mom's medications, and she has been very responsible about keeping up with everything, especially the dermatology cream. Also wanted to let you both know that she asked me to take her to her follow-up visit with the dermatologist. She indicated that once she's established a relationship with a physician, she thought you and I could take turns with her medical appointments. It seems that the advocacy recommendation applied primarily to initial visits.

On another note, how much do we know about this driver? --E

Maxie's phone, still in her hand, rang. Seriously? This wasn't even funny anymore. Her thumb was already curved over the decline button. Then she saw *SAFTA* in bright letters across the screen. Her thumb shifted to the green accept button. "Is everything all right?"

"Sure, sure. I just wanted to tell you that I made another appointment. For my stomach."

"I know. It's in my calendar."

"So I was thinking. Maybe you want to take the day off from work, I don't know how long the visit will take. And, and, that way, you don't have to rush from your lab, in that coat you wear, with those plastic glasses on top of your head. You can relax a little? And you know what else, I want to take you someplace nice after. You can dress up, put on a little makeup. Like the fancy ladies.

"You know, when Saba was alive, and the kids were little, never I could do things like that, like the rich fancy ladies. I had to work, and we had, *feh,* who had the time to go to lunch in middle of the day? But, these ladies here, Bernice, she's always talking about it, how she would take her daughters to, to—the Plaza. For tea. Once in my life, I'd like to do that. With you. So nice, how you come and take me to the doctor, let me take you out fancy."

This day just kept going on and on.

"You sure, Safta? It seems, I don't know? Extravagant?"

"Sure I'm sure. Or I wouldn't have asked. Only you know, you have to dress nice. Fancy-shmancy. Like going to a party. But classy. Maybe that black dress we bought together? But not with those army boots. Put on a pair of stocking, some nice shoes. And makeup. And your hair. So nice you look when you wear it down around your shoulders."

Of course. Fancy-shmancy. "I'll arrange with the driver to take us straight from the doctor."

Perfect. Just perfect.

CHAPTER TWENTY-SIX

Goldie

HARRY'S SITTING IN THE LOBBY like he's waiting for me. Maybe he was, because he waves at me a pink piece of paper, where I see big red hearts and *Valentine's Day Dance* in silly happy letters. This place, they can't figure out if we're in pre-school in diapers, or in high school with dances, or in college with lectures. A bunch of *alte kackers*, we don't come with instructions. But Harry, a happy man, has it figured out. From lemons, the old story, make lemonade.

"Are you asking me out on a date, Harry?" Every day the same dance. *Feh*. I know how it ends.

"Now you're talking, Goldie. I'll pick you up at 2:30."

Such a dance—they need to squeeze it in before five p.m. dinner. Half the people here, asleep in their soup by six. But Harry, his face is all lit up, his eyes on fire. Without any words, a whole conversation.

2008

"MORDY," I SAY, "YOU FEEL, THE SUN IS OUT." So nice, as nice as it gets. I loosen his scarf so he can feel the warm breeze. "We'll sit here a while in the sun, then we'll go across the street. I'll make us soup. What kind do you want, the chicken or the vegetable?"

His face, still so handsome, his hands, still big, grip the sides of his wheelchair.

"All right, I think today I'm in the mood for vegetable. I'll put the bread in the oven, nice the way you like, so the butter melts into all the little holes."

A flicker maybe? Or it's the sun, the way it makes shadows across his face. With all the medicines and treatments, there's no wake-up pill? I make nice his hair, not so much left, and for sure, he makes a sound, a nice one.

"All right," I tell him. "Let's go tell them I'm taking you out from the grounds."

The wheelchair, not so easy to push. "Mordy, how am I supposed to do all this?" I make like I'm laughing. "You're the strong one—"

Stupid, Goldie. Must be I'm tired, the chair so heavy. But so much quiet, it gets to me. I take a big breath. It's not his fault this is happening. Not his fault.

"Let's just stop for a little." I put the brakes on the chair and sit on the bench under the tree, facing him. I hold his strong hand against my face, like how he would do if he was here, *really* here. "Mordy," I say. "Mordy, Mordy, Mordy," I make a little song, music, always he likes music.

"Our Maxie, the last grandbaby, starting already college next month. Columbia University. So hoity-toity. By train from here, maybe twenty minutes, a half-hour. She'll be so close, finally. We'll make *Yom Tov* for her, we'll go back to the house." I let myself get excited from the dream. "I'll take you to shul, Norm will sit with you." Norm, the son-in-law, he's all right. "So, wake up, Mordy, you hear me. There's what to be excited about. You'll see, we shall overcome." That song, it sticks in my head. "Nu, enough sitting. Sing with me, Mordy, *We shall overcome, we shall overcome.*" Like it was written for me, even though I know it's about slavery and the black people, that song—I sing it, too. What, nobody has a private patent on *tsoros.*

Just a little more pushing up the ramp now. "Hello, hello," I call. "I'm taking him out now. We'll go across the street to the apartment; I'll bring him back by six. You don't worry about supper, he'll eat by me."

"How you doin', Miss Goldie?" The nice one, Fabienne, is at the desk today. Good. Such a pretty voice she has, like music. And her hair, with all the braids, beautiful. "You be takin' him across de street, you sign de papers."

She rolls her eyes, not like the other one, the big boss so *fabissen*, like she sucks lemons all day. This one smiles at how stupid it is that every day I have to do this. But it's the agreement. We needed a lawyer to figure this out? They prefer he should sit all day, every day, in the same room, staring at the same walls. No dignity in that space—crowded with everyone else in the same boat, some even worse. So much noise, everyone sounding out their aches and pains. If you weren't already sick, this would make you so. If only Mordy—he'd tell them.

I close my eyes. "Yeah, Fabienne, I'll sign the papers."

"You do good, Miss Goldie. Taking him out, bringing him home. In my country, we don't do what dey do here. You like dat place you rentin' dere?"

Do I like it? *Feh*. It's small, it's dark, it's on the bottom floor, no sun. I asked for any of this? I'm there to make sure he gets out every day, gets sun, gets decent food. I play him our records. We watch, at least on the television, he sees the old movies he likes. And I keep busy, that's the important thing. You have to keep busy.

"Maybe this weekend, my daughter Esti will come. We'll take him home, to the beach."

Months maybe since I got Mordy home. I'm sure—I know—Mordy, he can hear, he can tell. Always gentle, never angry. Never mean. Never yelling with the noises and the faces. Like he just wants to come out, to come back. So I have to make sure it's all the way it needs to be.

We have to overcome, that's all.

2017

"GOLDIE? GOLDIE? So, I'll come to your room at 2:30." Harry is looking long at me like he wants to say more but knows already that it's better not to say too much. A smart man.

"Miss Goldie." Fabienne is still here? So *tsemished* I'm all the time lately. "You best take good care of yourself, too. You be important, too."

Yes. I need to take care from me, too. I can get dressed for a dance. That I can enjoy.

In my closet, I don't even know why it's here, what Esti was thinking when she packed it for me, a black dress with sequins. In two pieces, a skirt with pleats and a big blouse like how I like, that hangs over it. And a long red flower against the black material, and the leaves on the long stem, all sparkly. Most important, all elastic, with no zippers or buttons, so elegant and easy. I'm so excited I even use hairspray. But no mascara—I shouldn't make myself look like a raccoon. The ladies here who wear so much makeup, they think they look good? They look like witches on Halloween. I have better taste. Always.

At 2:30 sharp, there's a knock on my door, and there's Harry, with his red bowtie, in a tuxedo. Of course. This man, ready always for anything. He takes a flower like the one he has in his chest pocket, but this one is with a pin, and he asks permission to put it on my dress. My heart starts like I'm a teenager again. His hands shake only a little bit, and afterwards, still bent a little over my chest—I don't know what comes over me—I quick kiss his cheek. All this with me in the doorway and him in the hall. He picks his head up and I see his face all red, and I feel mine is, too. But he only moves to the side and bows for me to come out to join him. He makes from our two walkers a kind of chariot-like, and even if it's rude that we take up the whole hallway, we link our inside arms together and hold onto the walkers on the outside ends. If anyone else is behind us, too bad for them. Tonight, well, this afternoon, me and Harry, Mr. and Mrs. Rockefeller.

So cute they made the reception room. There are hearts on the walls, and chocolate candies in red shiny paper scattered on top of pink tablecloths on the tables they arranged in a big circle. Even there's a singer in an evening gown with long gloves singing with a piano player, like Billie Holliday or Ella Fitzgerald. Very special.

Harry and I, in front of everyone, we're still linking our arms until he brings me to a table and gets for us two glasses of champagne. With his walker he can't carry the champagne, but I see him talking to one of the young staff. He walks with Harry and brings the glasses to our table.

He smiles when he sees the flower on my dress, and pokes Harry, "So this is what the big deal was about." He does with Harry what the kids do, with the hands like fists they knock each other.

And oh, how the music plays, and how Harry sings along, and the wine, it makes me hot and giggly. And Harry, he takes my hand and I let him. He kisses my hand and I let him, and he tells me how he likes to see me happy, and I laugh.

I say, "I like you, Harry. I like you a lot."

And in front of the whole room, with Bernice and everyone watching, he picks his glass up in the air, all excited, and calls out, "It's about time, Goldie. It's about time."

And suddenly, the nice waiter and the singer are talking, and she turns the pages in her music book, and now like Judy Garland, loud and fast, she's singing, "I'm Just Wild About Harry." Nearby at the other tables, some people clap. And the music plays, and we dance with our walkers, and mainly we look at each other and smile. And I think: This is being still alive.

So we're with the crowd, and we're waiting, and when the elevator stops at my floor, Harry says he'll walk me to my room, and I don't even care that the people in the elevator may be thinking all kinds of things. Wasting time thinking, a luxury I can't afford.

Suddenly, I'm nervous. The room is all soft and yellow from the sun setting, and I'm embarrassed how the light lands on all those amber pill jars that Esti arranges on top of the chest of drawers right when you walk in. I need to advertise like this? And in such big letters she wrote out the whole schedule, and it sits there on display for the whole world to see, which never they did because never before I had outside company in this room. Also, Esti and Norm hung on the wall behind the couch so many pictures from over the years. Me and Mordy, our whole story is up there.

"You want a cup of tea, some coffee?" I ask Harry. Always so easy to talk to him, but now the words don't come.

"No, nothing. I'm fine. Thanks." He looks around the room.

I face him across the tiny table, one of those little round ones like at a coffee shop, the only one that can fit in the room. His bowtie came a little crooked, and the flower in his pocket is starting to droop.

"Goldie," he says, just when I say, "Harry."

We both laugh but not because anything is funny. None of this is funny.

"Harry," I say again, "let's not make from this so much a big deal. We're not teenagers, we had our Big Loves already. But I like how you make me laugh. I like how you like to sing and see the best of everything."

"Goldie, no." Harry grabs his heart, exaggerated like in an old movie. He rolls his eyes and shakes his head. "Are you giving me the *Let's Just Be Friends* speech?"

"See," I say, laughing. "Always the jokes. Thanks." Then I get serious, I want to say this. "No, I'm saying that I'd like to be more than just friends. That's all."

And Harry, he smiles that smile where I can see how he must have been the kid in school that everyone liked. The one with the fast mouth and quick answers.

"Good. Me, too. Goldie, I can kiss you? A real kiss?"

We both stand up, slowly, the only way we know how, and Harry takes me in his arms, and kisses me how I haven't been kissed in a long, long time. And his mouth, it's different from Mordy's. It's not like how when Mordy kissed me and I lost who I was, I just became one with him. Harry, he's here, but he's also still separate from me. A part of me is still with Mordy. But, of course, that is how it should be.

Harry turns to leave and blows me another kiss—more kisses in one day than I had a whole year, maybe ten years—before he goes singing down the hall, Gene Kelly with a walker. I can't help it, I'm smiling. What can I say? He got the girl. *I got my girl, who can ask for anything more.*

That man.

CHAPTER TWENTY-SEVEN

Goldie

AS SOON AS HE SEES ME PUSHING that wheelchair button that opens the door, he's running inside to help me. And then, the car, he left it running with the heater on, so nice it feels. Some of these cars, they smell from cigarette smoke or those smelly trees they hang from the mirror; always I think that's dangerous with those things dangling in your view but no, his car smells like how a car should if you keep it clean.

This driver, not so bad. Every time he comes now he's wearing his suit. Maybe the only one he has. Double breasted. Big brown plaid. Big shoulders. The pants, pleated, fall all the way to his shoes. Fancy shoes. Wingtips. Each time a different tie. Very interesting his ties. Sometimes fat, sometimes skinny. Very stylish, the whole getup like from an old gangster movie. And even his hair always looking wet, pushed back, I can see comb-marks and he wears sunglasses and a hat. But a real hat, not that *fa'cackta* beanie—this one felt with a brim, like the men used to wear all the time. Still, no word about making from me a picture. Just he comes on time, he's polite. So far, so good.

"Good morning, madam," he says, reaching over to hand me a cup of coffee. This he started to do, too. Seems he's a maven from coffee. Who knew from all the fancy beans and brews? Nescafe my whole life, now, names I can't even pronounce. And so tasty. "Have you called Ma—your granddaughter to let her know when we'll be arriving?"

Also, very polite how he talks to me. I get the treat of seeing his white teeth.

"Madam, might I suggest that you call her now, before you lock your phone away?" He looks for a minute, then quickly away from where my purse is under my sweater and I'm about to close the belt, which he again pulled out for me.

"Don't worry from me. I know what I'm doing."

He holds up his phone, he thinks from here I can see it? "According to my phone, madam, traffic is moderate at this time, so we'll be there in approximately twenty-five minutes. In case you have not yet called, or if you might want to update her."

So fancy, he talks. Such showing off. "Your phone can tell you that? How does your phone know what's going on with the roads?"

"Through satellites. They track the traffic." He looks at me in the mirror. "It's called GPS. Each phone knows how fast it's traveling, and reports back its location."

What's he talking makes no sense, the phone tells you where it is, then why I'm always losing it? "I don't believe it."

"It's science that they developed. It's very sophisticated."

"In labs, like in Columbia University? You know from this?" Really, this can be very useful, to let people know when you're trying to meet them somewhere. I can use this information right now, for Maxie. "All right, give me a minute, I'll call her. You can drive the car while I'm talking."

Also, a wonder. To talk from the car. All the time when Mordy drove, I'd file my nails for something to do, instead of just sitting like a piece of lox spoiling in the sun. This modern science, like magic. But then I realize the driver so close, he can hear everything I'll say.

"Maxie," I say when she answers. "*Ikh bin in di mashin, ikh vet zeyn bay di shpitol bay 10 iklokk*"

"Safta?"

"*Ja, ikh bin aoyf meyn veg.*"

"Safta, why are you speaking Yiddish? Is everything all right?"

"Ikh bin fayn, fayn, nor dem shofer."

I see the driver is sitting very straight. I whisper, "We'll be there at 25 minutes after 10. He told me he has the science in his phone that lets him know how long the drive takes, even it can tell the traffic, he said."

Maxie whispers back so it's hard to hear. "You know, Safta, it's not like you were telling me something personal, you can speak in English. Besides," and I hear her waiting to tell me what she's about to say. "I'm pretty sure he understands German so he can probably get most of what you say in Yiddish."

He speaks German? *Varum?* Now I'm stuck with the phone in my hand, I can't put it away in my purse because it's stuck under the seatbelt.

"*Du sprichst Deutsch*?" I talk like I don't know what I'm saying isn't English.

"*Ja.*"

Now he gets quiet? This is when he needs to be talking.

"*Ich habe in der Schule gelernt*"

So he learned in school.

Not only he speaks German, he speaks High German. A show-off.

"So why are you a driver if you have all this education?"

Now is when he'll tell me how he's really a painter who wants to paint me. To tell the truth, I'm wondering why it's taking so long. Every time he comes I'm taking special care how I look. But still, he says nothing. Of course, I'll say no. But why still he never asked?

"Because I need to eat," he says, smiling into the mirror.

Feh, he thinks I'm stupid? "This is the best you can do? I heard you're supposed to be a big shot artist. This is how you have to make ends meet?"

"You do what you have to do, madam."

"Enough with this madam. You're driving me a lot," I say. "You can call me Mrs. Mandell."

Even after all this being friendly? Nothing. He says nothing.

CHAPTER TWENTY-EIGHT

Goldie

ALREADY I LIKE THIS DOCTOR. His office looks how a doctor's office should—serious. No glamor pictures on the walls, just a few of those charts with the skeletons and muscles and body parts in different colors, with long explanations I always read and never know what I'm reading. And boring magazines, the good kind, like *Newsweek* and *Time*.

"He's a good doctor," I tell Maxie.

"Yeah, he was recommended by my colleague. Did you ask about him, too?"

"No." She shouldn't know from my research. I wave my hand around the waiting room, with only one other person waiting, not like the crowded subway station from that dermatologist's office. "You can see, he doesn't overbook, the nurse knows her business, you can tell."

Before Maxie even has a chance to answer they call my name.

Again, the same business with putting on the gown that doesn't close. This time though they do everything, they weigh me, they take my temperature, they measure my pressure, and the nurse, a young girl, everyone so young, smiles and makes nice conversation. She compliments me even on my blood pressure and I tell her how I like to eat vegetables, even though, lately, my stomach is upset which is why I'm here. She nods like she understands and tells me the doctor will come in soon, and hopefully everything will get taken care of.

"See," I say to Maxie.

We don't even have so long to wait and he comes in. A big man. Very big. I'm a little surprised, he could lose some weight. But he's young. Strong. A man should have an appetite. He has time yet to worry about his weight, and he carries it well.

He shakes my hand, "Mrs. Mandell?" he says to me. His voice is nice, deep. Like a bear.

"And you are?" He turns to Maxie. I like this very much.

"Maxie Jacobson. The granddaughter." When Maxie smiles, I think the whole world feels sunshine.

He looks at her chest, not dirty like, just to notice the badge she wears around her neck. "You work here?" he asks.

Such a *mensch*, taking time to talk to us.

"I'm a PhD candidate in Cooperman's lab."

His eyes go wide, I can tell with respect. "Nice, didn't they publish that paper on the role of MDM-2 protein in apoptosis?"

When Maxie nods, her face very surprised and I can tell, also proud, he says, "I'd love to hear more about it."

In front of my eyes, less than five minutes—already a date. Even I feel my stomach relaxing, like we can leave now. Mission accomplished.

"So," he turns back to me, "what brings you here?"

"Sometimes I have diarrhea. My stomach is upset all the time. And I'm in assisted living, so always I'm with other people and it's not nice to be uncomfortable in front of them, but my kids said I needed to be there because once or twice I felt lightheaded and passed out. But now I'm drinking more water, that happened last summer, it was very hot; probably I was just dehydrated. I'm only telling you everything because you're a doctor."

Maxie's face is twisting all different ways while I'm talking, but when I'm finished, she just stands next to me and puts her hand on my shoulder.

"Yes, all right," Dr. Berber says. "Let's figure out what's going on. We can't have you feeling uncomfortable, that's no fun." He comes toward me after putting on gloves. "Is it all right if I ask you to open your gown? I'm going to press on your stomach."

He does all the things, listens to my chest, knocks on my knees, looks in my ears and throat, also my nose, but he spends most of the time pressing on my belly—he wasn't kidding about that. His hands are big, strong, and I look at his face, but I can't see nothing in his eyes. I'm only afraid I shouldn't pass gas while he's working on me, and once or twice I have to hold back from making a noise when he pokes a little too hard. Just I want he should give me a prescription Pepto-Bismol or something so this embarrassing uncomfortableness goes away. Maxie, she's an angel. The whole time she's in the room but she stays quiet, so I shouldn't be embarrassed.

Finally, he smiles and says, "Mrs. Mandell, I'd like to talk in my office. I'll leave you alone to get dressed. My nurse will come get you in a few minutes."

He turns to Maxie, "You'll come, too, right?"

The nurse shows us where is his office with all the nice diplomas on the walls. Maxie and I sit in two chairs facing his desk, where I see the backs of picture frames. "Maxie," I say to her; she's looking very nice, I'm happy to see. "Go see the pictures on his desk, what they are."

"Safta," she says, "That's ru—I mean, I don't think I should. They're his personal pictures."

"Just go, look, pretend like you dropped something. I'm not telling you to go through his drawers or anything, just give a quick look at the pictures."

Maxie sighs just like how Tamar used to do, and it makes me smile, because just like how Tamar never listened, I know that Maxie will. But instead of getting up to look she wipes her hands on her tight dress, really, she looks wonderful, even though she's wearing boots, at least they're cute, red and sporty, very sharp. "Safta, this stomachache? Does my mother know about it? Does Esti? How long have you had it? Does it hurt all the time? Could you describe where it hurts? How?" Her eyes are big with worry.

"*Feh,* just some gas. And I did say something, why else are we here?" I point back to the pictures again. "A quick look, it can hurt anything? I want to know."

But just then the doctor comes in and goes to his desk where he opens my folder.

"Mrs. Mandell, Miss Mandell," he nods at both of us.

"Goldie," I say. I don't correct him that Maxie's last name isn't Mandell. "And you can call my granddaughter Max, Maxie. Short for Maxine."

"Thank you, Goldie," he says. He folds his hands together and looks up at my face. "I would like to run some more tests. I want to do an ultrasound, possibly a CAT scan."

"So, Doctor, since you get to know everything about me, I can ask from you a favor? Can you show me those pictures on your desk that are turned around?" I shrug like it's not a big deal. "Just it would make me more comfortable, like to know who you are as a person."

He looks surprised, then laughs. "Fair enough." He turns around the pictures and I see him with the ocean behind him, standing in sand and around him palm trees. He's smiling, in a beach shirt and a big straw hat, with his arm around a pretty woman also in a big straw hat, and in front of them three boys.

Feh.

He looks at Maxie: "Some of your grandmother's responses to my examination, along with the symptoms she described warrant further examination."

I look away from his beach and make him turn back to me. "What, what are you saying to me?"

He smiles. "We just need to get to the bottom of whatever this is."

CHAPTER TWENTY-NINE

Goldie

MAXIE PUTS HER ARM AROUND MY WAIST.

"You don't need to make from me such a fuss," I tell her. "We don't know anything yet; for sure it's nothing. Always it turns out to be nothing." I say again.

Maxie, her face is so white. This girl, she doesn't know from anything difficult, her life a walk in the park. As it should be. All children should have such lives. Not always they do, even if the parents try for them their hardest.

1938

I KNOW THEY WANTED FOR ME EVERYTHING GOOD. I was going to be safe in America. That's what they told me. So lucky they said, to be going to America.

They put me on that boat, promising they'd come soon. Mama, my mama, your bubbie, your *alte-bubbie*—I'm your bubbie—hugging and hugging me.

Stupid me, listening, believing them.

An ocean liner—sounded so fancy. Stuffed, every inch of it, with sick, sad people. Days of rolling and groaning, of everywhere smells of sickness and salt, of moans coming from all the lumps under the gray blankets on the cots that fill the whole space. Then, an excitement.

Everyone yelling, jumping, hugging, crying, laughing at the big green Statue of Liberty. So much bigger than how she looked in the picture Mama had shown me. One of the nice ladies who was in the cot near mine put her hand on my shoulder and read to me the poem about all the sad people we are. This poem doesn't make me feel any better. All around, people crying, so I also start to cry. I don't want to be here, to be one of those huddled masses like the woman read to me. I want to go back, or even just stay on this stinky boat. So much, too much happening. So much noises and smells and I can't understand anything anyone is saying. Everyone pushing, somebody in a uniform yelling at us to go here, go there, get in lines. The nice lady helps me, we stand together, she tells me not to cough or sneeze, or scratch anywhere. She licks her thumb and even rubs my face, to clean where my crying made a mess. She helps me put on my hat, and pin the sign Mama made for me to wear on my coat for just this day.

I can't even walk straight, my legs still all shaking from the boat, when a man in a suit, a skinny lady with a funny hat that looks like a cup on top of her head and a girl bouncing her blonde ponytail come right up to me and say, "Goldie Fischel?" The way they look at me makes me feel very small, like what I am is not what they were waiting for. They push forward the girl and they say to me, "This is Our Susie."

This Our Susie, she bounces her hair without any hat and her hair isn't so special like she thinks. It's not so curly or so blonde like Gretchen's and Dorli's my best friends used-to-be until I was no more allowed to go to school. Our Susie's hair is more the color of a paper bag, *nisht ahein and nisht aheir,* a nothing color, and I'm getting a very bad feeling that this America is going to be like David Copperfield, you know that book? But this time for me, real life.

At the public school they put me in a class with little kids because I don't speak English. The chairs and desks, everyone so small, I'm like an elephant taking up all the space in the monkey cage. I try to tell them that I already know the arithmetic and I can read, but nobody listens to me even I'm talking in my best German, not Yiddush like we talked at home. Our Susie pretends she doesn't know me as soon as we leave the house every morning. Every night when I go to sleep, I tell myself that it's another day closer to when Mama and Poppa will get here. They promised *soon, soon* they'd come, we'd all be together *soon*, in America. "Soon, soon." They kept saying again and again. I wish I could take backwards the time and say to them a better goodbye. Always I wondered, how long is soon?

Up in the attic, where I like how small and hot it is, I tell everything to Hount-Hount. I do this ever since that time when I brought him for that Show-and-Tell, when you bring something from home and talk about it, and even though the class is all six-year-olds, and this whole Show- And-Tell business is baby stuff, still I was very excited to show everybody Hount-Hount, who came with me on the boat. Maybe somebody would finally see me if I could Show-and-Tell with him how my life used to be like theirs, with a real house and real parents.

But what these little children talk about, dinosaur bones from museums and someplace called Rocket Feller Center with dancing rockets; I was afraid to show Hount-Hount with his falling apart stitches and sticking out stuffing, me, so much older and holding onto a baby toy. I push him into the corner of the shelf under my desk. When it's my turn I tell Mrs. Rubin I forgot, and because my English is still not good they think I'm stupid so I don't get into trouble. When it's time to leave I quick *shtup* Hount-Hount under my coat, before anyone sees and laughs. It's easy, since nobody ever looks at me, sitting way in the back. I explain it all to Hount-Hount that day after school. I whisper to him in German, careful nobody should hear. Our Susie told me that if I ever talked here in German they'll put me in jail. But still, at night, every night, I whisper to him anyway.

But that day, I remember always the Show-and-Tell day, all that day my stomach is hurting something terrible, and in my underwear, blood. So much blood. Pouring from me, pouring and pouring, all over my underwear. My stomach, like there's a knife in there, twisting and turning. All that blood—on my clothes. My thighs. Everywhere.

At Ellis Island they took one lady away when she coughed blood. Everyone on the line saw her go, and nobody saw her come back. What was gonna happen to me if they knew blood was coming out from there?

Every night, my fingers are all red and hurting from the soap I'm using to wash everything clean. And still the blood pours out. What's the point of all this washing, three days already non-stop I'm bleeding? Then, it stops, like how it started. I don't know how. Why. A miracle. The stomachache, the bleeding, like it never was. It all stops. Just stops.

Some miracle. So what? Back to first grade? To talking to a dumb dog doll—like it's my friend? Then, the real miracle happens.

Our Susie's mother is in the living room with a pretty lady who looks like from the movies. That they're not in the kitchen tells me that this lady has some real *yichus*. I know they're talking about me. I can tell from the way Our Susie's mother is whispering, and the words she's using, not like how she usually talks. Something I hear, unfortunate. Sullen. I don't know what these words mean, just that they're not good.

This fancy lady must be from the authorities. But it all stopped. I'm better. And I was so careful. Even so, what if Our Susie saw and told. "I'd be delighted to have her stay with us."

Delighted? Stay with her? Like in an orphanage? Maybe with other kids there like me? My age? Maybe also from Germany? Maybe better?

The pretty lady's name is Edith. She tells me she's also a cousin, like Our Susie and her parents. Well, she isn't, but Joe, her husband, is, and that makes more sense because he's normal looking. Edith is beautiful. On the subway on the way to her apartment she carries my suitcase and tells me that I'll like Joe. That they're "Newlyweds." She laughs and turns pink when she says that, and I can't believe this fancy lady, this Newlywed, is carrying my old suitcase, but she said she wants to, since I'm carrying my school bag.

Then she pats her hair which is up in a "French Twist" I know because she told me that's what it's called, with her hands that are in little gray gloves, that match her jacket and her straight black skirt and high heels, and stockings with a real seam that goes up her legs. I have to remember to close my mouth when I stare at her, and I watch how she sits with her legs crossed, and how her teeth are so straight and white and how she smells so clean, how she's wearing lipstick on a regular afternoon. When we come out of the subway, she reaches for my hand even though I'm really too old to hold hands in the street, but it feels so nice. I think she'll let go after we cross to the other side, but I'm happy when she doesn't and instead swings it back and forth and says we'll have "such fun."

For the next three weeks I'm pinching myself how nice she is, how nice my room is, how nice Joe is, how he makes us laugh and how he and Edith talk slowly and always explain to me things that I should be able to say them in English. Joe also looks a little like Poppa, a little bit like a box and his hair, I can see that soon he'll also be bald on top just with hair around the bottom and sides of his head. And this makes me happy, that secret backwards smile, that on Joe will be a real smile, not like on my Poppa. My poppa, he didn't smile so much.

Edith explains that because I'm in a new neighborhood I have to go to a new school. She tells me this like it's a bad thing. I feel a lightness like the sun coming out. A school where nobody knows me—a do-over, a chance to start again fresh. Edith shakes her head and makes a funny small smile when she sees how happy this makes me. The kids in this new school look more organized, more like how the kids looked at home, and the teachers here don't seem so mad all the time. After Edith goes with me that first day, everyone is nice to me too, since I came with such a fancy lady. And here they give me some tests and right away they put me into my regular grade.

Then, one day, everything going good-good, when that knife feeling in my stomach comes back. Worse than last time. I feel sticky wet in my underwear. This American dream I was letting myself have? Ha. For some, maybe. For sure not for me.

My mind fills with pictures of jail—must look how the boat did with all those cots, but this time somewhere on that island in middle of the water. My fingers burning and my stomach aching, again I fill my underwear with toilet paper. I'm scrubbing and scrubbing, but what will it help? I climb out the window where I spread out my wet stuff on the rails of the fire escape. In the morning, if I'll see the morning, I'll bring it all inside.

But I'm so weak from the bleeding, this slow dying, that I don't get up early enough. When I open my eyes, Edith is standing by the open window, holding my washed underwear. I want to die right then, not to see her looking at me. She's so beautiful in a long, flowered robe that reaches all the way to the floor, and underneath her toes are painted red. Always she looks like a movie star, and there she's standing, her hair all down around her shoulders, and she looks even more perfect that way, and she's holding my disgusting horrible underwear and looking at me with her big soft eyes.

"I'm sorry," I finally say. And even though I thought I could pretend to Edith that I'm strong and smart and fit in America, I know that I don't. "I'm dying." I wail like a baby. "I'm bleeding and it's not stopping, and my stomach is hurting and I'm sorry, I'm dying, I'm sorry."

Edith runs to me, and hugs me and she smells so good, and her robe is so soft, and she says, "Your mama never told you anything?"

Mama? What could she tell me? Besides, it's not like she's here. She's back there, in my life used-to-be. Which even that isn't there anymore to go back to. At least, according to the news Joe reads every night.

Edith wipes my tears and pulls back my hair, and says, she says, "Goldie, you're not dying. You're exactly perfectly healthy."

She starts then to talk, talking and talking, not making any sense but she still looks the same, so pretty and kind. Edith is like a godmother in a fairy tale, but what she's telling me is the most disgusting thing I ever heard. If even Edith can tell me crazy things like this, I can't believe in anyone anymore. She must see the look on my face, because then she says that one day I'll meet a man and I'll understand.

I shake my head and say never. Finally though, I need to know something. For sure, never Poppa and Mama did this. But Edith and Joe? She just said I can ask her anything. So I ask her if that's why she took me, so she wouldn't have to do that thing she told me with Joe.

She looks back at me all funny and laughs so hard, and hugs me tight, and tells me that I'll change my mind.

She's wrong but I don't say nothing, I just dig my face into her soft robe, feeling her arms holding me close. I want to stay like this forever. Here, exactly like this.

But after a while Edith kisses the top of my head, so nice like a real mama. Then she nudges me to get up. She leads me into the bathroom and shows me where are these special pads to put in my underwear, and the special soap to use and where I can hang my wet things. She tells me that she has the same thing happen to her, every month, it's called having your period, and it's all part of being a woman. It's all natural, part of life, she says.

"See, Sheyfe, a natural part of life. Nothing to become all hysterical about. When you're young, when you're old, all different stages of life. No reason to get so excited. Now, just make the call to the driver to take me back to the place."

2017

"Ma, it's—surreal. It's—she just sat there, talking about her period. Her period?! I mean, it wasn't just her period, she talked about Germany, and Our Susie, and Edith and Ellis Island—all of it. She was only eleven and she, and she—did you know all this? She thinks, she says, it's nothing, but he wants her to come back for tests—and all she wanted to do was look at his family pictures—like nothing he said registered. She thinks it's nothing, a natural part of life, she kept saying."

"Cancer. Of course, it has to be cancer."

"Yes, yes. I'll tell her. I'll tell her exactly that."

"Love you too. See you soon."

She takes a long time with the call but finally comes back to where I'm sitting. My Maxie. My Sheyfe. With her long curls and green eyes. So cute. Always so cute.

"Safta?" she says, her fingers pulling on her necklace. My necklace. "I called my mother. She said to tell you she's coming home."

All these years in California. What I did. Breaking up my family—to keep it together. Tamar, she told me, "Ma. I'm happy, I'm learning, I'm growing. I'm—" All of a sudden shy. "I'm applying to law school."

Law school? A girl? My Tamar?

"The professors there, so many of them went through the Holocaust, like you did." She looked down. "Only worse, and I didn't know about the quotas, how—I want to work with immigrants and refugees, like you and Daddy were. I want to help and and—"

I did this, this Brandeis education.

"I already have an internship this summer. In California," she told me. "Berkeley," she said.

Even I had heard of this place, where all the free love was for sale.

"Home?" I ask Maxie. "That's what she said? She said *home*?"

CHAPTER THIRTY

Maxie

EVERYTHING IN THE COMPRESSED living space crowded in on Maxie. Safta's pictures on the walls, the too-big couch that she'd insisted on. Esti and her mother's high school and college graduation pictures. Their wedding pictures. Maxie's pictures, toothless at her older cousins' Bat Mitzvahs. Then as an almost adult at their weddings. Babies. Maxie with her caps and gowns, as early as kindergarten, smiling between her parents.

All of it so large, as Safta's life was getting so small.

Maxie felt clammy inside the tight black dress and cling-wrapped pantyhose she'd worn in honor of Safta's tea—at Safta's command. The little boots pinched her toes while she watched her grandmother carefully remove her skirt, unbutton her blouse, hang everything up on hangers, each action taking way too long. Then she'd had to turn away, unwilling to bear witness to her grandmother in her white cotton panties, the leg bands hanging open around her thin creped legs. She would preserve her image of Safta in her floral skirted bathing suits, her legs like tree trunks, not these withering stalks. Her shoulders wide—strong—not this collapsed fleshy torso with distended breasts distorting a former-era bra, not this wrinkled sun-spotted skin, those flaccid spaghetti arms.

Maxie didn't know what to do or say, the cruelty of time settling into a helplessness—heavy molten lead that reached to the tips of her fingers and toes. But she'd recover. Unlike Safta, whose cancer cells would multiply—were multiplying, rampaging out of control.

"Sheyfe, enough. I'm tired. You're busy. Go home. We'll do the tea another day."

"Safta, I'm so sorry." Maxie shuddered at the banal nothings issuing from her mouth. She had no book of instructions, and Maxie, rule-follower, needed guidelines.

"*Feh*, for what do you have to be sorry? Nothing, nothing. Look, it's getting late, I need to rest before dinner. Then I have to get my face on, right? For all the activities here. So go. Go. You need money, change for the train? You have tokens?"

Tokens? Maxie took one last look at the picture wall, the ones taken when there were subway tokens, and pay phones, and stockings and garter belts. Red lipstick and bobbed hair. Despite all the glossy artifacts, a past that wasn't really all that great. But it was Safta's past, and it would be gone.

T-Jam's car idled in the circular drive outside Safta's building. He'd driven Maxie and Safta there after the gastroenterologist examination. After Safta told, and Maxie heard, that intense story. After Maxie's mother declared her intention to come to New York. They were in the after now. The new now.

She knocked on T-Jam's window. "You waited?"

He flipped his sketchpad shut, clicked his mechanical pencil and pressed its lead tip against his opposite hand. He tossed both into a tin cookie box stored in the compartment between the front seats. "I figured you could use a ride back to the city."

Maxie felt her skin doing something unfamiliar. Not unpleasant. But she didn't know what to do next. Normally she sat in the back seat with her grandmother. But surely not now. She heard the lock unclick and she pulled open the passenger door, sliding into the seat quickly. It all looked different from here. She could see his cupholder with his phone in it, papers, mints. It was surprisingly neat but smelled like him. That characteristic paint smell. And a trace of caffeine. And something else. Functional and male.

"Is she all right?" His voice was low as he put the car in gear.

"Probably not," Maxie heard herself sounding normal even when she felt so gutted. "We'll find out. They're gonna run tests."

He offered nothing in response, neck taut as he reversed the car onto the road. They didn't speak further. He pulled up in front of the brownstone in Washington Heights where she rented a top floor apartment. Maxie slid out, but then stood with her hand on the door, lingering.

"T-J—can I call you that?" She waved her hand in a circle as if to include the car. "This driving. Your clothes, why? You haven't even mentioned it to her right? Sitting for you? I don't get it."

He took a while to answer. "So many indigenous tribes, they won't allow photographs, eh?" Canada slipping into his voice. "They're right. Stealing someone in a moment in time. It's a theft if it's done without regard. This," he shrugs, "it's setting the scene. Requesting entre."

"So this, whatever this is?" Maxie pointed her finger in another large arc, indicating his attire, "It's not ironic? I mean, it's cute. And I'm sure Safta is loving it, but how does it work?"

The dimples made their appearance. "You like it? At first it was—well—what did you say, ironic? Yeah, I guess. But I'm digging it now. I feel the clothes, the look. And putting them on, it—it makes me want to hold doors open and—yeah. It started with being about me, kind of a way to scam your grandma into feeling comfortable with me, but it's become who I am around her. And it's—yeah. It's not so much like she's the object now, I mean, she is. But it's immersive. The only way she'll trust me to paint her accurately. Fuck, the only way I'll trust me to."

Maxie tried to take it in. "You do this for all your subjects? You—get into character?"

"Everyone is different. With your grandmother, it was your idea, You told me to do it—-in not so many words. I got into it. Good advice."

Maxie sighed. "You may not have all that much time to—" and couldn't finish her sentence.

T-Jam was fast—out of the car and standing in front of her, both her hands in his, his dark eyes fully focused on her face. Her legs give out like some old 1950s starlet, she in her Breakfast at Tiffany's dress, he in his Atticus Finch suit—like they'd fallen into some stage set in an alternative time. She's in his arms and he's whispering in her hair, pressing her to his chest, and she folds herself into his large warmth like a protective cape and they go up the steps and she fumbles with her keys, and they're in her bedroom with their clothes strewn and twisted on the floor, her dress tangled with his suit jacket, his tie knotted into her pantyhose, his mouth locked onto hers, her tongue exploring his, her fingers pulling at his hair, releasing it from its Brylcreem hold—his rough hard worked hands unlatching her bra, cupping her breasts. Her breath coming faster and harder. His legs between hers. The smell of paint, of hair product, of soap. Of him.

Release.

Release.

Release.

Regret.

Maxie Jacobson came back to herself—her hopeless, helpless, exuding neediness all over the place pathetic self. A mercy fuck. How sad did he think—know—she was? And—and, oh God, it had been so good. For her. But for him?

"Do you wanna get a cup of coffee or something?" She could explain. Excuse. This wasn't who she was. This wasn't what she did. He was just working—she respected his art. And she'd—she hadn't meant—she didn't mean. Maxie pulled the blanket to her chin.

Watching her, he shook his head. "I get it. Let's not blow this out of proportion, Dr. J. We let ourselves get caught in the moment. What did you call it, in character? A one-off, eh?"

Sure. Yeah. Right. He was right. Be cool. One time. No sweat. He wouldn't even remember. She stayed under the covers while he collected his costume.

"This ride wasn't on the clock, by the way." There they were—those dimples.

Maxie lifted her pillow, pressing her face into it, waiting until she heard her apartment door close on his way out. But, once he was gone, holding onto it still. Damn, that smell. She couldn't even pretend to want to push the pillow aside. Instead she wrapped herself around it, one leg curled under, the other over it. A little mercy can go a long way.

CHAPTER THIRTY-ONE

Goldie

"HOW LONG HAS SHE BEEN LIKE THIS?" Tamar is using a softer voice than ever I heard. Respectful?

Esti, looking normal—nice like always. Tamar—in a dress like what the rice comes in. Probably she paid for it a fortune, too, it's not cheap to look so poor.

"She must be scared." Esti says back to Tamar. Like I'm not here?

I almost hear Tamar rolling her eyes. "Her? Scared?"

"Wouldn't you be?" Esti's voice, bossy. Scared. Bossy because she's scared.

"She's not me. Or you." Like we don't all know this? "She—oh, forget it, we're not accomplishing anything here. Ma, Ma, you hear me?"

"Yeah, I hear you. The way you're yelling, the dead could hear you." Here, not so much a joke. But nothing even hurts. For it to be something, something has to hurt. Common sense. Even the test, also it didn't hurt.

"Good, get dressed. I didn't come all the way here to watch you sleep."

"We have someplace to go?"

"I wanna check out the facility. Let's go to lunch."

Not the dining room, Bernice and her table. They all saw me and Harry at the dance. "Why? You're thinking of moving in? What do you need to see it for?"

"C'mon Ma. I mean it, get up. I'm hungry. I'm not gonna stop nagging you." She's holding up the brochure from the plastic folder that came with the room. "C'mon, there's a lot going on. Let's check out tonight's movie."

"No, no movie." Always at the movie everyone watching Harry instead of the screen, singing all the songs, saying all the lines. Me hiding my face. "The seats there, you fall asleep and then it's too hard to wake up and come back up."

"Okay, no movie. Deal. Just dinner. Let's go. C'mon."

She's going through my closet. The dress, the black dress with the red flower. It's right there, in the front.

"I know how to get dressed. I'll be ready in five minutes. Go, just go."

They think I don't see how they smile at each other like a big accomplishment they achieved. *Feh,* I have to go downstairs eventually, better at least to have them with me. Two pretty girls, young and smart. Okay, maybe one a little strange, but for sure interesting. Maybe interesting enough for the Yentas to talk about her instead of me. Her hair, a mess, all different colors gray and brown, half long and short, half curly half straight. And on her feet sandals like it's summer, never mind the burlap sack dress.

For sure, a conversation piece.

"Goldie, how *are* you?" The way Bernice presses on the *are* when she says it, like her *kishkes* are coming out from her mouth.

"Fine, fine." I look at the daily menu, like something interesting might be there.

"Hi." Tamar pushes out a chair. "I'm Tamar, Goldie's other daughter. Why don't you join us?"

Why don't you join us? Maybe a hive of bees, wasps, we should invite, too?

"Leave her alone," I say to Tamar, not even looking at Bernice. "I'm sure she's busy, Bernice here, she's like the mayor." Now I smile at her like a crocodile smile. "She's always involved, a joiner. She doesn't want to sit with us."

As I'm talking Bernice squashes her fat *tuchus* into the chair Tamar provided.

"Au contraire," she says. Like she's the queen of style or something?

"Delighted to meet you," she says to Tamar, and I watch how she registers Tamar's getup. Big surprise. "Your sister is like the mailman, always here, rain or shine. Such a dedicated daughter, your mother must have been a wonderful parent when you girls were growing up, to warrant such attention."

"Oh, yes, our mother is one of a kind," Tamar says, and I know from sarcasm when I hear it. "I live out of state, but my daughter is nearby."

"Oh," Bernice says, like opening a birthday present, this information. "She's the pretty one who comes and goes, with the long curly hair? I see her with her boyfriend, he's so handsome—you don't get to see a young man all dressed up like that anymore."

"What are you talking? What boyfriend? The man with the car? He's my driver." I turn to Tamar. "See what happens when you live in a place like this? People with nothing to do with themselves make up stories from everybody else."

"Goldie," Bernice smiles like we're best friends. Then she picks her hand up in the air to signal that she'd like a cup of coffee, who does she think she is. "If you weren't so busy with Harry, you would see for yourself."

"Girls, I'm not hungry anymore."

Tamar is looking from me to Bernice. "Ma?" she says. "What is she talking about?"

"Well," Bernice starts.

"Excuse me," Tamar interrupts her. "I'm talking to my mother. Ma? Is there something to what she's saying?"

"Nothing, nothing." I bang on the table to make my point, maybe a little harder than I meant. "He's just a driver, nothing with him and Maxie."

Tamar turns to Esti, who shakes her head no, she doesn't know from nothing. "That's not who I'm asking about."

"Harry," Bernice says.

"*Please!*" Both girls say to her at the same time. That makes me feel good.

"All right." I look down at my hands. Such old hands. "There's a man, a friend."

Bernice makes like a choking noise, then Tamar gives her a stink eye and she looks away.

"Ma," Esti says. "That guy? The one on the phone—the one you danced with? He's your *friend*? I thought we talked about this?"

"Not everything in my life you have to know. He's a nice man. Funny. Smart. He shows me things on the computer."

Both girls are looking at me. Like how they used to sit together on the couch, watching Disney, their eyes so big. The only time some peace and quiet. Except Esti's eyes get tight with worry. Tamar's are laughing.

"He likes to dress nice. Always with a fancy watch and cufflinks. All the time he sings. He likes for us to dance." They look at each other nervous. "His life with his wife wasn't like me and Daddy. He likes for me to tell him about how we were, me and Daddy."

"Oh, for goodness sake," Bernice makes another noise.

"Ma, go on," Tamar says.

I point my finger at Bernice. "Not in front of her."

Esti is already up and bringing my walker. "Let's go in the lobby."

"The courtyard," I say. "It's nicer there. Private like." Where I sit with Harry.

While we're walking, I figure I have to start talking before they come at me with all the questions. "So what, a man likes me. Such a surprise?"

"But, Ma, he made you fall. And now you're compromised. I'm not sure about this place, what kind of supervision, and care? You can't just be carrying on—"

Compromised? What's she saying? That I have a reputation? Always this girl finds what to worry about, even I don't know what she's talking about. "What are you saying? That they're gonna talk about me? This place, all kind of shenanigans going on."

"No, I meant, physically, your health."

"Don't worry from my health."

"Oh my God," Tamar interrupts. Good. I didn't like where this was going. Tamar is pointing at where the computers are set up. It's that guy, the fat one with the messy beard who always stares at Esti. At every girl visitor. He's busy at the screen, watching his dirty movies. Every day the same. New people, guests, they get all upset, tell him to stop. They run from the room. They call the staff. It helps nothing, like a cockroach he comes back. The rest of us? We turn off our hearing aids. Take off our glasses.

Tamar, she's stopped, watching the *alte* pervert. She pokes Esti. Esti rolls her eyes and pulls her along.

"We went to a dance," I tell the girls, back to the main story.

"Ma," Tamar says. Now she's all worked up, too. "There's a lot of talk here about dancing. Is that all you're doing? You have to be careful about STDs. Just because you don't need birth control doesn't mean you can have unprotected sex. What are the policies here, regarding—relationships? Do they accommodate you? Provide counseling? Condoms?"

Esti cuts her off. "Condoms? We have no idea who this guy is. He could be a—a, some kind of con man. You saw that guy at the computer. Do they even vet people here?" Esti's neck showing her veins. I keep telling her she's too skinny.

"It's a facility, not a homeless shelter." Tamar waves her hand like whatever Esti says doesn't matter.

"They may take, I don't know. You're never here, now you fly in offering condoms? I'm here. I see what goes on." Esti's face, very red.

"Sure. Right. Saint Esti. Then how come this is such a surprise if you're monitoring everything? Listen, all I'm saying is that she's got a right to her own life, right? If she likes this guy, why shouldn't she have some fun? It's not like she's gonna be ar—" Finally Tamar shuts her mouth. Really, she puts her hand over it.

"Exactly," Esti says, like she just won. "Do you really want her to get all involved with a stranger now?" She had the upper hand, but now she's giving it up again by getting excited. It's her nerves. "What if they—get married or something? It happens. It could be a racket. Maybe he's a, a—?"

Married? I cough, I snort elephant noises. Do they listen to me, the subject of all this big discussion? Not one bit.

"If they wanna get married, they'd sign a prenup. Why would they wanna get married, what point is there to that? Besides, we can protect her assets." Tamar the lawyer.

Now a prenup I'm signing? Maybe not a bad idea, I don't like that account, where he put my name. Can you sign a prenup if you don't get married? Maybe something else they call it?

"What the hell is wrong with you? This is Mommy we're talking about, and you're writing her off, signing documents?"

"You're the one who brought up marriage. I'm just saying. Listen. Why don't we at least meet the guy? We could convince them both to run background checks, for his sake, too. He's at much at risk as she is, right? Would that make you happy? We can ask the staff here for his references. Look around. He's probably a harmless lonely old man. Who appreciates Mommy."

According to the clock on the wall, the bowling is about to start. Not real bowling with those heavy balls. No. Here we stand in front of a television and hold onto a remote control. First, it makes a cartoon picture of you, and then that picture does what you tell it with the remote. Not only bowling. Also tennis. And Ping-Pong. All on the television. So busy the staff here, and the words they use, a whole language like we don't know where we are in life? Vibrant Life Plan. Continuing Care Retirement. One day even, Esti should never know, a whole lecture: 'A Guide to a Fulfilling Sex Life for Seniors.' Such interesting things they talked about, much better than the usual book club on Tuesdays. So I know what Tamar is saying. But that's my business, not theirs.

Meanwhile, the girls still going back and forth, I push my walker to the game room.

CHAPTER THIRTY-TWO

Chat Group: Driving Arrangements

Members: Maxie, T-Jam

MAXIE

Hey. This is about my grandmother's status. You know about the last dr. visit—that they're running tests. My mother's come to help so she and my aunt will take over my grandmother's care. Not sure if they'll continue with the driving arrangement we have in place. Wanted to let you know.

T-JAM

I'm sorry to hear that. About your grandmother. I wish her well.

MAXIE

Thank you.

MAXIE

...

...

...

MAXIE

about the other day - I was upset. I didn't. You're very gracious. Kind. So thank you for ... everything. And I'm sorry about your whole painting thing. Her sitting for you and all.

MAXIE

...

MAXIE

...

T-JAM

Nothing to thank me for. We were both there. I, it was great.

...

MAXIE

Well, yeah, it was. But I – no obligation, right? I mean, it happened the one time. And I don't regret it, not at all. But I don't want you to feel – obligated or anything. Well clearly you don't. I just mean – well, we have – had – a working agreement.

T-JAM

don't get all stressed about it. You paid me, we had a deal, that ride didn't count. Off the clock. And not getting my portrait, that's on me. Your grandmother's a very cool lady. You know, she even told me to call her by name.

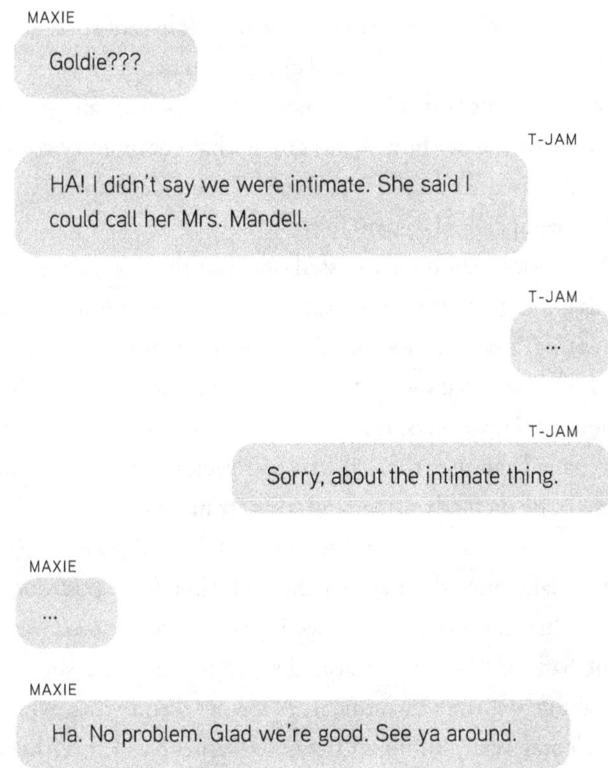

MAXIE
Goldie???
T-JAM
HA! I didn't say we were intimate. She said I could call her Mrs. Mandell.
T-JAM
...
T-JAM
Sorry, about the intimate thing.
MAXIE
...
MAXIE
Ha. No problem. Glad we're good. See ya around.

Glad we're good? See ya around? Sure, yeah, cool. Like she just fell in and out of bed with people all the time. She might be the last single woman in the world who never ever swiped left—or right—she didn't even know which way it worked. She'd thought about it, sure. It's not like she never masturbated. She was normal, totally normal. It's just, well, she—oh never mind. At least she wouldn't have to see him all the time anymore. Just bumping into him on campus, ugh, with that Jessie slobbering all over him. With his dimples and shoulders and hair, his tatted arms, his paint smell.

Good. That was done. Now what? If her weekends and any spare time wouldn't be busy with Safta stuff? Maybe she should sign up on Bumble, or Tinder, or—find out what the rest of the world had figured out. *Get a grip, Maxie. Focus. Breathe.* Who was this person who had invaded her head? Now was not the time to become the adolescent she'd never been. Was she living her life in some kind of reverse trajectory?

Even blowing off Cooperman—Dr. Cooperman—when he'd stopped by to ask her how it was going, that community consortium that she'd joined, and even had received some departmental funding for. She'd campaigned so hard for it.

One session. She'd only missed one. But those kids, their families. The kids undergoing cancer treatments, it was their normal. They were so accepting, brave. Innocent and unaware. It was the parents who needed support. That's what the consortium was all about. They were attorneys, social workers, researchers, all volunteers, there to talk and walk terrified families through the intricacies of what they were up against. To be their advocates, and support network.

And, well, aside from feeling good, it looked good, too, on her CV. Especially once she'd be out there hustling for a post-doc. Maxie Jacobson checking all her boxes, meeting all her goals. *Check, check, check.*

The Safta stuff—she'd allocated space for that, and she'd been accurate about the time investment. A few weekend visits, which were easy, welcome really, filling in the hole Daniel had left. Otherwise, it had been a few hours here and there, walking across campus to meet Safta at her appointments. That's where the driver was so important. The driver. *Enough.*

Only one missed session. She pulled up the website on her phone and added her name to the list for the upcoming meeting. She'd bake cookies or something. She'd make this right. She was back. Her phone pinged. Two messages. Scrolling: the first is an auto-reply to that thing she'd just submitted. The second? *Oh, no. Shit, no.*

From: Esther Abramson<Estia@gmail.com>
To: maxj; TamarJ
Subject: Driving - Mom

The arrangement with the driver has been working out very well, Ma speaks highly of him. Since Tamar and I are taking over Ma's care, can you pass along his contact info?

Shit. Shit. Shit.

Chat Group: Driving Arrangements

Members: Maxie, T-Jam

MAXIE

~~Hey so, bet you didn't expect to hear from me s~~

MAXIE

~~Hi, again. I promise I'm not stalki~~

MAXIE

~~hey, so what I just said, well nm, lol!~~

Just be straightforward. It's business.

MAXIE

Hi, again. this is awkward. My aunt just emailed. She wants to maintain you as a driver. Can I forward her your contact info? You can say no.

T-JAM

Sure.

Sure? Sure?

S.U.R.E. How to unpack that?

CHAPTER THIRTY-THREE

Goldie

"FINALLY, A MINUTE TO MYSELF. These girls, Esti, Tamar, the two of them together, like a team. All the time in my business. Did you call the doctor, did you schedule the appointment? Did you read that article I printed out for you? Are you taking your medicine? If I'm not already sick, this this, interference, will make me so."

Harry looks at me while I'm talking, nodding along like he's listening, but I see the edges of his mouth turning up in a smile.

"What, what's so funny?"

"Goldie, do you hear yourself?"

"Of course, I hear myself. I'm not deaf. Not completely anyway. I have enough other problems."

He tucks his napkin into his collar; this is a habit of his I could live without. But, also, not the worst thing. He says, "And where did your girls learn to be that way, do you think?"

"Where did they learn to be what way? How should I know? Tamar, out in California all those years—in that Berkeley—that's where she learned all her nonsense."

"And you don't think you had anything to do with it—this way your girls are 'all in your business,' as you put it?" Again he smiles so big. *Feh.* Men. They think they know everything.

"Harry, if you're trying to tell me something, just say it. Stop with all these, I don't know, insinuations." Sometimes I surprise myself with the words I know.

He reaches for a piece of bread, buttering it nice and slow. The napkin hanging on his chest is looking stupider every minute. Me, I'm holding onto my spoon very tight.

"Well, as I recall," he finally says, putting his buttered bread on his plate. "This whole thing with the doctors started as a plan for you to find a match for Maxie? And when I said that Maxie was a grown woman who could make her own decisions, didn't you tell me that you were her grandmother?"

"Yeah, so what does that have to do with anything I'm telling you now? We're not talking about Maxie, which by the way, that whole project only gave me all kinds of aggravation. We're talking about my daughters, Esti and Tamar, and how they're all busy bossing my life."

"Because?"

"Because what? What's your point?"

"Goldie, my point is—don't you think they're doing to you exactly what you always did to them?"

"I'm their mother." I say loud and slow, like he's an idiot. Which, right now, he is.

"I rest my case," he says. "You're the grandmother, you control Maxie. They're the daughters, they control you." He takes a big bite from his bread.

I don't even want my lunch. What does he know about anything? Telling me that my girls are acting to me like I do with Maxie—*feh.* It's not like I tell her what to eat. What to think. Sure, once in a while, I told her how to fix her hair, what to wear.

Harry is now eating his soup, making a big deal not to say anything. Good, he already said enough.

CHAPTER THIRTY-FOUR

Maxie

A SMALL HAND ATTACHED TO A MINIATURE PERSON whose missing front teeth only made his smile more enchanting, was pulling at Maxie's jeans. Definitely a biological (hormonal?) reaction. Had to be. Survival of the species. Irresistible. The last thing Maxie would ever have expected. Meanwhile, she allowed herself to be pulled toward his masterpiece, a sheet of paper where a yellow triangle took up the entire left corner of the page, crooked yellow rays extending from it all the way to the something or other, a large green bug? That was as tall as the stunted brown and green blob (a tree?) alongside it. When did kids figure out perspective?

Maxie laughed out loud, why would they have any, when she—but then his proud face fell, the smile inverted. "I love it!" She practically shouted. "Is it the Hungry Caterpillar? Is he going to eat that tree?" God please, don't let it be a cancer metaphor. Such a confounding combination of fragility and resilience.

And sure enough, he pointed, explained, earnest about his drawing. Warming to Maxie's enthusiasm, basking in her now effusive encouragement. More than anything, she wanted to take a picture of this child, at this moment, this hairless child and his picture, and post it to her Instagram. But no. Aside from who knows how many rules that would break, it just wasn't right. They weren't here to be exploited, made public, props for her self-indulgent self-aggrandizement. But she so wanted to capture this feeling, the complicated minefield that was childhood.

She looked around the room. Most everyone had left. She straightened the tables, locked the confidential files away, and offered the last of the cookies to the boy's mother and father, who'd stayed behind to help. They had so little, yet always brought homemade snacks to every session they attended.

"Goodbye, Miss Maxie."

Miss Maxie. Maxie Jacobson, scientist. Community advocate. Generous, full hearted, sensitive. And still rocking the size 6 jeans. She had so much. Didn't she? Of course, she did.

She checked her phone. Esti—God, why couldn't they figure out technology. She kept texting about paying T-J. Just Venmo it, goddammit. But Maxie took Esti's checks, made the deposits on her phone and then Venmoed the payment to T-J. Nice way to stay under his radar.

She walked out the door and down the street and, as if summoned, there he was. The recent object of so much discomfort. It really was T-Jam Bin Naumann just a few yards away, outside some shop, like he was waiting for someone. Someone he was used to waiting for. His body language—long suffering but resigned. Suffering yet another satellite in his awesome orbit?

Cross the street and continue walking? Who did he wait for when he wasn't waiting on Safta? When he was dressed like his normal hipster self, without the Gregory Peck/Cary Grant affectations? The woman who walked out of the shop waved away his annoyance. She was tall. Like him. Confident, long legged. Like him. The comfortable way they talked to each other, the ease between them, blatantly obvious.

Of course, he'd be with a woman like that. That day, that one day that she was *still* mooning over, meant nothing. She knew that. Maxie had a life, too. A solo, fulfilling one. She had her, her, oh, who cared? At least she didn't have to stand outside shop doors waiting for anyone.

No, she was only standing out in the street in full daylight spying on T-Jam Bin Naumann. Not spying. Not her fault if they lived in the same damned enormous, small city.

"T-J!" She called, waving, striding—no, strutting—toward him. There. Not spying, at all.

He looked away from his companion, an unguarded smile still on his face, his loose curls flying free.

"What are you doing way up here?" The smile not quite disappearing, in fact hardly changing at all, like it had been captured in a time-lapse photo. His posture and face giving nothing away as he looked around at the busy Harlem street while Maxie felt herself going through a series of facial and body realignments.

"I, uh, I do some, there's a gig, a committee, we meet monthly. On the weekends, or in the evenings." She pointed somewhere further north. A gig? Like, what, playing chords with the guys? A gig?

"Cool. Oh, let me introduce you."

Maxie finally got to look directly at T-Jam's partner. Gorgeous. Beyond. Regal. She had a long, luscious eyebrow raised. Her dark eyes were enormous, her hair, ridiculously thick and shiny black hung like a curtain, no, thicker, a tapestry framing her shoulders. And her mouth, what human being had a mouth that wide, lips that full, and damn, another perfect dimple?

Not Maxie, that's for sure.

"Jazz," he gestured toward her. "Jasmine." His other palm opening toward Maxie. "Dr. J: Maxine Jacobson." He looked at his feet. "The woman, you know, I told you about. The one—the driving thing."

Maxie held out her hand eagerly. "So nice to meet you." He told her about her? She could feel herself going red all over. What could he have said? Why? Did they share everything? Or was it so insignificant that he casually mentioned, "Oh, that woman with the grandmother, the one I drive, I felt sorry for her, so you know?" Who knows what these beautiful people did and said?

Maxie heard an idiotic laugh coming from her own mouth. "T-Jam has been so great driving my grandmother and all, he goes all out, puts on this suit." Shut up. Shut up. "Sorry. I'm late. So nice to meet you. So nice—"

Jazz takes her hand. "Please. Nice to meet one of T-Jam's friends. We rarely do." Her eyes were bright, laughing. She actually had laughing eyes. Her voice like velvet over sand. Dark, deep, husky and musical. The purples and deep greens of some mysterious desert spilling from her throat.

She was a princess, alongside Maxie's pea. This magnificent creature was looking at Maxie and waiting for her to say something. Anything. "Yes, well, my family" family—plural, not personal, "is incredibly grateful to him. He's been a godsend." Godsend? She'd paid a fortune for his services.

"Godsend! Great! Yes, that's the general consensus." Jazz grins, dazzling bright. "At least our mother would definitely concur. The jury is still out among his sisters. We just get the godlike petulance."

Sisters. Sister? Mother? She was his sister? His sister?

The alluring mouth. The dimple. T-Jam's sister. A shared mother.

Jazz was looking straight into Maxie's eyes. Was she nodding? Meanwhile, T-Jam seemed to be growing—shorter? He was—shrinking. Petulant. Adored. Coddled. A precious man-child.

Maxie heard an idiotic laugh. Her own.

Jazz was talking again, "So, this committee you're on?"

T-Jam was watching her, waiting along with his glorious sister. "Oh, I'm working on this—" Maxie caught herself in time, before she went into supercilious mumbo-jumbo clinical jargon. "It's this thing, reaching out to help families whose kids are—it's a group of researchers, social workers, and attorneys, really. They're so overwhelmed and we try to help them inform—our healthcare; what's new, what's available, trials, to make the entire process less mystifying. It's so terrifying and complicated, for them." She cut herself off. Not the time nor place nor people for her soapbox. "Canada. You're Canadian, right? Universal health care. So much better. More humane."

Wait, was she even Canadian? Where was T-Jam from? Really? Bin? Naumann ? That was clear as mud. And the T? The Jam?

"You're a doctor, T-Jam never said."

Not answering the question about Canada then. Turning it back to Maxie. Why would T-J discuss Maxie's professional status with her? Maxie felt herself going all hot and cold again, all the while Jazz—Jasmine—smiling and looking between the two of them. Enjoying herself.

"Well, not a real doctor," she was quoting Safta? "I mean, not an MD, I can't practice medicine, well, won't practice medicine. I haven't completed my PhD yet, but I'm on the research side of things. I'm there to—" This was getting painful. "Well, never mind, you don't want to hear all this. It was really nice running into you. I have to go."

"Lovely to meet you, and I'd love to hear what you're doing." That smile, blinding, kind of terrifying, like driving into the sunset. "T-J—let's do it. Go out some night. I'll bring Tess." She gave T-Jam a nudge. Then turned back to Maxie, "Tess is my partner. She's a journalist, well, trying to be. But she could write you up, you know? Get you some broader visibility? That's how these things work, right?"

"Sure, yeah. That would be great. Great." Maxie nodded her goodbyes, the street around her a blur of color and light. What an extraordinarily pretty day.

CHAPTER THIRTY-FIVE

Goldie

T-JAM? T-J? WHATEVER HIS NAME IS—looks at me with his midnight black eyes and snow-white teeth, not the smallest bit embarrassed that he's working and I'm the boss. With the three of them taking up the whole back seat, I have to sit up front with him. Now they can see how he just leans over to close for me the seatbelt, what we already established he does. I make like to push his hand away, the girls need to see I can do for myself, but only I push after I feel the belt is closed. So what? That I use his help, which I never asked for, the girls, not even Maxie, need to know this. Otherwise, who knows what they'll decide they need to do for me, 'for my own good.'

"I told you to bring them? You can't bring a whole *minyan* to come with me to the doctor."

For sure Tamar is behind this, I don't need to blame this beatnik.

"Yeah, you can." Tamar starts, proving my point. And that she heard everything.

Maxie interrupts. "Ma," she says, all polite. "We should listen to Safta." Such a good girl. Then she says, "Safta, today's meeting is important."

"We don't know that. Don't make from molehills, mountains."

"My mother came all the way here to be with you."

"I asked her to?"

"Ma!" Tamar cuts in. I'm surprised, for Maxie she usually has the patience. "Maybe it's not for you, okay? Maybe I needed to be here, all right? Me and Esti. You don't get to decide this for us. We get to say if we're here for this meeting. You're our mother. Non-negotiable."

"I'm not incompetent!" I yell back at her.

"Nobody is saying you are." Esti taking charge. "Nobody ever would say that about you. Ma, please, this is for us. Can you please just let us be here for you?"

Outside, everything gray. Apartment buildings and shops line the dirty sidewalks behind big garbage piles filling the street. Overhead trains going—noise, such noise and dirt. This is the pollution that makes people sick. That's making this climate change they keep talking about. Everywhere people, so many people, rushing, rushing, not seeing what's in front of them so much they're running to get somewhere else. Like those mice in the cages, spinning, spinning. Trapped.

1960

In the night I wake up feeling like I'm choking. And during the day? Up and down the steps, six flights up and down.

"Goldie," Mordy calls from the bedroom. "Bring the girls to me. Rest a little." They run around him circles, *Daddy, Daddy*. For them, a treat he's home. So funny that he's in bed like a baby. They make him tea parties and bring him dolls. They collect his curls into little rubber bands. Tamar shoves her doll's baby bottle into his mouth. We look at each other over their heads and don't know to laugh or cry.

That phone call, the rush to the hospital. An intersection, a light, a truck, Mordy's car—the whole side smashed in. Six weeks, the doctor said. They told us he's lucky. A full recovery, they promised. "He's young, strong as an ox."

"Mordy," I said. "How are we going to manage?"

"There's going to be a settlement, we'll be all right."

Esti, seven years old, comes with a book. "Sit nice," she says. "Crisscross applesauce."

"We can't sue? You were hit, Mordy."

"This is the best way. You can't fight the truck companies. Hersch spoke to their attorneys. No fuss, they said they'll pay straight out. Cash. It's better, otherwise years it could take, the attorneys walk away with everything. No lawsuit."

He's right. To go to court against a New York truck driver? Everyone says better to keep quiet.

"How long before we get it?"

Never we finish a conversation though. "Daddy, Daddy," all day long the girls so excited he's home. When he reaches for the crutches they run to him, "Daddy, Daddy. Use us. Lean on us."

"Let Daddy rest," I finally tell them. "Come, we'll go to the library."

Tamar drops everything and stands by the door.

Esti says, "I'll stay with Daddy. He needs to nap."

Such a *mamela,* that one.

Tamar skipping down the steps. "I like magic books and princesses. But not the scary witches. I like the one with the princesses sneaking out and dancing until their shoes tear. When I'm big, I'm gonna sneak out to dance, and you and Daddy won't know, and then I'll also marry a swan. Did you ever see a swan? Can I? One day—"

At the bottom of the steps that *mekhasheyfe* waits like a spider in her web. She blocks the hallway. That she calls a vestibule. *Feh.*

"Tamar, shh—remember, here we play the quiet game."

It helps to keep quiet? Not at all. The *mekhasheyfe* knows everything. She saw how they had to carry Mordy upstairs, how he's not going out since. She jumps at us from the dark. I close my coat tight. I should be skinny, like the refugees off the boat? And my girls, always they look pretty with the flowery dresses I sew for them, from the leftover slipcover material. It's her business?

I make myself smile, polite. "My husband, he's—" she's going to make me beg. In front of my little girl. "He's laid up? We're just waiting, another week—"

Her eyes, two black pebbles shiny bright from her happy meanness. She hands me an envelope, all ready. She wags her finger in my face. "I'm not running a charity organization here."

In front of my girl she does this. Six million we lost, and this one lives?

I crumple her envelope. "Come," I take Tamar's hand. "We're going to the library, no?"

Beside me Tamar is out of breath. She tugs on my hand, "Mommy, you're going too fast."

"Oh. Just we want to get to the library, right? Before all the best books are taken."

She lets go of my hand and runs the rest of the way, not stopping until she's inside and sees for herself that the children's shelves are full. Her face like a small movie goes from afraid to relieved, then a question mark, at me.

I feel like I'm two inches tall.

The librarian, who knows Tamar well already, tells her they're starting story hour, so quick crisscross applesauce—everything all right. She's lost in another world. She won't remember this. I hope.

Meanwhile, a whole hour of quiet. In the next room there are full shelves, a whole wall, with records, not books. A wonderland this library. There's a sign, it says in big letters, "Career Training." From records a career?

I thumb through them, how to win friends and influence people, how to build shelves—this you can learn from listening to records? Then I see under the letter "S" *Stenography*. The cover says from six records I can finish a whole course. This makes sense: You don't need to do nothing but listen. With Mordy at home busy with the girls, I could sit and—One of the mothers in Esti's class is a school secretary. She was telling us how the hours are great, the benefits so good, the summers off. No *shtupping* into the train to the city during rush hour, no fancy suit with heels, just a local public school. Even a pension, she said.

"You need a college degree?" I asked her.

She shook her head, no. "Just a test," she said. "Stenography. Typing. Some basic bookkeeping."

I can pass tests. Benefits? A pension? School hours? Home when the girls are home? Holidays, the whole summer off? I start to breathe faster. Even I'll still be able to help in the shop.

I collect all six records. "I can have these?" I ask at the checkout desk. For sure, for records there's a different system. These aren't just paper books.

"Due back in three weeks." The librarian takes my card without looking up.

Two records a week. Easy. Also, boring.

Now the music in our house is that man's slow voice, like he's on the wrong speed. "*Dear Mrs. Car-pen-ter, comma, We...are...de-light-ed....*"

The girls giggle, and Mordy calls from the bed, "*Dear....Mrs. ... Man-dell, comma, We...re—quest....your....com-pa-ny at our Tea Social this af-ter-noon...*"

And the girls, "*Mo-mmy, comma, we're hun-ga-ry comma, please period.*"

Mrs. Carpenter can wait. But at night when they're sleeping, back to Mrs. Carpenter.

Nobody is gonna wag their finger at my girls. Nobody is gonna give them envelopes.

2017

THREE SETS OF EYES STARING at me from the back seat of the car.

"So, what are you waiting for?" I ask. "You're all coming or what?"

CHAPTER THIRTY-SIX

Goldie

THE WORDS ARE LIKE IN A CIRCLE FLYING AROUND MY HEAD.

One word I heard. Just one.

I'm here and I'm not. Everything fuzzy around the edges, the faces, the colors, everything loud but nothing I hear. The world around me like a movie that is going silent to sound, from black and white to color, then back.

"This thing on my nose," I hear myself, like words from somebody else.

"What?" They all turn to look at me. Surprised. Like I'm not here. Already.

"This thing on my nose?" I repeat, like a stupid bird what repeats all day long. "This thing, this." I point at the middle of my face. "I'm not, I don't have to do nothing with it now, right? I mean, this cancer, it's, it's," I wave my hand. "So my nose, it doesn't matter anymore."

Liver, they said. It's in my liver.

"I don't want you should do anything, you hear? I'm not going to suffer with the chemo, with the losing my hair, with the vomiting all the time."

"Ma," Tamar says.

"Safta," Maxie says at the same time.

Esti, she's quiet, tears filling her eyes.

That nice Dr. Berber, who I wanted maybe for Maxie, but already he's married, he says, "It's a lot to absorb. Why don't we make an appointment for next week, or later this week, after you've had time to take it in, think about it? I work with an excellent oncologist. You'll have a team."

"I come in for nothing, just, just," I look at Maxie who's pulling on her long curls like she doesn't know what to do with her hands. "Just I wanted to—and all of you, you find things wrong with me. That wasn't the plan."

"What plan?" Tamar looks at me.

Cancer. My turn.

"How much time?" I ask the doctor. Again, everyone gets quiet.

He stands up and comes around the desk to stand next to me. He speaks slowly, carefully. Like to make sure I can hear him, like he knows I'm not really here. "It depends on treatment options."

I look at him, only him. The rest here, they don't need to hear this. "No suffering. Just to go. Without pain."

"There are things we can do. We will do."

He reaches, for my hand, and I let him hold it, like it's a dead fish, not connected to me. I say, "Not the chemo. Better not to live than to live like that. I had a good life. I'm ready."

"Ma," Esti says. "Let's listen first."

"What's to listen? He said it all already."

"But—" Esti starts.

"If I may," the doctor has a nice voice. Overall, he's very nice. Why does he have to be married? Why can't he fall in love with Maxie, then I could know that's taken care of. And why is Tamar again looking like she's wearing potato peels? I can't go yet. Still so much I have to fix here. And why Tamar never talks about her husband—something wrong there. And Esti, she has to stop crying and taking care of me so much. What will she do when I'm not here?

"I still have what to do," I say out loud.

"The first thing is to meet with Dr. Harris, an excellent oncologist," Berber says. "Then we'll have more data, a better sense of what alternatives we have."

"What kind of name is Harris?" I ask. "I want a Jewish doctor."

"Ma!" Again, Tamar all excited. "What do you, what does it matter?"

I don't have time to be polite. "I want to know everything about him. How old he is, is he married."

"What the fuck?" Tamar says, then covers her mouth.

"I'm dying, I get to ask what I want."

Maxie stands up. "Thank you, Dr. Berber. You'll send this doctor, Harris, the onc—" She can't say the word. Then she does, stronger. "The oncologist, all Saf—my grandmother's records, is that right? We'll have a meeting, all of us?"

"But you, you, you'll still be a part of it?" I ask Berber. "I shouldn't just get shuffled around like like—"

He holds tight my hand, all day long he must be used to this kind of thing. How does one stay a doctor when this is what you deal with all the time? And an oncologist, like the angel of death. *Feh.* But my time is short, I have to find for Maxie—I have to—but not an oncologist. That won't be a life.

"I'm on your team, Mrs. Mandell."

"Goldie," I say to him. "We don't need to stand on ceremony. That's for when you have time."

CHAPTER THIRTY-SEVEN

Goldie

TIME.

Time.

Waves. When you're standing in the perfect spot, in the perfect position. You slide in the water like it's the most natural thing in the world, the wave lifts you, carries you, fast and cold, flies you to the shore. You catch your breath and laugh and get up and go again. I need to catch them, every single one. Hold onto them. These waves will carry me all the way. Waves that change everything. All the good times. The best times. I'm seeing them all.

1947

ONE LOOK AT HIM, THAT'S ALL IT TOOK. This one I would hold onto, all the way.

A whole week I was on pins and needles, finally it's Sunday and we're going on a date. All my friends came to help me pick out what to wear. Not like I have so much to choose from, really, just they came over to let me talk about him. To wish me luck. Each one, even Shirley, giving me a hug on the way out. "Six months, Goldie. In six months, a ring on your finger."

I can't stop smiling.

I see him from outside running up the steps. He shakes hands with Pa, who's special going late to the shop. How tall Mordy is next to him, how he stands so straight. How he looks Poppa straight in the eye, answers his question, directly. In Yiddish.

This is a boy who is a man. He saw more things already in his short life that nobody should ever see. Almost I wish he was in his Army uniform, stupid thing to think, with the war just over. I walk down the street with my head high. If the whole neighborhood is gonna watch, at least I'm giving them something worth seeing.

Mordy walks on the balls of his feet, like to get somewhere fast. "Prospect Park, it's near here? We can rent a boat. I thought, since we met on a boat?"

A boat? A scene like from the movies. And how he handles himself so comfortably with the guys at the boat-stand. A *Greena* and a regular guy. Perfect just for me.

I'm sitting in the boat like I'm Cleopatra and he's rowing me down the Nile. Sweat is collecting on his face and he neatly takes his shirt off, and folds it over the bar on the boat. His muscles bulge with each stroke. I'm tasting again every kiss from the drive home only a week ago. I tell myself to look around at the trees, the water, not just to stare at his arms, his neck and chest when he pulls on the oars.

He stops and smiles. That smile. My face is all hot, good he can think it's from the sun. He goes back to rowing, and I go back to watching him row. The whole time in back of my head my friends, what they said, *six months a ring.*

When we pull up to the dock, a little man in a uniform is standing, his foot tapping on the wooden boards like he's waiting for something to happen. Big patrol, watching the lake? Then, even though we're in the water right in front of him, Mordy helping me from the boat, this *shmoe* holds up like a cone loudspeaker and yells into it, "Police. You're under arrest."

Under arrest? We robbed a bank and this was our getaway boat? And why is he yelling into a loudspeaker when we're standing right in front of him?

He puts down the loudspeaker and comes over to us, his hand on his belt now, and he orders Mordy to drop the oars, which he was already placing on the dock like we were told to do. He says, "I'm arresting you for indecent exposure."

Mordy puts his shirt back on, he says he's sorry. He didn't know. Why would he, always the guys in the neighborhood have their shirts off on the hot days. This is not a question in the citizenship test.

The fat-faced policeman says Mordy has to go to the station.

The last time Mordy saw his father he was going to a police station. But this is America.

I can explain to this man—this police officer of stupid—that Mordy is a war hero? The way his face curled up when he heard Mordy's accent? I keep quiet.

Mordy smiles at me like from under his eyes, and my whole body relaxes. He'll know exactly how to handle this *shmegegie* cop. "Goldie," he whispers, when the cop is turned around. "Think of the story we'll have of our first date. A story for a lifetime."

Such a lifetime.

The bungalow in Rockaway Beach, in the middle of the rows of tiny shacks that fill the whole street. We can stay until the season ends, the landlord said. He likes that we're there so early, in March, like to protect the properties. This, or share Poppa's apartment until we save enough for a deposit and a month's rent for a place of our own. So what if there's no heat in those bungalows. For us, no such thing as cold. Until July, before the summer people come, the whole beach to ourselves. Every night, no matter how tired we are from Mordy working and taking the classes that the Army gives for the soldiers who came back, and me in Pa's shop and the extra bookkeeping, we go to the beach. Our own *Gan Eden*.

Afterwards, in the outside hot shower. Hot from the shower and cold from the air and salty from the sea.

That's a honeymoon.

Step by step, one foot then the other. The years roll on, like the waves, that almost you don't see or hear them anymore. Almost.

And then, alone, you're back on the shore.

CHAPTER THIRTY-EIGHT

Goldie

HARRY'S MAKING FROM THIS SUCH A MYSTERY. "Wear something comfortable," he tells me. "But be ready to paint the town."

I need to tell him. But now when he's planning this big date? A little more I can wait. Nothing happening so fast.

"A nightclub?" I ask. "A show?"

"No," he says, "nothing too fancy. You'll want to be comfortable."

That cream-colored wool suit I bought that day with Maxie. What better occasion should I save it for? Only no new shoes. You find a pair that works, that don't pinch, you stick with them. Of course, a salon appointment for my hair and nails. My hair. No chemo. I told them.

Harry is also wearing tan pants, but with a white shirt and a blue sports jacket. We make a good picture. We're about to leave, when Bernice sees us in the lobby. I should be surprised? Probably all day she checks the books where everyone has to sign out what they're doing. Anyway, she makes at us all kinds of oohs and aahs, and then like we're sixteen years old, she pulls out a phone and says, "A picture. Let me take a picture." Harry, always a good sport, puts his arm around my shoulder, so what can I do? I smile at the camera. Bernice shows us the picture, which now you can see right away, not like waiting weeks for them to come back from the developer. In the picture, Harry is just putting his arm on my shoulder, and I'm looking at him. And what I see? A smiling girl out on a date. And my outfit—perfect, very smart.

The next picture, the one where I posed? That's where I look like I'm going to the dentist.

Outside, I don't believe it. A fancy black limousine. I tell Harry about my deal with T-Jam. "Goldie," he says, "please. Let me take you out in style."

I want to tell him it's stupid to spend so much money when a car is a car. But I see Harry's face, and I understand that maybe a car isn't always only a car. Men, boys, always they have a thing for the cars.

At least it's a normal size, not like the ones that go on for a whole block. And then, the driver who comes out? *Himself*—with the suit and the tie and the hat. And that *chutzpahdik* smile.

"Harry," I knock into him like accident on purpose. "How?"

"I asked him the last time he dropped you off. The limo was my idea though. I know a guy."

Of course, he does.

"Madam, Monsieur," T-Jam holds open the door. I see around his neck a camera. "Before you get in? Would it be all right to photograph you this evening?"

"For your painting?" I ask. What, if I wait for him, it'll never happen.

And I can't believe, this big shot with all the ideas and the smiles and the chutzpah turns all pink. "That would be wonderful," he says. So sweet, I can tell he really means it. "But, no. I can't paint from a photograph. But I might try a sketch if the light and setting is right. You won't know I'm there."

"Sure, sure," I say, smiling big. "It's taken you long enough."

Once we're all settled, the walkers in the trunk, the seatbelts locked, I take in the luxurious arrangement. This must be how the Queen of England feels every day. I even wave to Bernice, that stupid half wave twisting my wrist like I'm opening a jar in middle of the air. Her mouth hangs open at the front doorway.

"So," I say to Harry, leaning back into the soft cushions, "now you can tell me where we're going?"

His smile is all mysterious. And maybe a little shy. "You'll see."

We drive over the bridge, and along the West Side Highway. I thought for sure we'd get off at midtown, to go to Broadway, but the car, it keeps going straight.

Docks. I see lots and lots of boats, big ones, small ones.

"A sailboat, Goldie. A sunset cruise. Private."

"Harry, a boat. Beautiful." I blink hard. "Just beautiful."

Like a sign? *Feh.* Sometimes the wave just comes when it comes, perfect.

Two men wearing all white and starched clothes run down the ramp to set up the walkers, to help us out. Then one goes with each of us up the ramp, helping us over the bumpy parts. How Harry thought of this whole production. Once we're on the boat, the captain, in an elegant sailing jacket, greets us with champagne. The wind is in my face and running through my hair. Harry puts his hand over mine, on the handle of my walker. We shuffle over to the deck chairs where there are blankets folded neat at the bottom.

I drink my champagne. I drink it all. Every single drop.

"Whoa," Harry laughs. "Don't you want to pace yourself?"

"No, I want it all," I tell him.

I want it all.

THIS BEAUTIFUL NIGHT, being here like a princess. Not a princess, a queen. Not looking through a window, coming in the back door. I'm here, it's me, Goldie Mandell, in my Lord and Taylor wool suit, with this fancy man with his cufflinks, watch and champagne. The men on the boat, the captain, all here to give me whatever I want, blankets, pillows, more champagne. They're here, but also hiding not to get in my way. My way. Like I'm a *macher.*

This is what they call, arriving. I've arrived.

To what? Better not to ask. Best to live in the exact moment I'm in.

From the water, where we're now sailing, the big white sheets all puffy and blowing, I see Manhattan, pieces of it. This small island to hold so much. All the big important buildings, *shtupped* like onto a postage stamp of land, they had to grow up, not out. So many people, so many stories. From the richest of the rich to the poorest of the poor, all squeezed together. Everyone's story the most important one, to them. The next person, the one they see every day on the train maybe, or even who lives across the hall, or who sits across the aisle in the office, they each have what they think is the most important story, too.

And up there, He watches this theater he created and laughs? *Vey is mir*, in *mien alta yerin*, I'm an old-age philosopher?

Good to get out. Every day in that place, with the same people, the same walls, the routines and activities, you lose the bigger picture. But what is this big picture? Here, I'm at the end of my story, and I'm just another little dot? From Germany, through Ellis Island, growing up in this mean city, making a life. Creating a family.

Now, on this boat, all fancy with a man I know from a few months. Suddenly this man to be so important at the end of everything? A whole new chapter at the end of the whole book? Like the period at the end of the sentence, just a tiny dot. That marks the story finished.

"Goldie," Harry says. He's smiling, like he's also thinking deep thoughts. I didn't know he could. "You look very pretty, the way the light is hitting your face. Where are you?"

I'm falling apart and this he calls pretty?

"Harry," I answer. "This," I wave at the city view. "It's so much. It's everything. I lived here almost my whole life, you know. To see it all laid out like this, it's—" My voice starts to break. I need to pull myself together.

Harry opens his arms. He isn't coming to me though, he stands there, waiting, smiling a small smile, his eyes like they're hoping.

I push my walker to where he stands. When I let go, he reaches out both his hands, and I take them in mine. One step, one step. Closer, closer. I can smell his cologne, of course this man wears cologne, better he smells than me. Another step, and then he is holding me close, and I put my head on his shoulder. My eyes, I want to say it's from the sea air, but these are tears that are coming from inside me. Even with my poufy hair I let my head lie on Harry's shoulder, and I'm surprised how strong it is underneath my cheek.

He kisses the top of my head. How long since anyone did that? He tightens his arms around me. We stand like that, looking back on the city.

"Me, too, Goldie," he says. "I lived here all my life, too. I walked those streets, took those trains. Went to those shows." Then he adds, more quietly, "went to those clubs."

He sighs, shaking his head. "We're not done yet though, eh, Goldie? Look at us. We still got some gas in these old engines. Meeting you, Goldie, you're my second chance."

More like his last chance. This is not a winning hand he's holding.

"Harry," I have to let him know. "Harry, this night. It's perfect. But you shouldn't count on me to be your chance."

"Goldie, no, let go. Live a little." He says, his smile falling a little.

"That's all I have left, Harry. A little, just a little I have left. To live."

When his eyes tell me he doesn't understand, I explain more. "Those doctor visits? If you poke enough, they find something. I had some tests. The results aren't good."

"Aren't good?" Harry repeats, his face turning white.

"They're bad, Harry. Very bad." A second passes. "The worst."

He looks out at the water, then when he looks at my face, I see the softest, kindest eyes looking back at me. "Then we make it the best days of your life, Goldie. Every single day. Would you let me do that for you?" He looks again at the water. "For me? Would you let me do that for me?"

I feel like a weight coming off my shoulders. To have this companionship until the very end, this I never could even think to hope for.

His eyes are shining bright. He leans his face to me, and he's kissing me, like he means it. And I'm kissing him back like I mean it, too. The tea from the bottom of the pot, bitter, but also sweet and strong.

CHAPTER THIRTY-NINE

Maxie

MAXIE INHALED, scanning her computer screen one last time, hardly noticing the cloying, slightly rotting smells that suffused the lab. The lab. *Her lab.* Her place. Her space. Pausing over one problematic PowerPoint slide, she hit save, and closed down her computer. She stretched her arms and legs, loosened her neck, finally stood up, remembering to pull her protective glasses from the top of her head and rest them alongside her laptop. After exchanging her lab coat for her outside jacket, she walked past her samples, checking that the lights were on, the machine purring gently. Last one out—shut off the lights, and lock the door.

She looked at her watch and picked up her pace. Plenty of time. Definitely enough to walk— *stomp* her way home. She needed to regroup. Damn Esti. Damn email. The one piece of technology Esti had mastered. Silly Maxie, believing that it would be easier with her aunt in charge. At least she had a deeper appreciation of her mother now. She pulled out her phone to reread it. It hadn't gotten any better since her first reading.

From: Esther Abramson<Estia@gmail.com>
To: maxj; TamarJ
Subject: Advocacy - Mom

Maxie,

I need Safta's paperwork. Tamar says you're too oversubscribed but as her former advocate, you still have all her documentation. I need you to get it to me ASAP! ORIGINALS WITH SIGNATURES. DON'T SCAN AND SEND ELECTRONICALLY! The most efficient way to handle is for you to hand deliver them to the driver so we'll have them in time for tomorrow's appointment.

Please confirm receipt and acknowledgement of this email.

Aunt Esti.

DELIVER? ASAP? CONFIRM RECEIPT? Former advocate? Goddammit. Even her font choice was obnoxious. And what was wrong with just scanning and emailing?

Never mind. Deep breath. Just walk. A beautiful night, the sky just tinting gray after the late sunset. Her mother always warned her not to walk home alone, in the dark, but that was so New York in the eighties. Besides, it wasn't full dark yet. Still, her apartment key was in her bra. Just in case. Can't hurt. Thanks, Ma. Thanks, Esti. Thank you, thank you thank you.

This was just such a friggin'—*oh, shit.* Maxie tried and failed to catch herself before her knee collapsed beneath her. All those fucking enormous tree roots all down Riverside Drive. Momentarily stunned, she barely registered the spasms shooting up her thigh, through her ass, into her lower back.

"Dr. J?"

There he was, T-Jam Bin Naumann at his uncompromised and unapologetic best: Birkenstocks and socks, beanie and curls, hairy, tatted legs and arms, a knight atop his twenty-first century steed—a bicycle he gallantly threw to the side in order to lean over and offer her a hand up. "I was just on my way to meet you, for the papers. The ones you texted me about. You all right?"

She blinked. This one was her best yet, her daily conjuring of meet-cute events. Script perfect. Angry confused heroine. Dashing, unperturbed prince. She blinked again. Still there. "I'm fine. Just fine." She put her foot down, forcing herself not to grimace. Hopefully.

His left eyebrow shot up. "Doesn't look fine. You're hobbling. C'mon, I'll give you a ride back to your place."

"Really, it's all right. I just tripped, wasn't paying attention." Setting her foot down, she clenched her teeth as the pain shot straight through her. Again.

He reached for her elbow. "You have a lot of your grandmother in you, you know?"

She crossed her arms, "Ha. Hardly. She'd never—" What? She'd never what? Never want someone, something, so much, and not have any game.

"It's not a bad thing. C'mon, let me get you home."

This time she nodded. He bent, she draped her arm around his neck, he held onto her waist, and she hopped hugged her way to his—*bicycle?* That's right—the bicycle.

"You're kidding?"

He shrugged. "It works. C'mon. You must've done this before?"

T-Jam mounted his bike from the back, one long leg on the ground, the other swirled in a graceful arc over the back wheel and onto the other side. It was like a dolphin cresting a wave. Maxie studied the sidewalk. Holding the bike steady between his thighs, not that she was paying attention, he reached forward to guide Maxie toward the top-tube before wrapping his arm around her waist to lift her onto it.

Yes, she had done this before, and it was as deeply uncomfortable as she remembered. Maxie knew to keep her legs extended and out of the way. Not easy under any circumstances, worse with a bum knee.

But chagrined and hopeless, she wiggled back cooperatively, and T-Jam leaned forward, his arms circling her to reach the handlebars. He began to pump the pedals, her head pressed against his chest, bouncing to his thumping heart as he strained. She smelled his scent and she was fourteen years old on Larry Gold's bike, aching and glorious, *does he like me? Does he like me? Does he?*

God, she was still such a sap.

Then T-Jam was carrying her up the steps but looking the other way when she pulled the key out of her bra. He brought her to her couch. "Where do you keep your plastic bags. I'll get you some ice."

"I don't have any. They're evil." She shrugged.

He looked in her freezer and came back with a bag of frozen veggies that must have been in there since 1995. "Try this."

She pressed the bag to her knee, relishing—needing the cold to numb the heat that was burning the surface of her skin.

"Anything else I can get for you? Some water, pillows?" He was all over the place, pulling pillows from the opposite end of the couch, propping her up. She pressed her hands into the soft cushions so he could get the pillow behind her back, anything to get him out of here before she jumped his bones. Again. Her hands brushed against the remote, buried deep within the folds— that's where it had disappeared to—but no. Not this. Not now. Maxie's single-life support system for rainy days and lonely nights sprang to life on the television screen. Picking up right where it had been left off—somewhere in the middle of *Dirty Dancing.*

All the heat in her body rushed to her face. How many rainy Sundays, Maxie and Tamar, tucked into the couch, Maxie's head on her mother's chest until she pushed her off with a groan and a smile. The two of them, shoulders swinging, hips swaying. Not with Patrick Swayze. With Baby, all nose and frizz and longing. "Maxie girl," her mother would say, her own frizzy hair, not insignificant nose and toothy grin all right there, Sunday afternoon accessible. "I swear, this was my life, the Catskills, the Goyish boys, except, well, we never got to spend a summer luxuriating like that. Maybe mine was more Dirty Dancing meets Saturday Night Fever." Even her eyes dancing, excited. Young. Her Berkeley Immigration Lawyer Mom.

Even with the ice numbing her knee, Maxie was hot all over. Why couldn't it have turned on in middle of some PBS documentary? Because this is who she was. In her home. Her Home. She didn't have to defend it. She didn't have to defend anything to T-Jam Bin Naumann. Of course, she didn't. But she was going to anyway. "I love that movie." She shrugged, fussing with the ice pack of peas on her knee.

"I watched it." she swallowed, unable to stop herself, this was what she did, what she was going to do, dig herself in deeper—shut up, Maxie, just shut up—but her mouth was on autopilot, "the first time with my mother, when I was, I don't know, ten, eleven years old. That movie, it was, Baby was, that scene where she carries the watermelon.

She carried a watermelon? No. No. Rewind.

"You could feel Baby's hope, you know? She was idealistic and the world was on the brim of stuff. And there was all this sex in the air. And all this class stuff going on at the hotel."

Maxie felt herself morphing into that watermelon. All pink and round and full of stupid black pits. She tried again, "but she was just an earnest kid. Who wanted, who wanted *more*. She was on the cusp. She wanted life. She put herself out there. All she wanted, dreamed of, was, you know, to fly out of her corner? Have the time of her life?"

Maxie stopped, finally, refusing to look up. So she looked at the screen, where Baby was unbuttoning Johnny's shirt. Oh, God, if only this couch would open up and swallow her whole. Damn that remote. One dumb movie, not a treatise on American White Elitist privilege. She liked dumb movies. She pressed the lumpy bag to her knee.

"Well, that's me. Your turn. Is it exhausting?"

T-Jam looked confused. "What? The bike riding?"

"Being so cool? Is it a lot of work?" she continued, hearing herself, hearing the sexy beat of the movie soundtrack. Where was her off switch?

"I don't know what you mean?" He shifted, looked around. Eyes landing on the screen where Johnny and Baby were in the woods, hiding from Baby's father.

Maxie finally turned off the TV, the silence much worse than the music track had been.

"Oh, c'mon. You're walking charisma. You've even got my grandmother wrapped around your finger. You're the poster boy for hipster chill. *Chipster.* The clothes, the attitude, the art, the paint streaks, your hair." Not to mention the dimples. She punched the pillow on the couch. She'd fallen for it, all of it. "I like dumb movies, okay? What do you like? Ingmar Bergman marathons?"

He tilted his head to the side. "Not really. Too many metaphors. And subtext. Obscure symbolism. Two hours at a time is my limit." He looked at Maxie and laughed. "Gotcha. No, I like movies. Not just "films." Doesn't everyone? I'm gonna let you in on a secret: My sisters watched 'Dirty Dancing' all the time. Soundtrack of my teens. Then I'd hide in my room and practice dancing in front of my mirror." He had a faraway look, a small smile.

"You know, I imagined getting out of my corner, having the time of my life." He was quoting her? Quoting the movie? "Wondering if I'd ever touch a girl, ever dance with one, ever meet a girl who got me so twisted up in knots that I'd—I'd dress up in a suit and drive her bad-ass grandma all over town, and she'd never even know."

What did he just say? But he was looking at her, like really, really looking at her. Like she had to say something. Anything.

"But, but—you skateboard?" *Skateboard?* "You, you, play hockey—I've seen you on campus." Now she was admitting to stalking him? All right, yeah, she maybe *had* done the odd Google search. "Your hair!" His hair? That fall had done something to her head. Her precious head.

Oh, God. The dimple, seriously flashing now.

"All right, Dr. J. Let me set you straight on how—what did you call me? *Chipster?* On how chipster I am. One. Skateboard? I started skateboarding 'cause my mom was always late getting me from school; she had trouble with the culture—getting used to—anyway, so I'd walk home, and it took forever and I'd get picked on, you know, for being—it was a tough neighborhood. The cool kids all had skateboards, and I convinced my parents it would be practical, wheels. I saved what I could, small stuff little jobs here and there, and there was this, like secondhand store, and I convinced the owner to let me sweep out his shop. Wheels. Things got a little easier after that." He shook his head.

"Hockey? Same deal. It's not cool to be a guy who likes to draw—hockey made me all right. Unsuspicious. And then I started doing the drawings on their equipment, and their posters." He looked at the wall now, finally taking his eyes off her. "And it helped, you know, for getting into Uni. Out of Germany. I wanted—" He ran his fingers through his hair, but gave up about half way through the tangle. "What next? What are we up to? My hair?" He shrugged. Then he leaned forward, and she nodded, not sure she had. The back of his hand was soft against her forehead and he brushed away some stray curls that had fallen loose from her ponytail, then his thumb lingered on her flushed cheek. "Don't you get it, Maxie Jacobson? Why are you all in knots?"

Knots? Didn't he know that his eyes, looking at her that way, worked like magnets uncoiling every last shred of resistance she never had anyway?

"You could do anything, but you take care of your grandmother. You smile with your whole body. You turn red when you're embarrassed. Which is all the time. You have no idea that you're beautiful. That amazing hair. You believe in your research. You're the last one to leave your lab at night. You're on that do-good committee and you don't have a single plastic bag in your apartment. You watch movies with your mother. Who wouldn't?" His voice turned soft, "If they could?"

Any minute now, harps would start playing. Why not, since none of this was real? Stuff like this didn't happen, characters like T-Jam Bin Naumann don't exist except—except in dumb movies. And Maxie Jacobson didn't believe in fairy tales. In happily-ever-afters. She was a scientist. A real person. A real, but oh, my. What was he doing now?

Resuming his squat beside her, balancing himself in the perfect yoga position with utter nonchalance, he yet again raised his chipster quotient. And he was *still* talking. The reel was still unspooling.

"That day when we came here from your grandmother's place. When we," and now *his* face turned pink. T-Jam Bin Naumann was blushing, and Maxie wasn't. Because none of this was really happening. But why was her heart beating so hard? And so loud? "It was—how I knew it would be. But you freaked out. You didn't want me in your space. I got it. I don't belong in your world."

Oh, but he did.

"You wanna know why I never asked your grandma to sit for me? Coz I wanted it to last. And it kept getting harder, the more I got to know her, to know you, the more I wanted to—"

Enough. Either this was real or not. She reached out, sure she'd fall into vapor, and, yes, she fell off the couch, yelping when her knee banged the hardwood floor. He was still there. He was still there. He had her knee in his hand, rubbing it, not at all helpful but no way was she gonna tell him that, tell him anything. Too much talking. Instead, she sealed his mouth with her lips, choreographing the deliciously dirty—the glorious dance she'd always believed she'd perform. Someday. One day. This day.

WHEN MAXIE WOKE UP, her naked back pressed against T-Jam Bin Naumann's equally bare skin, she thought, "If he's really here. If he reaches over. If he kisses me. If he wants me—"

Before she had a chance to complete the thought, his dimples were flashing and there he was. "I have to leave," his mouth pressed against her ear. "I'm sorry. I have a date with your grandma."

Maxie stretched, smiling. Then shot up. *The papers. Safta.*

CHAPTER FORTY

Goldie

THEY TELL ME NO SALT. They tell me no sugar. Cancer, they tell me, loves sugar. It feeds on the sugar. So why no salt, I ask. They tell me, not good for my heart. My heart? It's my liver that's sick.

They tell me. They tell me. They tell me.

Esti coming around all the time with these concoctions. Every day—lentils. With turmeric, she tells me. What's turmeric, I ask her. It's good for you, she tells me. She makes me hot tea, green tea, with this turmeric and ginger. The smell alone makes my *kishkes* turn. A little honey I can have, I ask her? What difference does it make now what I eat? But this I can't say to her, so hard she's trying. So hard she always tries. Later, I'll eat it later, I tell her. My appetite not so good right now.

Tamar, she comes with candies. Cookies. Try them, she says, with such a big smile. "You made these?" I ask her. "No," still with the smile. "Just have one."

Better than the stuff that Esti brings, but something about those candies, those cookies. Like all of a sudden I'm feeling myself, watching myself from the inside out. "You put something in these?" I ask her. "I feel like, I don't know, like I'm underwater, swimming. Everything like in slow motion."

You like it, Tamar asks, her smile even bigger. No. I tell her. I don't like anything what's happening.

Maxie, Maxie. So sweet. She comes, she doesn't bring food, thank God. She sits, she holds my hand, like she doesn't know what to say. I should help her? So hard she's trying to figure things out. My Sheyfe. Why she makes her life difficult, she can do anything, have anything she wants. Except that. I see how they are together. She thinks I don't know. I know. So many choices, she'll make the right one.

Harry, he's like a light shining in this tunnel. He brings me French fries. He watches with me movies and tells me jokes. He takes me out for walks and brings me flowers. All the time flowers. We talk. All the time we talk. Who knew what I have to say is so interesting?

CHAPTER FORTY-ONE

Maxie

MONDAY MORNING AND MAXIE had no idea where her phone was, or even if it was charged. No beeps, buzzes, or alarms. T-J's soft breathing the only sound in the room.

Saturday morning—a lifetime ago—they'd prepared breakfast. In her small kitchen they'd squeezed close at the tiny counter, scooping out mangos, dipping warm tortillas oozing melted cheese into spicy salsa, biting into the rich meat of ripe avocados. Maxie tasted nothing. It was the most delicious food she'd ever eaten.

What was this extraordinary man doing in her home, in her bed? In her body? A hand, his hand, reached over, piercing a mango spear that sat on her plate, lifting it to his mouth.

One plate. One bed. One body.

Words don't come. Their language is silent.

On Sunday, finally, they forced themselves to go out. They walked around Manhattan holding hands. Tight squeezes, little pinches, confirming they were still attached. Maxie's body different, new, somebody light, funny, and alive in T-Jam's presence. It jumps at his touch, its eyes see things in vivid color, admiring every plant, laughing when the street vendor explains how the painted eggs are filled with confetti that spills when they're cracked over someone's head.

Maxine watched this stranger, herself, lift an egg and crack it over T-J's head, saw the pastel bits of paper, tiny round discards from a hole punch, cascade around him, settle into his hair and onto his shoulders. He's so beautiful, his features balanced so perfectly on his face. She saw a hand, her hand, reach to touch his cheek.

He kissed her, confetti littering the cracked concrete. He took her hand, leading her away. "Let's get out of the city."

He drove, she navigated. Up the Hutchinson River Parkway, then the Merritt Parkway, somewhere in Connecticut. A state park. She followed him; wordless, confident he would lead. They climbed higher, forcing short quick breaths, rapid heartbeats. When they rested on a large boulder, he took a knife and the last mango from his backpack, sliced off a large chunk then stabbed it, guiding it into her mouth. She swallowed, sticky sweetness running down her chin.

T-Jam tells her about his family. Running away from Syria, growing up in Germany. Landing in Canada.

"Your name? The T? The Jam? The rest of it?"

He shakes his head. Looks away. "No. I don't go there." He softens the blow, filling in by talking more about his family. His mother is a twin. "My father's brothers are twins. Twins skip a generation. We could have twins." Her cheeks grew warm, her mouth opened to a small O. She raised her hands to cover that traitorous cavern, to revoke the words.

Silent, T-Jam cut another slice of mango, another offering.

On the way down, she fell behind. The incline is too steep, the drop too treacherous. The sun was setting and the air had a nasty bite, pricking at her neck. They'd gone too far, hiked too high. Why had she followed him? Goosebumps formed on her arms, her feet missing her hiking boots, ached and pinched. A mistake.

Backpack on his shoulders he stood like a statue in relief against the tall trees. She forced a smile, nodding. Wondering if they'd ever find their way out. T-Jam waited for her to reach him, pointing downward with his chin. They were ridiculously close to the road, less than twenty yards away, directly above his parked car. She looked at him, her jaw dropping. He smiled a wicked smile, one she hadn't yet seen. Wrapping his hand around hers, he kisses the inside of her wrist.

Back at her apartment, back in her bed. They talk about everything and nothing. T-Jam laughs out loud. Often. He sketches constantly. He thanks her for making him comfortable in her home. For not fussing or cleaning up on his behalf.

"I'd have cleaned if I'd known this would happen. Still, it's not that bad." She waves her arm at nothing.

He lifts his eyebrow and hooks his finger under the bra that's hanging off the back of her chair, looks over at the jeans bunched on the floor.

"Oh that, well, yeah, but you can't—"

"Shhh." He puts his fingers to her lips, cups her chin. "I welcome your lingerie in every corner of my life."

Now they sit at the desolate looking table, the mangoes and avocados gone, the tortilla scraps brittle in their basket. Sketches of her sleeping, reading, wrapped in a towel washing her face are spread willy-nilly across various surfaces. Two days ago? Three? Another lifetime?

"Thank you." T-Jam says.

"It was—nice."

He leans forward, his expression earnest. Focused. T-Jam Bin Naumann. "It was much more than nice."

She put her finger to his lips. Keep it light. Don't crowd him. Don't be needy. Her laugh sounds hollow. "I'll see you on campus?"

The refrigerator hums to life. Two sets of eyes, two tense bodies turn toward the round-faced old-fashioned clock hanging above it. T-Jam pulls his backpack onto his shoulders and just before he walks out the door he pulls Maxie into his chest.

"The T is for Tawfiq, grace, guidance; favor of God; success. The Jam is short for Jamal, beauty, gracefulness. Bin, of course, is son-of. And even though he gave us all Arabic first names, my father chose Naumann, Germanizing our family name, celebrating his status, his family's status as New. I don't tell this to just anyone, Maxine Jacobson. I'm in this for a lot more than a weekend."

CHAPTER FORTY-TWO

Goldie

Time to get dressed and go downstairs. Bernice sits down next to me. That's the trouble with coming down for the *pish-vasser* tea and the stale cookies. Everyone else comes, too.

"How come we're not playing cards anymore?" she asks me. She saw what Harry was like when we played. She thinks I'm going to talk to her about it?

"Oh," I tell her, "the staff, the administration, they put a stop to it. You didn't know?"

She looks all surprised, how come I know something she doesn't.

"They have a rule. No betting. They say it's not allowed in the facility, it's illegal, or something. They can get into trouble." I shrug my shoulders. "I know, craziness, right? Like our nickels and dimes are big money. But it's in the rulebook. They say we can play private like, in one of our rooms, but not out in the shared space." This is true. At least, maybe it is.

Another of the ladies, I think she was jealous when we started playing, always everyone here all upset about something. She caught me in the elevator one day and told me we could get in trouble "with the authorities." Like this is what they'll pay attention to? They can better pay attention to our lunch menu, I told her. But now I remember what she said, and I repeat it to Bernice.

"Maybe we can do something else?" she says. "Maybe," she looks around the room, "maybe we can do sing-alongs with the piano? Does anyone play?"

"Ah," I say, "Look who's coming. Harry, come, come, sit." He can deal with her. She'll be all over him the minute I'm out of the picture. I know it like I know my own name.

"Harry?" Bernice turns all soft and girly. She thinks with her pink sweater he's gonna mistake her for a cute teenager? "You're so musical. Do you play?" She points to the big piano in the corner.

"A little," Harry says. "I can pick out a tune."

This Bernice, she lights up like a bulb. "Would you play for us at night, sometimes, Harry? Since we can't play cards anymore? They can't have a rule against that, could they?" She puts her hand on his arm. "I'm a bit of a singer, you know."

Who cares? None of us can hear. But I get an idea. "What's that thing, that the kids do? They had it at my granddaughter's bat mitzvah? With the machines? And the screens? Kaka, kara, something?"

"Karaoke" Harry says, excited.

"That, yeah," I say. "Bernice, you should ask them about that."

Bernice gets all perked up. A lady with a job.

Chat Group: I don't know how this thing works

Members: Harry, Maxie

HARRY

Hello. My name is Harry Silver. I am a friend of Goldie's. In the place.

MAXIE

Is she all right? What happened?

HARRY

Everything is fine. I didn't mean to scare you. I got your number from Goldie's phone. I know the best way to get in touch with you kids is this texting stuff. But this typing, it's killing me. Can we meet? My treat. There's a coffee shop on Broadway and 232nd? I don't want to talk in front of Goldie. It's a surprise. A good thing. Nothing to worry about.

MAXIE CHECKED HER WATCH, equal parts curious and dubious. And equal parts concerned. If he thought for one minute that she would divulge any of her grandmother's closely guarded health secrets, he could just, well, forget that.

The diner was a classic, though. The waitress was even in a pink dress with a white collar, her pad sticking out of her pocket. With a nameplate. *Doris.* Of course. The booths were covered in some sticky vinyl and the tabletops were splotchy Formica. Sure enough, no question about it, that had to be Harry, that old guy in a tweed overcoat and a fedora making his way out of the Access-A-Ride minivan that pulled up in front of the hydrant right in front of the front door. Yep, definitely him pushing his walker to her table, waving at everyone behind the counter.

"Thanks for meeting me." His voice was pleasant, a little pebbly. "Did you order? Get anything you want. On me. I appreciate you came all the way up here."

"Well, you asked." Maxie shrugged.

He sat down across from her, looking at her intently.

"Nope. Nope." He finally said. Disappointed. "Your grandmother's right, you're a beauty. To tell the truth, any gal under fifty looks pretty good to me, but you really are a looker. But, I guess I was thinking, hoping, that I'd see more Goldie in you. A fellow gets to wondering, you know."

Maxie started to collect her things.

"Hey, wait, I see you're upset. I didn't mean to offend. Just, when you care for a lady, you wonder about all the years you missed, you wonder what, never mind. I promise you, I don't mean anything insulting." He shook his head, "I'm outta practice. I, can we start over? Hello, I'm Harry Silver." He held out his hand.

Maxie shook it, watching his face the entire time.

"Hi," he smiled at their waitress, squinting at her nameplate through his glasses. "Doris, if you could get me a coffee and one of your cheese Danishes? They're so good. Thanks so much." She immediately poured him a coffee. "Thanks so much, I appreciate that. No rush on the Danish, Doris, whenever you can."

Doris beamed. Doris smiled at Maxie, too, like serving them coffee was the highlight of her day.

"Thanks again, Doris." Harry actually tipped his hat to her.

Maxie raised her coffee to her mouth. It was delicious.

"All right," Harry smiled, pouring milk from the little steel jug that sat in the center of the table. He stirred his coffee for a long time. Still stirring, not looking up, he said, "It's this karaoke thing? That we're having next week at the place. I wanna do something special for Goldie. I could use your help."

CHAPTER FORTY-THREE

Goldie

FINALLY, IT'S HERE, THE KARAOKE NIGHT. Of course, it's not really night, they're doing it on the afternoon of March twenty-first. The first day of spring. Also, my wedding anniversary, but this I don't mention. Still, a celebration to make it to another year. They made for us even a special meal, for the karaoke, not my anniversary, of course. Roast beef, with real potatoes, not the stuff that comes from a box. Thank God, I have all my teeth to enjoy it.

In the room that they this time made into a theater, I'm sitting, relaxed. I'm not singing. I'm just in the audience. But Harry, he says to me that I should just wait to hear what he has prepared. He won't tell me, says it has to be a surprise. I'm sure whatever it is, it will be very nice. And even if it isn't, I'll say it is. Nobody here is a Frank Sinatra, you know.

Bernice is standing at the door to the reception room, *vey is mir*, she looks like a cake. She's all pink and puffy, her dress all layers of ruffles, her hair in big soft curls, and I can't believe it, she's wearing gloves like the Queen of England. She's giving out programs, there was a whole committee working on them. With all the retired talent here, there's a lot that can get done.

When she sees me, she gives me a smile, a real smile, "Oh Goldie, just wait." She puts her hand over her mouth, like she has a big secret. "Oh, oh, I mean, never mind. Nothing. Silly me. Here, I saved you a good seat."

I look at the program, it's long. They have ten people singing, and there, at the end, I see Harry Silver.

Next to his name I see the number two. Two songs he's singing? That Harry, he never knows when to stop. He's the last one, they shouldn't walk out before he's finished. Maybe I don't have to worry about that, probably they'll be already sleeping in their seats.

Lauren, finally I got Perky Breasts' name, starts the show with a few words; we all clap when she's finished, I don't think anyone is listening. Everyone is all nervous for their performance, or for their friends who are performing. Bernice opens up, singing, of all things, likes she's Doris Day, "Sentimental Journey." She's good. I even force myself to stand up when she's finished, we're all clapping so hard, all of us lost a little bit in our own sentimental journeys. The applause lasts for a long time. A few of us, even me, I'm not ashamed to admit, wiping away a few tears.

Sadly, after her performance, the rest, not so good. Some just make us laugh. But all in good fun. Everybody, even the usual *kvetchers*, is in a good mood. This whole show is better than I thought it would be. In some ways, I'm feeling better than I did for a long time. Like being a kid again, everything I'm seeing like it's fresh.

But with each person who finishes, even though I'm smiling and clapping, my stomach is getting more and more upset. Not from the cancer, no. This is a good ache, because I'm scared for Harry. What if he's terrible? But I tell myself, lots of them were already terrible. And still we clapped. Making him last, it's like I'm chewing on nails. More like I swallowed them already and they're in my stomach going round and round, scratching up who knows what little is still left of my insides.

Finally, it's his turn. He walks out, nice and calm, and takes a seat on a stool, one foot on the floor, and the other bent on the lower rung. He's wearing all his fancy clothes again, even he has his scarf. No tie, his shirt open at the neck, with the silk hanging down next to the lapels of his jacket. I breathe out. He's going to be just fine.

He holds his hand up to his forehead, like blocking the sun, and I understand that the lights are in his eyes. He looks this way and that before he starts, and people are starting to get restless.

I feel everyone turning their face toward me. I wave, a small lifting of my hand, but that does it. Harry nods to the guy at the machine and starts to sing.

Oh, how I wish he hadn't looked for me. What does he sing? Frank Sinatra. And not just any Frank Sinatra, what did he choose? *Taking a Chance on Love.* As soon as he starts, everyone claps. And points. At me. My face is burning. And this song, about cards, and taking chances. Like written just for him, and he's pointing at me. He's singing to me. Straight to me.

And Bernice, all her cake layers bobbing up and down, smiling and pointing at me, in case anyone still doesn't know who Harry is singing to. I can feel all the eyes in the room on me, and it's like the nightmare when you go to school naked.

Finally, the song ends, and everyone claps, and Harry even points to me, and everyone claps more. I feel myself sitting in the chair, like this will never end until Bernice gets up on the stage, and says, there's a special surprise.

Good, everyone looks away from me, and I start to breathe normally again, when what do I see? Maxie, my Maxie coming out on the stage. And she's schlepping along another stool, and she's sitting down next to Harry.

"A duet," Bernice is saying.

I start to feel all hot again. The music starts, and now I have to grab my hands tight together. Where did they come to do this?

It's beautiful, how they sing together. But this song, the one from *Fiddler*. He sings to her about love, about marriage. About raising children and struggling for a living, making together a life.

And Maxie answers the familiar lyrics, funny, pushing him away, then pulling him back in. Until finally, their voices together, harmonizing. Their life. Their love.

This man. This man.

If only Mordy was here, to hear how his granddaughter sings. How Mordy always sang. Not Frank Sinatra, not his style. But this, this song, how Mordy and I loved this song. I let myself go there, back to Mordy singing to me, me with my terrible voice a *tzherbrochen toph* singing back. What twenty-five years, fifty, sixty, an eternity, always I love him.

I look up, don't even hide my tears, and Maxie is smiling through all the applause, and after that silly song about taking chances to fall in love this Harry, he sings to me, about Mordy, with Mordy's granddaughter, Harry bows to everyone. Bows to me.

In one lifetime, lots of different ways to love.

* * *

Maxie backed off the stage, it was Harry's night. Harry and Goldie's. She hadn't been sure when Harry asked her to sing that song with him. It was, she knew, *everyone* knew, Goldie and Mordy's song. His argument?

"When you like a girl, you need to make the grand gesture, you know. Your grandmother, she loved your Zaidy. A good man, the way she tells it. And I respect that, of course I do. But I'm here now, and for the time that she has left," he looked down. "I want to make her happy."

The look on Safta's face. Stunned. Upset. Then, pure joy. Here was her grandmother. She had a man crooning to her. Serenading her! Against all odds, she was fully alive.

Maxie inhaled the air rich with the first day of a New York spring. The promise of possible. She began to hum. She laughed and started to sing. She looked right and left, then twirled. Bowed. Waved an imaginary cane and tapped.

Taking a chance on love.

Chat Group: DINNER???

Members: Esti, Tamar, Maxie

ESTI

Dinner? She – HE - wants to take us out to dinner? I have her on this macrobiotic vegan gluten free diet. I've made sure the cafeteria there is on board, actually, I've been bringing her stuff. How can we go to dinner?

MAXIE

I don't think the menu is important It's Harry He wants to take us all out They've like, I don't know, like they're declaring that they're a thing

ESTI

Now?!

TAMAR

I think it's great. It's where hope and optimism overcome adversity. There are studies about this.

MAXIE

Ma! I'm a scientist!

ESTI

What are you even talking about?

TAMAR

State of mind can have an effect. If she's open to being happy, who are we to poo-poo it? I'm not saying she'll overcome her cancer by falling in love, I'm not nuts. But it can be a distraction. It can keep her from getting depressed.

ESTI

Getting involved now? It's just gonna–all these complications?

TAMAR

What complications? She wants to live–it's great. Awesome I think it's awesome.

MAXIE

I don't think what we think matters. It's what she wants.

TAMAR

Maxie, you're absolutely right. When did you get so grown up?

ESTI

I give up.

CHAPTER FORTY-FOUR

Goldie

THIS MORNING I GET TO THE DINING ROOM FIRST. I don't let anybody else sit down, even though the table is empty. I tell the staff I'm waiting for somebody, seat reserved. I put a napkin on the chair; they should see it's taken. At this point in my life, to get so excited like I'm still a girl.

The nice waiter that helps Harry always with his big ideas comes to the table. "Good morning," I say to him, smiling big.

"I'm so sorry, Goldie, so sorry."

My stomach, right away it makes a knot. No, I'm being stupid. He can't know about the cancer, I didn't tell nobody here. Harry and I, everything now, just we concentrate on having fun. Only the happy.

"What, is the orange juice sour?" I say, trying to make a joke that doesn't sound funny.

The waiter puts his hand over mine. He's giving me something he wants I should take. I look at what he's trying to give me. Harry's silk scarf.

No. No. The room starts to feel like under water. I can't breathe.

The waiter sits in the chair, Harry's chair. "I heard the paramedics when they took him out. They said he was smiling."

Sure he was. Harry, taking his final bow before the show drags on too long. "Leave 'em wanting more," I can hear how he'd say. "Go out with a bang."

Slowly, slowly, I lift my hand and let it reach for the scarf. But I stop, put my hand on the table, pick it up again, how many times do I do this? Finally, my fingers curl around the silk.

I squeeze the soft material. I want, but stop, not with everyone around, to press my nose into it. Just one more time to feel, to smell him. My person. In this place, my person.

The smell of his cologne reaches me anyway. Then his blue eyes behind his glasses. They smile, and his cufflinks sparkle and it's a whole Broadway production up there, all the angels singing, dancing. *Everyone Wild About Harry.*

Chat Group: NO!

Members: Esti, Tamar, Maxie

ESTI

They just called to let me know

TAMAR

That's it. That's it. We have to get her out of there. Now!

MAXIE

No! NO! NO! Not Harry. NO!

CHAPTER FORTY-FIVE

Goldie

"He just—died?" Maxie looks at me, then at the floor. "But he was fine, so alive. He sang, he joked, he was—" her voice drifts away while her hands go every which way like they don't know what to do, like she can pull Harry back from wherever he is.

I can't answer any of her questions, because I have all the same ones. This place. I keep asking, "Can you tell me when the funeral is? Where it is? The family, they'll be sitting shiva? We want to go."

Nothing. They tell me nothing. I don't understand. "A person, he had a life. He had friends, family. He's not just, I don't know, like a thing. You can't tell me anything? Where he is, how, how, how to say goodbye?"

"Mrs. Mandell, Goldie," Lauren Perky Breasts puts her arm around my shoulder. "It's what he wanted. What his family requested."

"I don't believe this. Any of this. This is not what Harry would want. He would want a party, a big celebration, not to go like, like, a cockroach in the dark."

For once, this Lauren looks like a real human being. "I'm so sorry," she says, that phony smile she always holds finally melting away into her face. "I know you were close. But there's nothing we can do."

No. Not nothing.

Nothing to do when every day just waking up is a miracle. You move on, even you forget. You light candles and say prayers for relatives you never met. Every year you bang on your chest and you say you remember. But this man, he was here. He took up space. And that space, it deserves to be respected.

"I don't understand," I say to Maxie, "Like he didn't have a footprint? A fingerprint. He had children, never I saw them, but he told me. Always he said they were coming to visit. Not right, this isn't right."

He made life in this place a life. Less like a waiting room.

"His room," I say, getting an idea. "Somebody has to come to empty his room. Always family comes." You live here just a few weeks and this you know. That last visit, the faces how they all have the same blankness. The shoulders slumped. The lines around the eyes deep and the mouths tight. If you walk by you hear sometimes laughing, crying, but mainly quiet, just the thud, thud of a whole life going into boxes. Bags in the hallway. Better not to look. But I always try to stop, to say something. To let them know the person they knew, they loved, we saw them, too.

"Let's go. He was on the fifth floor." I quick turn my walker. "You go ahead, quick, get the elevator so it will come by the time I reach it."

But the fifth floor hallway, all quiet. His room, the door open, and inside, empty. Maxie quick squeezes my hand. Her frizzy hair flying every which way, and her eyes, so big, so sad, wet. Her pretty face, her little mouth turned down, her lip all quivery.

"Give me a minute alone," I say, and slowly, slowly walk into his empty room.

1938

MAMA STANDING ON THE DOCKS, her hair like it was imitating the water, all in waves crashing around her face.

Even the kerchief she had on her head couldn't hold all that hair. Her eyes, like two small islands lost in the ocean. And she kept holding onto my hand, pulling me into her chest, wrapping me in her arms, and I just wanted to go already. They told me in America I would be free. Go anywhere. Do anything. I'd be able to go again to school and I'd have friends and the streets would be lined with gold. Real gold? I asked. And they laughed, nobody anymore laughs but from this they did. And no more being afraid of just going outside, they told me. And they were coming. Soon, they said. Soon. Just I should go first and get it ready for them. So of course, that's what I wanted, to get started and go already. The ship so big, so many people, so many things to see and such strange smells to smell and so much to explore.

But Mama wasn't letting me go, until finally Poppa made her. "It's time," he said.

At last I was free. I ran up the wooden plank and into the ship to see whatever there was to see. Never again I saw Mama.

First Edith told me, so I should be prepared. How Mama was weak. That she got sick from the hard work. The cold weather. Then when he came, Poppa told me that's what happened.

I tried, I tried to remember her. To have what to hold onto. Poppa, he didn't have anything of hers to give me.

2018

But Maxie, with her crazy long curls flying every which way, and her soft eyes, so sad, more blue than green. Always I thought she had Mordy's eyes. Today, today I see Mama. Something from her I had all along. Even I gave it to my children and theirs.

CHAPTER FORTY-SIX

Goldie

WHAT AM I SEEING? Bernice in middle of my kitchen? What they call here a kitchen, a shelf in the entryway, with a microwave and a tiny sink, next to that refrigerator that fits nothing.

What's she doing here, all made up, her hair in a silver puff? From all the way across the room I can see the layers of color around her eyes, and the rest of her skin, all smooth without a single spot. Sure, it's in creases and folds, and her neck—like one of those little dogs with all the loose skin falling on top of itself but still, she must spend hours every day putting together her face. Of course, her nails—perfect. Like it matters?

"Your door was open," she says. "You don't lock it?"

"I have anything anyone wants?"

I should ask her why she's here? Truth is, when I first came, I wouldn't have minded maybe her friendship. But she had her group, and when I tried to talk to her she made like she didn't hear me. Only I became interesting when Harry was around, but now he's gone. Also.

So now she comes, maybe, to offer me comfort? Too late. Now is not the time to make friends.

"You need something?" I ask her.

She heard I'm sick? She's checking out the apartment for somebody else already? Or maybe herself, she wants to be on a higher floor?

On the sunny side of the building? I don't know where her room is, never she invited me.

She looks around like there's something to see. All our rooms are the same. Maybe we have *tchotchkes* from our homes, but to anybody else, junk. It's all junk.

She comes all the way inside, facing the couch to look at the wall with all the pictures. She points to one of me and Mordy on the beach, that first summer. "That's you? And that was your husband? A movie star?" She stares for a while, nodding her head like she's adding something to a to-do list. "And what did he do for a living?"

I shrug. Sure, with his million dollar smile she's probably thinking a lawyer. A successful businessman. But he wasn't educated. He was learned—he could tell you anything from anything, he read, all the time. A good mind. But, education, no, he wasn't so fortunate. A refugee boy.

"Family business," I tell her. Mandell's Slipcovers and Upholstery. Not the biggest American success story.

"Oh?" she asks, her face all-curious.

"We sold it years ago."

A small lie. We shut it down.

"And those two women, your daughters. So devoted. Especially the one who comes every day. And that granddaughter, wow."

"Which one?" I ask like I don't know who she means. I should make it easy for her? Esti's girls come too, with their little ones, on Sundays, maybe once, twice a month. They take turns. "So many grandchildren, great-grandchildren, it's hard to keep track. Like Grand Central Station how they come and go."

I hear these words coming from my mouth like somebody else is in charge. She never has any visitors, and I'm rubbing her face in it. All the time now I'm mad. At her. At Harry. At Him.

Meanwhile, she's still here, still talking, still about the grandchildren. "Oh, yes, adorable." Bernice tries to run her pink-tipped fingers through her silver hair, making like she's fixing it, but it's all glued together too tight to move, so she ends up just patting it. Stupid. "But I meant the one who comes more often, the pretty one with the hair."

"They're all pretty with hair." Like worms in my head, coming out from my mouth.

Even though her face tells me she's uncomfortable, she keeps going anyway, like she has a speech prepared. "The one, you know, the one who brings you home all the time? When you leave to go out with that driver?"

"Maxine," I say. My voice letting her know this is the end of this conversation.

"She takes after your husband. The eyes, and all the curls." She says this like it's a big compliment she's giving me. Like this will soften me up.

That I have a pretty girl is a shock? That I had a handsome husband? Even once I was like that, pretty and young, not always this *fa'bissena* old lady, this creep I don't recognize.

I say nothing.

"Goldie, why are you so—so? Listen, I have a grandson. He doesn't come to visit, my son, sons, they're not like your daughters. Divorced, the older one. And his boys, like they hardly know I'm alive." Her voice trails off, and under all that makeup the lines that show through aren't from smiles.

She forces herself to keep going. "A crazy idea. I just thought, she's so pretty, and so—" Conversations here are like that, everyone getting lost in the middle "—involved." She finally comes up with what she wanted to say. "So involved with you. I just thought—when you said she was single, I thought, a granddaughter like that, she could make my boy, maybe, my grandson, happy. Maybe help him grow up, become a mensch. Visit his grandmother while—"

Visit his grandmother while?!

This Bernice, she thinks she still has plans. "*Mann Tracht, Un Gott Lacht*," how Pa used to say. To think she could just come into my house. Picking over my bones before they're even yet in the ground. Trying to steal what's mine. Always the same.

1949

SHIRLEY, MY FRIEND. Always first in everything, but this time, I beat her. Me, Sadie the Married Lady. I even ask Mordy if he has some friends like from the Army, maybe her Mr. Regular Guy would finally show up. We have a party, Mordy's friends, my friends, now bringing their own Mordys, and Shirley. She makes this entrance, wearing a two-piece bathing suit, smoking cigarettes that dangle from long red fingernails. Even she has big sunglasses and her hair is all short and curled. I smile like it's normal how she looks. I tell her she'll catch a big fish, and she makes like a dirty joke about big fish and small swimming holes, and I laugh again because I'm married. I understand. Maybe even I brag a little, how big Mordy is, everywhere. So what, we're having fun. Private grown up girl fun.

We're all having a good time, drinking the beer that I bought special for this fast company, and Mordy goes inside to get some more, and Shirley goes with him, and I stay outside with the rest of the guests, and almost forget all about them. Almost. Then Shirley comes out alone carrying two six packs, and I'm thinking it's funny, where's Mordy?

I tell myself, not important. But for the first time ever, when Mordy comes to me after everyone leaves, I'm like watching and not participating.

"Mordy? Shirley. What happened? Mordy, tell me what happened."

He rolls onto his back, his hand to his forehead, his voice like a big sigh, "Nothing. I promise."

"Not good enough." My body feels tight, shut down. Like a brick.

Little beads of sweat start to shine through his needing-to-shave stubble. That's when he's the most handsome to me, when his face is all scratchy and dark. The private face only I know. But not now. Now there's something dirty between us.

Mordy breathes out, long and slow. My body goes from a single brick to a whole walled-in prison.

"I went inside to get more beer." *Vent inside.* My heart bangs like it wants to shatter me all over the place. "She followed me. I wished it was you." *Vished.* "I was maybe a little drunk from the beer, and you were so cute in your little dress over your bathing suit, and I just wanted to hug you and squeeze you."

Vas, vere, vanted. Every V from his mouth cuts like a chisel, pieces of me flying off, ripping away from this nest that was mine and Mordy's.

He turns red. "Be inside you. Like it never stops, that movie in my head." He looks at me, waiting I should tell him that it's the same for me, because it is. But I can't. I'm all locked up.

"Shirley," I say instead, and I'm surprised how flat my voice is.

Again the deep breath. "She followed me inside, in that little," he gestures up and down to show how her bathing suit was split in half. "And she squeezes past me to get to the 'fridgerator and when she bent down to get the beer, she like, blocked me so I had to see, and she, her," he points again to his chest, his mouth so tight it's pulling on his skin, his cheekbones sticking out at sharp angles, his eyes like holes, seeing something he doesn't want, "all hanging out, everything. I could see all the way down to her—"

Her headlights. Always Mordy and I laugh about my sweater so bright, how my yellow headlights knocked him out that first day he saw me. They blinded him, he said. All he could see the rest of the day. Something private just between us.

We're in bed on our backs, staring up at the ceiling. The only noise the in and out, in and out from our breathing.

"Goldie. She was shoving them in my face, the kitchen so small. And I had all that beer and I was thinking about you, about us, together. And then, she turned around, and leaned over again, to get the other six pack, and this time, her whole *tuchus* was sticking out she was standing so close, and I couldn't, all I had on was a bathing suit, so little between us, and, and—"

"*Ven de schmekel shtait de saychel geyt.*" I spit this at him.

"*Nein,*" he answers, also in Yiddish, then back to English: "Yeah, my *schmekel* stood up, but my *saychel* didn't go anywhere. I kept my head. You outside, so cute. And there I was, not even able to control my own body. She turned around, fast. She saw. And she laughed. 'Goldie wasn't kidding,' she said. Laughing, saying your name. I pushed her so I could run away. Just I wanted to go back outside, to breathe, to see you, to tell you I was sorry. But I was trapped, like a stupid animal." He puts his hand over his eyes. "Finally, I was, you know, relaxed enough, able to go back outside. And there you were, in your little dress over a normal bathing suit, just like I knew you would be, and I was ashamed. So ashamed."

He's still staring at the ceiling, his neck so tight he looks like from stone.

She makes from my marriage a cheap joke? I feel like a red-hot fire going through me and jump from the bed—our bed—scratching myself, dirty, like bugs are crawling all over me.

I invited her, that friend, into my house.

Mordy jumps up, grabs me, holds me tight. "We're safe, Goldie. You and me. We're still you and me Goldie. Always."

Never you're safe. Never you know who, where, when, the threat will come. Never you can relax. The nest you make in the highest tree. Even then, something can fly down from the sky and destroy it all. Mordy is still holding me, promising me that we're okay. Telling me he's sorry. I want to cover my ears not to hear him.

The worst thing is thinking of Mordy, my Mordy, as weak. His arms, holding me, so strong. How he fixes things, takes them apart and puts them together. How he solves problems, how, even silly things, like when my ice cream was melting too fast because the sun was so hot, he licked it off my arm like the most natural thing in the world.

He's just a person. I'm just a person. Tests, there will always be tests. Maybe passing the tests, the fighting to be strong for each other, that's what marriage is? Not just licking ice cream.

Mordy is still waiting for me to say something. You have to work together to make it as good as it can be, not just good enough.

"Me and you," I say back to him. "We're in this together."

But that woman? Never she comes into my house again. Just because there are tests doesn't mean you have to take every one.

2018

"I KNOW WHAT YOU WANT," I say out loud to this Bernice, this other older Shirley with hair so silver that it's blue. With a face all sad and hoping behind all the makeup. She's still in my house. My house that she wasn't invited in. "You don't pick over my bones yet!"

"What? I just—"

I rush at her with my walker like it's a tank with a gun on top. "Get out, out!"

She puts her arms up in the air, running away from me. She leaves the door wide open; it's banging against the hallway. The room, quiet and empty. Just all the pictures on the wall.

CHAPTER FORTY-SEVEN

Goldie

I CAN'T REMEMBER HER NAME, never mind how come she's standing in middle of my room. Always she tries so hard to be friendly, it hurts to see how it's such an effort. Her voice is too loud, like she thinks she brings sunshine if she hollers. And yellow, every day she wears yellow. Today she has on a suit like Hillary Clinton always wore. Poor girl. It's a pair of pants, of course yellow, with a jacket and a yellow and black scarf around her neck, like she's a bumble bee. A little creepy.

She booms at me, "Mrs. Mandell?"

"I'm standing right here, you don't have to yell."

"You didn't come to lunch. I wanted to check that you're all right."

Often, I don't go to lunch, never she comes checking before. "I wasn't hungry." I look close at her face. "I don't have such a good appetite."

She blinks slowly, like the dolls the girls used to play with, that could open and close their eyes and even cry. From this I'm to understand she feels concern. "But, Mrs. Mandell, we, I, received a troubling report. From another resident. She said you became, you were *upset* when she came to visit. I wanted to talk, to let you know that we have specialists, counselors who can help you through this difficult time."

"There is no getting through this, it's one way—a dead end." I wave my hand at her. You'd think that she'd be smarter than this, she runs this whole place?

She flinches in her yellow getup. "You can't be aggressive with other residents."

"She barged in, wasn't invited. Ask her if she knocked. Trespassing. That's what she was doing."

Another lady comes barging into the room. Like a thunder cloud she storms in. "I'm her attorney. Anything you have to discuss with my client will go through me." She hands Miss Bumble Bee a card.

Tamar. This is Tamar. So strong. So sure of herself. Her crazy clothes, they make her look impressive. Different.

"My daughter," I say to Bee. "Also, my attorney."

Tamar says, "I understand that there was an invasion of my client's personal space this morning? I'd like to address the security measures that are in place to prevent this breach of privacy."

How she speaks. Such words she uses. Such a strong girl. Smart. I need to watch her, learn how to do this.

"Ma," she says, after Lady Bee leaves, breathing in deep like opening the window from a bad smell. "I don't even wanna know what happened. That Bernice—" She waves her hand like at a mosquito. Such authority, nothing scares her. "Anyway, listen. I have an idea." She gets a face like when she was a teenager, all excited. How she changes from one minute to the next, I'm having trouble following. "Let's go home."

"Home?"

"I want to go to the beach. Please. T-Jam will take us. Maxie, Esti, Norm. We'll make Shabbas. I'll cook."

"*You'll* cook?"

"Okay, Esti will cook."

"*I'll* cook."

"Okay, you'll cook. I'll peel. Listen, please, Ma, please. Let's go home. I want to go home."

All the way at the end of the world they call our house by the beach. Outside, the fishy air, and the sound of the waves hitting the sand. And in the sky, always the seagulls with their *geshri.* Like they're hollering to us, *ha ha*, you're here, too.

Home. Our home. I'm home. For the weekend, Tamar said. Whatever I can have, I'll take.

CHAPTER FORTY-EIGHT

Goldie

I THOUGHT SHE SAID WE WERE COMING just for the weekend? I shake my head, like this will clear it out? Important that Tamar shouldn't see how confused I am. Not to even know the day of the week?

But the way she's looking at me? Then says, "You're tired. The doctor said that's nor—well, to be expected."

"And why are you still here? You don't need to go to work? Back to California?" I need to show her I know what's what.

She gets up. "You want another cup of coffee? Some cottage cheese?"

"Why you're not answering me?"

She shrugs, like a stupid. "I don't know."

"You don't know? Tamar, you know everything, always. We can't both be stupid at the same time, bad enough just me." That just came out, oh well.

"I took a leave of absence," she says, like she didn't even notice what I just said.

To upset her whole life? "You can go home, Esti will call when it's time. I'm still here. Not going anywhere yet."

"Ma, it's, I needed a break." Now she's washing the coffee cups, when the dishwasher is right there.

"What does it mean, a break? From work, from life?"

"There was this huge case, it just ended. It was a horrible case, a young woman. I've been working like a lunatic." She finally stops with the dishes. There's something she doesn't want I should know. Always with the secrets, and frankly, I don't have energy for it right now.

"Okay, as long as it's what you want. Just for me, I'm not asking for anything."

"Of course, you're not." She throws the dishtowel down on the counter. Still I have to walk on eggshells?

2000

We're finally in Berkeley. Of course, I had to invite myself. *Please* and *thank you*, very polite the whole week. Time for Tamar to see her father. Time for me and Mordy to see the baby, not such a baby anymore, already eleven years old. Maxie, they named her. After Pa? I asked Esti. She told me, "No, after Maxwell's equations."

A relative from the husband's side? I don't ask. Even if I did, I wouldn't understand his answer. I never know what he's saying, but also, he hardly speaks. A professor. From physics. Like from outer space. At least he's Jewish.

The two of them, this California, Berkeley life. I don't say anything, how she dresses in grain sacks. She has a nice figure but what she wears? Once I asked her, "You go to the office like that? I thought lawyers wear nice suits?" So terrible I asked her that? "And your hair, if you styled it, you know, and maybe colored it?" A mother can't tell her daughter the truth?

She comes home late from her office, she's tired. "You want I should make supper?" I offer, nicely. Really, it would be a relief from what she feeds us, we're not rabbits I want to tell her. I keep quiet. I ask a student I see with a yarmulke where we can get some decent food. Even I take a taxi to Oakland and find the kosher store where I buy some pastrami and corned beef for Mordy. "Look," I tell Tamar. "I found us what to eat. I'll roast some potatoes."

"Are you sure that's the best food for Daddy to be eating?" It would kill her to say thank you?

And the husband? He reads the paper, he doesn't talk. Two days, three days I don't say anything, but this is too important for politeness. "You know, maybe if you put on a dress that showed your figure, he'd look up from his books sometimes. A man likes a woman who's a woman. Maybe get home at a normal hour and fix yourself up a little bit before he comes. Also, you saw how he likes the pastrami we bought? And all the brisket he ate? Maybe make a nice supper once in a while? The place falls apart if you leave work an hour or two earlier?"

A whole lecture I get about women's rights. What oppression? You love a man, you do for him. He does for you. It's called a marriage.

One thing I can say, she's a wonderful mother. How she has patience to listen, to talk to Maxie, to ask her questions. And Maxie, like a little grown up she says what she thinks. Such ideas she has, and Tamar nods along. Not just nods, they talk whole conversations. So much she knows, about places, and events going on around the world. I watch them, and it makes me feel good. Only, why can't she see how I want to be with her like she is with Maxie?

But, quiet, I eat the quinoa, whatever it is. I add a little mayonnaise—also that I bought in Oakland—it should have some taste, and the kale instead of normal lettuce, and the tea that tastes like water you boiled the vegetables in. For Mordy I make a pastrami on rye. I make one for Maxie, too. She loves it, licking all the mustard from around the edges. For the husband, I leave one in the fridge. He can figure out for himself to take it. I don't *mish arayin* between a husband and wife.

"So," I say to Tamar. "It was an interesting visit." That's for sure. "I'm glad we came. It was good to finally spend some time with Maxie. She's something special."

"Are you actually giving me credit for doing something right?"

Where did that come from? All week long I'm holding my tongue. Maybe once, twice I told her to fix her hair, a crime I committed? I quick turn back to my suitcase, folding again a sweater that's already folded.

"Ma, stop. You can't do that. It's all right for you to criticize, to tell me everything I'm doing wrong, and I can't say one word to you?"

"Sue me, I came to visit. That's too much for you to handle, one week with your mother and father?"

"That's not what this is about. It's how you're so manipulative, how you pull strings and force your opinion on everyone around you. You know it."

I know this?

"I know that you're a fancy shmancy lawyer who has no time for her parents, that's what I know. You move as far from us as you can, and maybe once a week, if I'm lucky, you call. And then, what, we talk for two minutes—always you're so important, so busy. And that's good. I'm proud of you, but I don't understand why you're always angry. I'm your mother, I can't once in while say something? You think we'll be here forever? You think here in this California you don't need parents?"

Good I stop myself before I say more. But so much I want to say. To ask her if she sees anything different about Mordy, to tell her that family is everything, that I miss her, that she should come home already from this fake place. But I don't say none of this, because always I hold my tongue. A parent shouldn't mish in.

"You're proud of me? What are you proud of, exactly? That I was capable of becoming an attorney, without you calling anybody up to make sure it would happen? That I have a great kid, and a full life that you don't control? That I'm surviving without you monitoring my every move?"

All of a sudden, my big shot Tamar starts to cry.

"Tamar, Tamar? Are you sick? Is he bad to you?"

"Ma, stop, just stop. Please. I know all about it. The secret deals. The lies."

"I have something to lie about?"

But the way she's crying and looking at me. I sit on the bed, the open suitcase shaking from how heavy I sit down. She knows? How? Such a long time ago, she was so young. I was afraid. For her. For Mordy. What did it hurt? Only me it hurt. Nobody else.

"For you, it was all for you. So you should have a life." I wave my arm around the room, at all the strange wall hangings from trips she went on with her family. Trips not to New York to see us. "Daddy and I, we couldn't afford to send you away to school. You were smart, a good student. Was it so terrible?"

"But it wasn't about that, right? It was about him—you didn't think I could make up my own mind? I wasn't about to become a housewife and have babies—his babies. How could you think, after watching you and Daddy, what you went through, what you were to each other, that I would be that stupid? Didn't you know, couldn't you tell that I appreciated, I understood—I wasn't a dumb kid, Ma."

"How did you find out? You were so happy, so proud?"

She makes a face like she can't believe how stupid she is. "I believed it all. Funny thing was, Junior and I had already broken up. He was—who cares? Then, winning that scholarship, it was the best thing that ever happened. I thought I earned it. I deserved it. It was like an award for all the hard work, for breaking up with him, for trying so hard."

This I didn't know. And maybe, who knows, if I did know and none of this happened, was it so terrible that she got to go to Brandeis? This Berkeley I could live without, but I never stopped her from her dreams. Except one. Not a dream, more a nightmare I wanted to save her from. And I did. I thought I did.

"When I was applying to law schools, you know I applied to Columbia and NYU, too. I thought I'd stay in the city, I always planned to." From one secret so many others. "I was filling out the applications, and they had this section for scholarships, and I went to fill in the one I'd won, the one—you know." The way she looks at me, like a thunderstorm. "And I couldn't find anything about it, anywhere. I found the documents, I saved them, especially the original letter. I called the number, the guy I spoke to back when I won it."

Her face is harder now, like a stone. "And at first he didn't know what I was talking about, then he says, 'Wait, yeah, it's coming back to me. Let me find it.' He called me back a few days later. 'It was a one-time gift. From an 'unnamed source.'"

"An unnamed source? I was pre-law. How long do you think it took me? I found her Ma. Toni Romano. I talked to her. I paid her back. Every single penny."

The wind is knocked out of me.

Like a judge she stares down at me. "Does Daddy know? Did he ever know?"

My voice so small: "Please, Tamar, I didn't know what to do. You were impossible, never I could talk to you. I just wanted, I just wanted—"

"You wanted what was best for you. It's all about you. You never even considered how demeaning you are."

'Demeaning?' I don't even know this word, but I know what it sounds like. I took something from her? I did it for me? I even once thought about myself?

This is what a grown woman cries to her mother? What did I do but for her?

"Look at the life I made for you, this you call mean? How long you gonna feel sorry for yourself? I did something so terrible, I got you to go to the best school, gave you the best chance. Years, years, I made myself sick over this secret, and all along you knew? You called her? You got yourself out from it. And never you could call me, and tell me? Never mind, thank me. For years you walk around like it's this big tragedy. I could never tell Daddy, never in my life I kept something from him. And I did it for you. And you, big important *pisher,* goes to law school, moves across the country, and still you're angry at me and my little life where every day, always, I think about you. And your sister and your father. *Feh.*"

I look around the little room, decorated like a museum. "Big deal you call before a holiday. For this we should be grateful? Poor, poor you—all the way to the bank you can cry." Then I imitate her voice for one word. "'Demeaning?' Nobody, ever, in this world gets anything without somewhere some help. Be happy you had a mother who cared. Such a sin I committed to give you a life. *Again.*"

I slam the suitcase shut.

"Still about you. Always." Tamar shakes her head and walks out of the room.

CHAPTER FORTY-NINE

Maxie

HE WAS LATE. Maxie wasn't gonna stress about it. No. Not at all. That was the thing about him, what you saw was what there was, no hidden agenda. No—oh, and there he was. On a skateboard. Hot damn. Yeah. She'd wait.

"Sorry, I'm late. I had to wait to get into the darkroom. Then it took longer than I thought it would. But, look. You gotta see these. Let's find a place to sit down."

He slung his arm around Maxie's shoulder, kissed the top of her head, then inhaled her scalp. "I love how you smell." he whispered into her hair. *Love.* He said it. He also said *smell.* Stop it, Maxie. No agenda. No stress. She buried her head in his chest, careful of the skateboard and his backpack. Careful. Always careful. They walked toward a bench shaded by an overhanging tree. Around them the campus buzzed—a great place to be alive, to be an artist, a scientist, to be. She squeezed T-Jam's hand. Felt his fingers wrap around hers.

He was excited. She could tell by his walk, the energy radiating off his skin in palpable waves. He pulled his backpack off his shoulders and carefully, extremely so, extracted a large envelope that he handed to Maxie, staring at her very intently while he did. Maxie tried to ignore his intense scrutiny as she opened it, wondering when? What? She didn't remember him taking any pictures. He wouldn't have done—no. Nothing like that. Why would she even think that.

She held up the first photograph by its corner, her fingers twitchy, her breath anxious. He was still watching her. She looked, then stared into her grandmother's face. Her breath caught. She was—beautiful. Wise. Ancient. Her face caught just before a smile, like she hadn't made up her mind about it yet. There was so much intelligence and thoughtfulness; something all knowing and resigned—no, that wasn't the right word—something accepting—in her expression. Safta's hair was blowing off her face, tossed by an unseen wind, she was staring straight ahead. Yes. Accepting. She looked to be on some sort of ship, Maxie could make out what looked like water, some chop, a railing?

There were more. A whole series. Harry. Dear sweet Harry. The camera had caught his jaunty vibrancy. Smiling. Debonair. Owning his space.

Then, another of Harry, where his smile had faltered. His eyes turned inward. Holding the picture felt ghoulish.

Then, Goldie and Harry, together on deck chairs. An empty bottle of champagne overturned in a bucket. The colors were dimmer, the sun had just set. They were holding—clutching hands. But at the moment the camera clicked they were facing away from each other. It was unbearably sad, and brave, and yet, the clutched old and spotted hands, their fingers, gnarled and bony, intertwined, told a different story. They were holding on. To each other. To that night. Caught for eternity.

Maxie let the pictures rest on her lap.

"Hey," T-Jam pulled her toward him. "Hey, hey." He wiped away the tears she hadn't known she'd been shedding.

"Has she seen these? She knows about them?"

"Not yet. She knew I was there. I drove them that night, and I asked if it would be all right if I photographed them. I—they never posed. Obviously. I tried to stay out of their way."

"They're almost too much. Too powerful."

"The first one, her face looking out—that's the image I always wanted to paint." He shrugged. "I don't like to work off photographs, it's not the same as a live person. But I get the feeling she'd allow it, if I asked. She even said something along those lines. Or maybe I can finally ask her to sit for me. There's something there, Maxie. Between her and me." He was looking at her. Intently. Asking her.

Maxie tugged on the necklace she hadn't taken off since Safta gave it to her. The one with the corny inscription Saba had written her on their first anniversary. "You think she should know about us?"

"Shouldn't she?"

And there was that other shoe dropping. Stupid, silly, absurd. What did it matter what her grandmother thought? How she'd react. But she would. And it would be awful. Because for Goldie Mandell—T-Jam Bin Naumann, Tawfiq Jamal Bin Naumann—wouldn't, couldn't matter.

CHAPTER FIFTY

Goldie

TAMAR, SHE SITS IN FRONT OF HER COMPUTER all day, so busy. If she's not staring at that screen, she's staring at her phone.

"Hello," I want to tell her. "Here, look at me. I'm still here."

To tell the truth, I miss Esti, always coming and fixing everything, even I never asked her to. And Maxie, my Sheyfe, too hard for her to come all the way here. Only I see her now at the doctor's office.

Tamar, even in the same room as me, who knows where she is, really. She's very busy putting Wi-Fi, hi-fi, something I don't know, in the house. What is it, I asked her? I don't see anything. A half hour later she's still explaining and still I don't know what she's saying. She tells me with this mysterious thing I can't see I can shop from pictures on the computer and order one, two, three, and the next day, nothing extra, it's delivered to the house.

"I'm supposed to give my credit card to the computer? And from a picture how do I know what I'm getting?" Crazy how these kids never want to be a part of the world. But I have to say, it's nice how every night we sit in the living room and Tamar turns on the new television they bought for me, so big, fancy, like a private movie theater. She pushes some buttons, and *schoen*, a whole list of movies to choose from, new/old, comedies, musicals, drama, anything you want.

This is all right to do from the house. Makes sense.

"Show me how you did that," I tell her, so fast she makes it all go by.

"I just did," she says, making all the pictures go up and down.

"No, you did it, but you didn't show me how. Do it again. Slowly. In case I want to do it and you're not here."

"Then Maria, or Maxie, Esti, somebody, will do it for you."

"I want you should show me."

She sighs, and again she waves the remote control and everything on the screen changes. Then she starts to talk very slowly and loudly.

"No, from the start," I say. "Turn the television off. Give me the remote. Also, get for me a pencil and paper."

"Please?"

"Please what?"

"Please, Ma, can you please say please?"

"I should say please?"

She blows her hair off her face. "Listen: Please, or no please?"

"Please or no please what? Just show me how to work the television."

She hands me the remote, like she's doing me a big favor. "Never mind. Here."

"What are you so mad at, it's so hard to help me?"

"No, Ma, it's not hard to help you." She thinks I can't hear from her voice the exact opposite?

Maybe she's going through her menopause, a little early? Or maybe her period, so long ago I forget how it could make you a little nuts. Oy, when it was the three of us in the house together.

"Tamar," I say slowly. "Would you please get me a pen and paper? Would you *please* go through all the steps so I can write them down?"

She gets up and comes back with a pad of paper and a pen.

"Are you ready, Ma? Are you comfortable? Would you like another pillow?"

"Yeah," I say, "get me—" And her hands go tight. "I mean, thank you. Yes, I'd like a pillow. Please."

I stare at her and she stares back at me—I don't know how long.

Then I see it, her mouth is twitching and then both of us are laughing. We're still laughing while so nice she fixes me up on the couch. I have my pen ready.

"Please?" I add, sticky sweet like syrup.

She shakes her head, but her eyes are still happy. "Here. First you press the on button." And then, she takes the pad and starts to draw a line here and a line there, and before you know it, it's a picture of the remote with a big arrow to the on button. That much I already knew, but she's drawing so nicely, and so carefully, her crazy hair falling over and hiding her face, almost I expect to see her tongue sticking out, and her fingertips turning red from squeezing the pen too hard.

And I sit and watch.

2006

USELESS, I SIT AND WATCH. "Mordy, what are you doing? This isn't the way."

"Sure it is." He smiles at me, too long, his eyes not on the road.

"Watch out!" I yell, my hand reaching for the steering wheel.

"Sorry, sorry," he says, straightening the car, all around us the honking finally quieting down. "I must be tired."

More and more little things, misplacing things, forgetting things. Nothing, nothing, no big deal. But they're adding up. In middle of conversations, he stops. I laugh, I tease. But not just once in a while this is happening.

"Never we go this way to Esti's neighborhood," I say. Not arguing, not accusing. Outside the window we're in his old neighborhood, in the Bronx, where he lived with his mother maybe forty years ago.

"No, no," he says fast, very fast, blinking hard. "I just thought it would be nice to you know, take a detour. See the old neighborhood."

Outside the buildings that are still standing are all boarded up and there are empty lots where other buildings used to be, full of weeds and garbage and broken glass and even more broken people, you can't tell what they are, men, women, children. Like a war zone. This is a place to stroll down memory lane? Memory. No. That's the place I'm running from, the darkness that I see coming.

But the signs—they're adding up. In the mail letters about bills not being paid. I look in our checkbook, and I can't believe, it's a mess. The next day I go to the bank. The money is all there, just no checks written. I start another checkbook Mordy shouldn't see, and I pay everything. If I see he writes checks, I take them and tear them up when I get to work.

Nobody has to know. I read about healthy food and habits. I make broccoli non-stop, even he makes faces and asks why. I cook more fish, brain food, no red meat, everyone says so. I tell him it's Weight Watchers. All of a sudden, *my* diet, after a hundred years I'm trying, now it's number one priority. Exercise time, I yell every night when he's ready to relax on the couch. "Remember, Mordy, how you used to do those pushups? Show me. So strong you are. You do pushups, I'll do sit-ups."

Our living room turns into a gymnasium. Jack LaLane, our new best friend. One day at a time, that's all. Some days he's the same as always. The fish, the broccoli, the exercise, it's working.

That rainy day, I'm waiting and waiting at the dentist's office. I call the house, no answer. I wait another half hour, but they're closing down for the day. "Sorry," I say to the receptionist, "my husband, there must be car trouble."

No umbrella, by the time I get home, I'm soaking wet. "Mordy," I call, "Mordy!"

He's in the kitchen, and the stove is on, but the water in the pot is boiled out. "Mordy," I say, my voice too loud. I think I need to yell to get through to him? This is not us, not me and Mordy. I need to calm down. "You forgot to get me? We made up you'd come. I had to take two buses. You see what's going on outside? I'm soaking wet."

How he looks at me—his hands making fists at the side of his legs, his eyes so full with so much sadness, his mouth, his beautiful strong mouth all turned down.

"Never mind," I say, "It happens. I'm not gonna break from taking a bus. And I'm not gonna melt from a little rain."

The afraid I'm seeing in his face, maybe he sees the same in mine?

"Goldie," he says to me, swallowing before he says more. "For a while, I knew this was coming. Call Moe. He has the papers. I set it up already. We need to make things right." He looks down, the second time in our lives that he can't look me in the face. "Call the girls. You need to let them know."

2018

TAMAR FINISHES HER DRAWING of the remote, with lots of arrows and boxes on the page. Underneath, with numbers, the steps I need to follow.

I go through them, it's a little tricky between the pictures and the little buttons, so small, that I need to push. Tamar stands there the whole time, not taking the remote from me. Letting me figure it out. Finally, I recognize the screens and I learn how to push the arrow and even push down so the movie I want comes up.

But also it happens that I push a lot that I don't want, and then I get all jumpy to make them stop, and to start all over again.

Again and again, until I get it right more than I get it wrong. Tamar looks so proud, smiling, happy with her work. Like me, with the broccoli and fish.

"Thank you." I say to her.

CHAPTER FIFTY-ONE

Goldie

ESTI AND TAMAR TOGETHER IN THE KITCHEN. Sisters. Without talking, they're like dancing. One picks up the coffee cup, one puts it down. Tamar is in shorts and a T-shirt. She's running, every day on the beach. Esti is in a sundress, with pretty sandals. But their legs, exactly at the same angle under the table. Not exactly the same, maybe from the bend of the neck, or the toss of the head, not even the same color eyes, or the same shape of the face, but something is there, something more, stronger, than the color of hair and eyes.

From nothing, from love in the dark, two kids ourselves who didn't know from nothing, just to try to be together the best we could be, this is what we made. The footprint we leave. They should only know from happiness.

"Ma, you're up?! Good. How are you feeling?" Esti stands up to kiss me.

These days, lots more kisses.

"Not so bad." I tell her. At least no more pretending *alts iz in order*. In some ways, a relief.

"Oh," she says, pulling from her bag a big pile of envelopes. "I stopped at the place on the way here. Here's your mail."

This one, always, always her feet on the ground.

"Thanks, good," I tell her. Always something to check, especially now with all the doctor visits. You have to keep track of these things, the way the insurance never wants to accept anything. Everything a fight. To tell the truth, I enjoy it. I have what else to do, stare out the window all day?

Tamar makes me a cup of coffee, and Esti gets for me cottage cheese, like how I like it. Then they sit and watch me eat.

"Stop," I tell them. "I know how to eat. Don't you have other things to do?"

Esti with her nice, manicured nails starts sorting through all the envelopes. Tamar, still here. Angry at me again, this time because I asked her about T-Jam and Maxie. Maxie, my Maxie. My Sheyfe. T-Jam. Maybe not a terrible person. But terrible for Maxie.

"Ma, this looks mostly like junk. Can I throw this out?" Esti shows me one envelope after another, flyers and junk mail. She holds up a letter, studies the return address, and shows it to Tamar. "Some kind of scam?"

Tamar reads it. "Ma, you wanna see this," she says.

I put on my glasses and when the writing becomes clear, I read something, something, Harry Silver, Bank of America, lots of numbers, Joint Account, Goldie Mandell.

And at the top and bottom of the page, Law Offices of Sheldon Nussbaum. And a phone number.

"Talk to me."

This is how an attorney answers the phone? He sounds like a—I don't know what.

"This is Sheldon Nussbaum? The lawyer?"

"Yeah, hon. What can I do you for?"

Do me for? This is how a lawyer talks? And I worry about Tamar's hair?

"This is Goldie Mandell. I'm holding here a letter you sent me. About Harry Silver."

"Ah, the mysterious Goldie Mandell. Thanks for calling. You must be some lady, the way Harry talked about you."

"You're his lawyer?" I ask.

"Was, honey. Poor Harry, he should rest in peace."

I answer automatically, like to the Kaddish. "Amen."

"So, you got my letter. Good, good. Just wanted to make sure you were aware of the estate. A bank account, it's not really an estate, but Harry, he had everything in order, all his I's dotted and his T's crossed. Wanted to make sure you didn't forget about it, or let it wallow, a bank account doesn't go into probate, nothing like that. It's free and clear, and all yours."

"I don't want it. Not a penny. Harry and I talked; he only wanted me to hold onto it while he was alive. I'm sure I'm not supposed to have it now he's, he's gone. I knew him just a few months. Can you tell his children? I don't know how to get in touch with them, they should have it."

"Goldie," he says, "I can call you Goldie? Harry didn't want that. He was very clear, it was for you, he said."

"What am I gonna do with it? I need it? I'm not gonna be around so much longer myself. He has kids, it's for them."

"You ever met the kids?"

"If I met them, would I be asking you?" These lawyers, every minute costs a fortune.

"Look, Goldie. I'm a family man myself. Harry, he was no saint. But those kids? I'm the one who told Harry. He only wanted to make things right. But sometimes, right isn't so clear. I told him, Harry, I said, you gotta put away a little something for yourself. They'll suck you dry, then leave you to rot. I didn't like talking to him like that, but sometimes, you just get a rotten hand, you know what I'm saying?"

"He messed up, but he got himself on track. That daughter, that mansion out in the Hamptons? And that son, he never figured out who his angel investor was? Harry, God bless him, a more generous man you'd never meet. Remind me? How many times did they come to visit him? Or even call?"

"All right, I hear what you're saying. But still, they're his children. Flesh and blood. What am I? A stranger from a few months."

"Goldie, what can I tell ya? Harry wasn't just a client, ya know. We went way back. I gotta respect his wishes, and his wishes were that you have this, he wanted to give it to you. You can do with it whatever ya want. You wanna write them a check, go ahead. You can. But I can tell you one hundred percent that Harry never intended this to go to those kids."

"I can't live with myself, knowing that I'd have something that I shouldn't. Please. Can you just send me whatever I need to sign, or I can come to your office, and sign it there, and then you know how to get it to them. That's what I want."

"Harry said you'd put up a fight. Here's the deal, Goldie. The money is yours, free and clear. He didn't want you to give it to them. He said you'd know what to do."

I'd know what to do? He's gone, leaves me all alone and tells me I'll know what to do.

CHAPTER FIFTY-TWO

Goldie

2008

THE GIRLS TOOK A BREAK. All night they'd been in the hospital, all week. Go, go, I told them. I'm here. Go home, take a shower, a nap. Nothing is happening here. And they listened to me, because this is how it was. How many rounds of this we'd already gone through? How many times already we said goodbye?

But this time, this time? I take Mordy's hand, still warm, large, and hold it against my cheek. "Mordy, you hear me?" I ask. Always I ask, and sometimes, maybe, he squeezes my hand. I'm never sure. The girls say they feel it. I think they want to. I know that's what I want. But I know what Mordy's squeeze feels like, and this; this isn't it.

His eyes, though. This time, they look back at me. So green, still like spring grass. I think, maybe, he tries to smile. Something is happening with his face, but who can tell? His body makes these motions, these jerks, stops and starts; I think a long time already since his brain is attached to all his parts. But, at this moment, those eyes, there's something there.

So I stand there and I talk to him, holding his hand until his eyes close, and that terrible breathing that hurts to listen to, is all I hear. My Mordy. With his curls and his smile.

I look at the Yeshiva boy. He sits in the corner of the room, out of the way. He's there, all the time. He came, he said, they told him,

Mandell, look out for Mandell. So he sits there, a nice boy. No bother. All day long he's praying, his body bending back and forth, his lips moving the whole time. He knows what to do, our own agent to Mordy's God.

"I'll be right back," I tell him. I need to stretch my legs.

He nods, still shuckling over his book. I go do my loop, one time, five minutes, around the floor.

That's when Mordy leaves.

All the time, all the years, I'm there, next to him. But he looked at me. He saw me. I know he saw me. And then he left me, when I wasn't there to stop him. To tell him, again, not yet.

The Yeshiva boy, he becomes like an energy. He knows what to say, what to do, what steps to follow.

I put my hand against Mordy's cheek, so calm. I close his eyes and a tear, one tear from his eye, spills onto my thumb. I press it to my lips.

One minute a beautiful boy selling raffle tickets comes into your life, and nothing is the same, ever again. And then, one minute, that beautiful person, not a boy anymore, somebody who is closer to you than your own arms and legs, the mattress you sleep on, the food you eat, the air you breathe—no matter how much he tried to prepare you—he's gone.

And for the rest of time, you're not the girl you were before you met him. You tell yourself, sure sure, you have all your parts, but you don't. For the rest of time, you're a cripple, missing those parts you didn't know how much you needed.

CHAPTER FIFTY-THREE

Maxie

"WHY DON'T YOU DRIVE?" T-Jam says, getting into the passenger seat. "I've never been out to the Rockaways."

Maxie slides into the unfamiliar seat, adjusting the multiple mirrors and seat positions. Making it right for herself. She'd hardly ever driven herself anywhere since she'd come to New York. She wants him to put his hand on hers. Or rest his hand on her thigh. Tell her it was going to be all right. She doesn't want him to touch her. She wants to turn the car around.

She floors the gas pedal.

With every mile closer to her grandmother's house, it feels more and more like this is a mistake. Why should she impose her life choices onto Safta? Best to keep it quiet, let her grandmother live out the rest of her life peacefully—as peacefully as Goldie Mandell ever could. There were no winners in this scenario, a lose-lose for everyone.

"You don't believe that." T-Jam had said.

How did he know what she believed? Who was he anyway, this interloper? "You do her an injustice if you're not honest with her."

She looks over at his profile, then back at the road. An injustice? Not to her grandmother. To him. He'd never understand that he was the snake whose charm seduced and perverted, that his presence threatened the core of the life Safta clung to so tenaciously and held onto with such ferocity.

"It's your decision," he'd said.

Ha. Her decision? She was part of a larger whole. The whole that nursed a constant state of generational neuroses and existential belligerence with its fist raised, halfway. *Never again*. If it's not too much trouble. *Am Yisrael chai*. We should be so lucky. But that was so yesterday. Now the upgraded Israeli version: Fuck with us, we'll fuck you back. Harder and smarter. And apologize after. With as much sincerity as yours.

As if single simple Maxie Jacobson's little life mattered. Who was she sitting in this car, hands clamped to the steering wheel, shivers running up and down her spine. With this man. To tell her grandmother that her puny little love mattered more to her than every conviction—and fear—her grandmother held onto all her life.

Safta didn't have to know. She could die, and rest in peace. And she'd never know how her own granddaughter, who she loved and nurtured—who she showed off and bragged about—betrayed every conviction she lived by.

Beside her, T-Jam took her hand. Squeezed it reassuringly. His touch, his smile. The smell of him closing off her airways.

The daily phone calls with her mother. "She keeps asking about you. She lives to see you." Tamar's voice not accusing. Not judging. Just conveying the awful truth of Maxie's avoidance.

See me, Safta? Can you do that? See me?

CHAPTER FIFTY-FOUR

Goldie

A LONG TIME SINCE I'VE SEEN MY SHEYFE.

Ah, here comes Florence from down the street. So nice how I sit on the porch here and see everyone. They stop by, ask how I'm doing. "Florence," I wave, "Maxie's coming. You know, Tamar's girl. She lives here now, not here. In the city, she has a big job. At a laboratory. How are your girls?" Her girls, *feh*. Nothing with nothing.

Oh. There's T-Jam's car. Makes sense he drives her. "Oh, never mind. She's here. I'll talk to you later." Florence waves back, pulling her stupid little dog on its leash. Like a little slipper, that dog, making a commotion. Good she goes away, she doesn't have to see T-Jam, not wearing a suit anymore. He's not part of the picture.

I watch him parking across the street. Back and forth? Always he drives so smooth, and now he can't park? Wait? Maxie's in the driver's seat? She's bending over the steering wheel. He's patting her head, putting his arm around her shoulders, she presses her face into his chest. He says something. She says something. Then their faces closer, closer. Right here on the street? Where everyone can see? What world do they think they're living in?

This is what she chooses. To tear my shirt, pull out my hair, to sit shiva like she'd dead. A ghost. It's the law.

My Maxie. She's alive. So beautiful. Kind. Smart. This is smart? This is kind? She turns her back on everything. Everybody. For what? For who? I can't watch this. I won't. Every day the world gets worse.

Hating and killing, shooting in schools. Fighting in the streets. Again swastikas on doors, smeared in cemeteries. *Never Again*? More like *Never Ends*. The next world will be better.

Can't be worse.

They're walking together, Maxie and that man, coming at me. Like milk and meat on the same plate. My stomach turns. The dots come. The darkness. This time, I don't fight it. This time it's time.

CHAPTER FIFTY-FIVE

Maxie

MAXIE CAUGHT HER GRANDMOTHER just as she collapsed. Tamar ran from inside the house, stopping in the doorway, her hand to her mouth.

"Is she, has she?"

"Call 911."

Her grandmother stirred in her lap. "Wait, no," Maxie called. "T-Jam." She turns to him, but he'd already taken charge. "He's a trained EMT."

It was surreal, T-Jam bending over her grandmother. He took her vitals, did what he did, lifted her like she was weightless, transported her to his car, assuring Maxie and her mother the entire time, "Her vitals are good. She's not in danger. But she needs to be checked out. Let's go." He kept repeating that to the two distraught women, ushering mother in front, daughter clutching her grandmother's hand in the backseat.

Maxie wiped away a few grayish reddish hairs from her grandmother's clammy forehead, careful to keep her fingers as soft and light as possible. Safta's hair was so thin, her skin so translucent. Tiny blue veins pulsed against Maxie's fingertips.

"Safta, Safta," her mantra. "Don't go Safta. Not like this. Please. This isn't your end. Please please. Don't go. Don't go."

Her grandmother opened her eyes. "Sheyfe?" she mumbled. "I don't understand."

"Shh, shh," Maxie soothed her. "You'll be all right. You passed out. We're on our way to the hospital."

Her grandmother's eyes opened wide, recognition registering. "No hospital." Maxie felt her straining against her. But she was so slight, it was more of a shudder than a strain.

From the front seat, T-Jam slammed on the brakes. "Red light. Goddam it."

Goldie's hold on Maxie's hand became tight. Her eyes opened wild. Her utterances urgent. "*Royt leyts. Myn Mordy. Red lights.*"

Squeezing her grandmother's hand, Maxie's lips move incessantly as city streets blur by. Safta was with Saba. Always with Saba. Safta's head lies heavy on her shoulder. With her free hand Maxie adjusts and readjusts the blanket T-Jam had been quick to place around her grandmother.

"*Ikh farshtey nisht. Vau zenen mir.*" Her grandmother's voice, so small.

"Shh, Safta, shh. Rest. We'll be there soon."

"Where?"

Her eyes closed again. Her breathing slowing.

Maxine Jacobson, still stroking her grandmother's forehead, stared out at the blur beyond her window as T-Jam drove the car. Her grandmother and this man, canceling each other out. She drew big red lines through both of them, variables in an equation.

Maxine Jacobson, with her degree, her apartment, her great hair and size six jeans. Maxie Jacobson canceled to zero.

CHAPTER FIFTY-SIX

Goldie

HE'S WHO COMES TO VISIT? "How are you?" he asks.

"Look around, you don't see where I am?"

He sits down, like to stay. He wants to talk? I'll talk. Leave her alone, you're not good together. You don't see you're breaking her heart. My heart. Me, it doesn't matter anymore. But her? You don't see what you're doing to her?

But this hospital room, the walls moving like in soft waves. The blanket heavy, the pillow puffy. Something they gave me makes everything fuzzy. I hear myself, but I don't feel myself talking. "Your whole life, you live, you work. For what? For the children. Everything for the children. You hold a baby, you feed her, diaper her, try to keep her safe. And then, such stupid things people do. To themselves. To each other. *Shalom Bayis*. You know what that means?"

"Shalom—like Salaam?"

Close enough.

"Mordy, my husband, whenever there was a fight, a disagreement, always he said, *Shalom Bayis. Bayis*, it means house. He said to keep the peace in the house. I'll tell you something." What do I care I'm spilling my guts to this, this, whateverheis is, it matters? "I would get sometimes mad at him. Always you give in, I'd say. To this one, to that one." I'm quiet for a minute. Remembering. How he'd then give in to me, too. With that smile. Like he knew something good was always on its way.

"I thought, you know, that if he was stronger, more—what's the word—that maybe he'd be more successful. I thought a man who opened his mouth more, maybe he'd be listened to. Make better sales." Always that's what I worried about. Sales. Me too, stupid.

Mordy, when he died, so many people at his funeral. All those *schleppers* he always rescued. They all came. How the Rabbi spoke. Not like when you go to a service and the hired speaker doesn't know what to say. "Even from the Army, men I never met, they came to his funeral. They told stories, about the Yid, who stood every morning in the corner wearing his Jew ropes, they called it. While they were on line for food, he stood in the corner all wrapped up in his *tefillin,* like taking his blood pressure, they said, all bent over, mumbling to his God. They'd be playing cards," cards, probably like Harry, "and if one of them started swearing, or talking about some girls, they'd poke him and say, 'Pipe down, the Rabbi there, he's praying for your soul.' And they said, he'd smile. Never get angry. Like he had his own mission there, separate from whatever the fighting was all about. For him, personal. Getting shipped overseas, back to Europe—for him, going home. To find his family. To make sense of the craziness."

I need to stop. But like my brakes aren't working. "A parent. A father. You only get one. Precious, a family."

Now the silence is heavy. Outside, we hear from the hallway, the beeps, the noises, the announcements, everybody in the hospital going about their business.

"I know," T-Jam says, his voice, finally, not laughing. His teeth not flashing.

I asked him?

We both sit, quiet. Well, I'm more lying down than sitting. His back is straight. His hands tight on his lap. His eyes, not looking for me.

Then his voice like soft and faraway. "They took him from his office, at the University. We didn't know what was happening. If we'd ever see him again. There was no one to trust," he laughs a not-laugh. "Probably somebody we knew turned him in." He shakes his head, looking now at the floor. "I stopped going to school; it was like we became contagious."

I hear him. I know from that blanket that makes you invisible, how it suffocates. How I stood behind the curtains watching my friends—not friends—going to and from school, playing in the street, hiding they shouldn't see me. Wishing that they even wanted to.

"Every day my mother walked to the prison, begging for answers. She prepared baskets of fresh bread, up all night baking, even though she knew, she had to know, it would never get to him. Maybe it wasn't even for him, maybe she hoped, if she gave it away, they'd tell her something. Anything. All that bread, I was so hungry." He looks at the floor, his hands now fists.

He's not here in this room now. I know, I recognize this.

"I spent hours praying, begging God." He shakes his head, "Making deals for my father to come back. To be normal. But when he finally came out," his voice now, it hurts to hear it. "He was broken, bent, an old man. I wasn't any taller, but I could stand over him, he was so small. They made him so small."

T-Jam runs his hands over his head, "He had all this thick black hair and he was strong. Tall. Broad. His face. They destroyed his face. It was like it had been shredded," he waves his hand over his face, "with these large black and blue and yellow patches." He closes his eyes, "Like a trail map, tortured lines through mountain passes. A map of what they did to him."

Then, like he remembers where he is, he lays his hands flat, his fingers spread apart, back on his lap.

"My mother kept smiling this horrible smile. Who did she think she was fooling? While my father, his eyes, even his voice was different, like a recording. 'We have to get out.' All he kept saying, over and over. 'This isn't our country. Not our home.'"

Poppa every day poring over his papers, the money in the clock. Mama pulling the yellow stars off the clothes where just she'd sewn them on. The ride to Hamburg in middle of the night. Every day a mystery. Trains in the night, walking in the dark. Strangers who became your angels.

"How did you get out?" I ask.

"I don't know. Turkey, we were in Turkey for a while. I was a kid, just going wherever they did. I remember it in pieces. Being cold. Tired. Hungry. So hungry." He taps his fingers on his lap. "So many languages, it hurt my head. Figuring out how to talk. Afraid of opening my mouth."

"But you got here?"

"My father had studied at university in Germany. He had connections."

Nazis holding still their arms in the salute. Black and red swastikas. Yellow stars. Marching, everyone marching. "Germany? *They* saved you?"

"They were still kind to Syrian refugees then. He was a university professor. We got there early."

Kind? Germany?

Mordy on the train station with his brothers. Waving goodbye to his Papa and Mama, who stay behind watching them leave on the terrible—the wonderful—Kindertransport. Me on that ocean-liner. Mama's hair blowing from her kerchief.

Outside I hear it's raining. At first just a drizzle, but very fast, it turns into a downpour. The room gets even darker and noise now from the rain hitting the window. I pick up my finger and point. "You can maybe open the window, let in some fresh air. I like how it smells, the city in the summer when it rains. Like everything getting clean."

He checks, but the window is sealed, always they lock the windows. He shrugs, like an apology.

"Your father, your family, they're safe? They're here now, too?"

"No. Not here." T-Jam looks out at the rain. "My parents are in Berlin, still. My brother—" He stops talking, then slowly he starts again. "I got to Canada on scholarship. There are programs for 'displaced Syrians." The way he says that, like dirt caught in his throat. "Some universities," he waves his hand, like there's some magic he wipes away. "One of my sisters, Jazz, is here, too. We were a normal family. Not charity cases. Except we were charity cases." His shoulders give a shrug. "Eventually I got here, more university connections." Now like he's back in the room with me. A little embarrassed. He doesn't look at my face. "No matter. Sometimes you have to take, sometimes you can give. I'll be giving, too, eventually."

We're quiet. Too much. We said to each other too much.

"I'm sorry for your troubles." I say, finally.

"And I for yours," he answers.

He smiles at me, those big teeth sparkling. Really, he's a very handsome boy.

In the corner, there's a flicker, a light? I see no—Mordy. There is his smile, the one with the teeth and the jaw. His face from when we first met, not when he was old and sick.

MORDY SITS ON THE MATTRESS, facing me. Never he comes to me like this. Maybe it's me who came to him? Even I can touch him, his face scratchy from needing to shave, his hair all dark curls. But the eyes, the eyes I miss the most. That's where I see right into his heart. My own heart thumping like an engine.

"Mordy, you see this guy?" I point to T-Jam. "Some *mensch*, huh? Maybe under all that mess. But for our Sheyfe, our Maxie? I, Mordy, tell me, Mordy, tell me. I see how they are together. But she doesn't know. She never knew from—Maybe too much we hid from them. She doesn't know, our *Sheyfelah* that all the kisses, the promises. *Feh.* Nothing. They make from us nothing." Mordy getting like more transparent, not so real anymore.

"Just Mordy, wait a second. Give me an *etza.* Tell me what to do. What's the right thing to do?"

"Mrs. Mandell?"

The mop with his curls standing over me. With those velvet eyes. Mordy. Feh. Not Mordy. Why I'm so alone here? He stands with his kind eyes. And his dirty fingernails with all the paint.

Those hands with the paint—his hands on my Maxie. All I wanted for her, a doctor who makes a nice living. Who comes from a good established family. A nice life. An easy life. To take on such complications? Mixing meat and milk? Why such a mess she has to make for herself?

What kind of life would they have? Would Maxie light Shabbas candles? Make a *bracha*, like Mordy always told us. Me, I forget, too, before and after I eat I'm supposed always to say something. But He needs to hear all my little kvetches? My please and thank-yous? It's the big things that matter. Maybe they tell us all the time to do these little things so we remember the big things? Maybe if you say, that's not important, that's not important, and soon, nothing anymore is important.

"T-Jam!" I say, loud.

"Mrs. Mandell, are you all right?" He answers, loud, too. Fast. Looking at all the machines I'm hooked up to.

"Fine. I'm fine. Just, tell me. What to you is important?"

"Excuse me?" his face confused.

"I asked you a question. Tell me, what to you is important? *De ershata zaich is tezeyin an erhlicher yid.*" I say to him, mysterious like. "An *ehrlicher yid,* Mordy always said. To be a *mensch.*"

"What?"

"Never mind, I asked you a question. What's wrong, you have nothing to say?"

"I—uh, important. Um, education. Family. Respect for yourself, for others?" he asks like a question.

"This isn't a job interview. It's a philosophical conversation I'm trying to have." Ha, I know some words. "I went to college two years. And I worked as a secretary in the schools, I had to pass a test, over twenty-five years I worked. I know some things. So tell me, what's important?"

He's quiet, like he didn't hear me?

"You believe in God? A God? Many Gods?" Who knows what his people follow?

He taps his fingers on his knee. "Not really." And he keeps on talking, like he wasn't ignoring me at all. "I think the most important thing that's happening right now—you really want to know? It's climate change. It's the single most devastating projection we're facing."

"Like the global warming? A heat wave? I'm talking about people, important between people."

"So am I," he answers fast. "Millions and millions of people. You see, there'll be no arable land. No resources. Everyone will fight for their small piece."

"Arab lands? You're talking about Israel?" I knew it. That Bin in his name. An Arab and a German. All my nightmares mixed up.

"Arable, not Arab. It means good land, for growing crops."

"What does farming have to do with what I asked?"

"If there's no ara—good land, there will be mass migration, it's already happening. And people who hold the advantageous—the good land—places like Siberia—will defend itself against the migration—it will lead to wars. The way it's being ignored—it's a complete willful disregard of hundreds, millions of lives. The final effect will be like all-out nuclear war, in terms of the damage to humanity. It's a crime, as big as any other—bigger than ever's been perpetrated. So much desperation."

"Siberia? In Russia, where they send people to die?" Always Mordy wondered if that's where his father ended. "So I'm lucky to be going now? While the going is still good?" I ask—I can make a joke. I didn't mean for him to get so tense, but maybe good to see this, too. He's a passionate man, I see.

He looks surprised. Then serious. "Yes, you may be."

This cancer, it gives you a power; everyone so afraid you're about to break. This one, he doesn't think I'm breaking. Or he accepts that I am.

Good.

He gets quiet again, but maybe only because he's getting prepared to make a whole other speech.

"Listen, you want to be with my Maxie?" I have to direct this conversation. I need the here and now, not outer space.

"More than anything else." He answers fast, for this he didn't have to prepare. He knows it like he knows to breathe.

Finally, we're getting somewhere.

"She's part of a package." What I wanted to say from the start:

"Before you fix the whole planet, you have to pay attention to your small piece of it, you hear what I'm saying? You think deep thoughts, but I just see this stupid job. But also, I see you're on time, responsible." Here I let myself smile at him. "And always you're nice with the walker and the seatbelt. And you tried at least with the suit." I stop smiling. "But that doesn't make a life. How you can take care of a family? That's another thing. You'll have children, Maxie is Jewish, the children are Jewish. You have to promise me, they'll be Jewish. We didn't survive this long for them to become some mix of everything and not know from nothing."

He looks me straight in the eye. "Respectfully, shouldn't you be talking to her, not me?" He pulls a big envelope from his bag and puts it on the table next to the bed. He salutes and turns to go.

The room too quiet now. Just the rain on the windows and the beeps from all the machines. I open the envelope with my shaky hands. Pictures. Of me. Of Harry. Sweet Harry. Such a special man. I run my finger over Harry's face, bring the picture to my lips. Feh. Like I'm a teenage girl? Still, no one here to see. I can let myself do what I want.

One more paper slips out from the envelope, like it was stuck. The paper is rougher. Thicker. Not a photograph like the rest. A drawing. Fast, sharp, skinny lines. Her face. Her hair. Her eyes. Her mouth. Swollen. Her lips full, almost like they're bruised, but smiling. A soft—a secret smile. I can hardly hold this picture, it's like burning my fingers. Her eyes half closed, like how a cat looks. I can't look away. Not for me to see my granddaughter like this. Not for anyone. Except. Except for the one who made her look like this, the one she looks like this for.

CHAPTER FIFTY-SEVEN

Maxie

MAXIE JACOBSON WAS NOT GREAT.

Never mind *The List*. The schooling, the funding, the apartment, the hair, the almost always size 6 jeans.

Sometimes even Maxie Jacobson could remove her stupid protective glasses and see things in black and white. Maxie knew all about mutual exclusivity. She understood incompatibility.

How many lab tests had she run trying to determine optimal conditions in which her specimens would thrive? How many studies, papers, had she worked on to consider catastrophic effects on threatened homeostasis? How much of herself had she committed to recommendations for reversing negative trends affecting once vibrant ecosystems overwhelmed by devastating disturbances? Oh, she understood the fragility of survival. She appreciated the need to reproduce, recreate, restore and maintain stability. At best, to flourish.

Safta's people, her people, had been annihilated, obliterated, torn down, wiped out, devastated, decimated, exterminated, ravaged, wrecked, and ruined. And yet, they endured. Denial wasn't an option. Assimilation wasn't an option, never really offered anyway, and always rescinded in any case. And utterly beside the point, since it was never welcomed. The push and pull of pride, versus arrogance. Of annihilation versus preservation. And she was worried about size 6 jeans?

But her Safta and Saba were the Grateful Not-Dead, their fortunate destiny and responsibility to live full lives, raise a family, carry on and carry forth. Now it was her turn.

Maxie Jacobson couldn't keep on ignoring her birthright. It was in her face, larger than life in the form of T-J's beautiful face with the dimples, the eyes, the hair, the teeth and the tats. And in Safta's diminishing presence, her thinning hair, her translucent skin, her prominent cheekbones and withering hands. Safta would be gone, along with the other remnants of her slaughtered generation, the ones that had survived that last major disturbance. But this generation, they were safe. Beyond it. Recovered.

Weren't they?

Trending news begged the opposite. It wasn't up to Maxie to carry the weight of her people. She was just one very insignificant person. What difference would she make? But everyone was one person. A mass of one persons. Behaviors. Patterns. Maxie wanted to live. She wanted to love. She wanted it all. But Maxie understood mutual exclusivity far too well.

CHAPTER FIFTY-EIGHT

Goldie

SHE'S LOOKING AT ME WITH HER BIG PRETTY EYES, but they're like empty picture frames, no light or life in them. Since she came for Shabbas, she's all limp like a doll made from rags. She sits there now like a caught fish. Even you throw it back in the water, it survives?

Am I wrong? How can I be wrong?

Hard enough for two people to love each other when everything is easy, when their lives have what in common? To build from two strange families, backgrounds? And all the suffering? The history? To ignore all that?

But we need to stay stuck in our histories? It's done so much for us, all the remembering? The banging on our chests? The always being afraid? Angry?

This beautiful, smart, kind girl. I know she doesn't hold from all that I tell her. But still, she's here. She comes. I won.

Big prize.

The Shabbas candles flicker in the slight breeze from the open window.

"Sheyfe, so what's gonna be?"

"I'm fine, Safta." She pushes around the chicken on her plate.

"You don't look fine. You look terrible. Tamar, doesn't she look terrible?"

"I'm thinking of moving back to California. I'll apply for jobs there, after I graduate here. The dream is a tenure track position. But it's hard, extremely competitive. I could, I don't know, I'll have to be flexible."

And back there in California, after I'm gone. She'll remember me. The grandmother who ruined her life? And then she'll make good decisions?

And I know for sure what good decisions are? Always I thought I knew. Now I start to have questions?

I have to say my piece. "You're lonely? The other one, the one you were with for so many years, you felt bad? That's why you got involved with him?"

"With *him*? He has a name, Safta. After all this time, driving you around, you still can't call him by his name. And Daniel, the 'one' I was with, has absolutely nothing to do with any of this. T-J is more of a—a mensch—than he could—oh, never mind. What's the point of trying to say anything." She balls her napkin in her hand and throws it on the table.

I take a deep breath. "First of all, I'm not breaking, you can tell me what you think. Second of all, I'm not stupid. I know you love, you think you love, this this T-Jam." I wave my hand. "You're an adult, Maxie. You have to live with the decisions you make. I'm not gonna be here forever. But at least while I am, let's tell the truth to each other, yeah?"

The look Tamar and Maxie give each other. See, I'm still ticking here. I continue, "I know what I'm saying. I still have my marbles. This, this T-Jam. I know he had his—with his family. Where they came from—what they went through. But Sheyfe, for you to walk into so much. Enough with one history, you need to take on another one?"

"I got it Safta. You can stop campaigning. Family. Family. The war. The history. I got it."

"Maxie," Tamar makes a stop sign with her hand, her face white, but her voice steady. "Let's hear what Safta is saying." She turns to me, "So, tell us."

"He's *nisht fun anzerier*." Sweat beads on my forehead and upper lip. I mumble, my neck all sweaty. "I don't believe this, in my house, on Shabbas, who knows how many more I'll even have, and this is what we're talking about." I need to steady my hands on the table. "They hate us, they all hate us. One day sure, they're nice. But as soon as there's trouble. As soon as it's inconvenient—puff. You can only trust, you're only safe, with your own kind."

"Stop. Can you please stop. He doesn't hate anyone. You're the one doing all the hating." My Maxie says this to me? And the way she looks at me. I'm not the one hating right now, not nearly as much as what I see.

Again, Tamar puts her hand on Maxie's. "Let her talk." Tamar looks at me with her smart eyes, such smart eyes she always had, even when she was a little girl. "Ma, what are you trying to say?"

"I already said it." Just I want to go to my room back to my bed. But I can't. "No," I shake my head. "You're right. I have to finish." I turn to Maxie, my Sheyfe, "You do what you have to do. But I'm not taking your unhappiness to my grave. You make your own mistakes. Not for me do you end this. But think of everything else that you're ending. They don't have to kill us if we kill ourselves."

Maxie

Maxie turns to look into the Shabbas candles, the flickering flames fighting to stay lit in the slight breeze. Carrying her grandmother's words.

"Millions died. For stupid hate. I won't sit *shiva* for *myn kint.* But the rules. We have the rules." Safta's voice is back. Getting stronger. "Maxie, you will call this man, your," she swallows, "T-Jam. T-Jam Bin Naumann."

Maxie hears the odd name scratching her grandmother's throat. Safta swallows and continues. "We will talk to him. All of us. Together. And maybe, who knows. Maybe an answer."

She looks straight ahead, beyond Maxie and Tamar then waves her hand in that way she had, the way Maxie had seen her do all her life—the one that indicated that the discussion, as if there had ever been any, was done.

"Always Mordy could find the answer. Just you have to look hard enough."

CHAPTER FIFTY-NINE

Goldie

LIKE BEFORE THE BIG STORMS when they tell you to evacuate, and we're all sitting here pretending like nothing is about to happen. The wind makes a banging noise against the screens. Outside the faraway sounds from waves breaking on the beach are like warnings that this isn't a normal situation. He's in his suit, but also he's wearing his socks and sandals. Like he's all mixed up. Like we don't already know this.

Maxie looks like she's about to take a test that she didn't study enough for. And Tamar? Today she has a big flowered scarf around her head, with all these tropical flowers, like I don't know if she's pretending she's a fortuneteller, a cleaning lady or *a frima yid.* Whatever it is, makes no sense. Like anything here makes sense?

We're all staring at each other. Listening to the wind and the waves. Tamar jumps in. Good. Somebody has to start. "Well, T-Jam, there is no precedent for this, but it doesn't need to be an impasse. Do you, either of you, have any idea of how to achieve some sort of steady state?"

What's she saying? That they're going steady we already established. But where are they going? Me, I know where I'm headed.

But Tamar. She negotiates. Makes deals. What she said she would do, all those years ago. First with dogs and cats, now people. An immigration attorney. Helping people, now she tries to help her own daughter, and this—this T-Jam Bin Whatever his name is. No. Naumann. I know his name. I know who he is.

Maxie looks at her mother. At me. Scared. No. Not scared. Not the right word. Like her mind is made up and she wants this to be over but she's not running away. Like she's gonna fight this out, no matter what.

So say something already. Make some sense from this that I can take with me. Let me know that I can rest, that this isn't something I'm letting just to happen, but something that I understand needs to be. So I can explain it to Mordy when I get up there. That he shouldn't think I made a mess of everything he worked for his whole life.

Something Maxie's saying about Ruth. Who's Ruth, in middle of all this? Precedent? She's talking too like a lawyer now? Why do I care from this Ruth? Oh, wait. Ruth. I know what she's talking about. The story about the girl who came from that other tribe, who stayed with her mother-in-law after her husband died.

1948

MORDY BRINGING HIS MOTHER all the way on the train from the Bronx. Like a visit from the Queen, her silver hair like a crown on her head. So proud of that hair, such a business how she put buckets out on the fire-escape to catch the rainwater, then heats it, and pours it over old sheets to filter it. Once a week only she washes her hair, but always it sparkles.

For this occasion, her hair fresh washed. Her pearls shining. She sits in our living room with Poppa, and I'm glad I spent the whole day cleaning. The best tablecloth I put out, from the best leftover material from the shop. I swept the floors and banged the curtains. I dusted, I scrubbed at the bathroom floor on my hands and knees. I baked. And cooked. Finally I fixed my hair and put on my best white cotton-lace blouse and blue skirt. Tasteful.

We're sitting in the living room with coffee, and carrot cake, the one I make so well, and it's not a surprise, really, but when Mordy pulls out the little box with the ring inside it, my heart goes crazy and I make a mess on my skirt with the cake crumbs and what comes from my mouth? "No, no. No."

Mordy says, "No?" and makes to put the ring box back in his pocket.

"No, *yes*! I mean, Yes."

His mother, her silver crown sparkling, smiles, even though there are tears in her brown eyes. My own Mama, what would she think, with her soft blue eyes and frizzy hair? Always so soft-spoken, she would have been happy for me. For sure. And Poppa? Our two families, now to become a new one.

He stands up, "A L'chaim." He leaves the room, fast, too fast, and it takes a little too long for him to come back with the dusty, half-empty bottle of schnapps we keep in a far-away cupboard. He pours large portions, finally emptying the bottle that had been waiting for years to be drunk.

The ring. Mordy puts it on my finger and the diamond is beautiful, tiny and delicate in a gold setting, like a flower. Mordy is so proud, he worked so hard to get it, more important for him than me that I had this ring.

Over the years, it needed to be stretched, then lately, made smaller, so always it fits just right.

2018

"Exactly." Tamar is talking. "Ruth was a Ger, a stranger. Boaz showed her kindness." Tamar smiles now at Maxie, like a private joke, "after she crept into his tent."

Ha! The best part of the story. Not just a good girl, a smart girl. She knew how to get the rich boy. I look at T-Jam. My smart girl, this is who she wants. What can I do? What did I do? Mordy and me, we had nothing. We had each other.

Maxie ignores the joke Tamar is making, and says, "*Dovid Ha'Melech*—King David—was their grandson."

And bigmouth Tamar, like she just won an argument looks at me, "Fresh genes, new blood, all in all, good for the Jews." Then she folds her hands in her lap, like she's finished. How many times I've seen her like this? I need to hear from him. Not them.

"Good for the Jews? Genes? What are you talking about? They're having babies already? First he," I point at T-Jam, "needs a bris."

There! I cut to the chase. T-Jam's face goes white and his hands shoot between his legs. "Mrs. Mandell—" still polite, but his voice is in a higher pitch.

"Safta! He has, he is, how could you?"

What? We have *a yur un a mitvach* to waste here? The clock is ticking, mine very loud.

"Genital mutilation. Safta, hardly!"

"Mrs. Mandell." T-Jam is butting in now. But I'm not done.

"Good your Saba isn't alive to listen to this, this—I don't even know what you just said. Whoever heard girls to make a Torah argument? Let's talk *tachlis* here. I need to know what's gonna be."

"Mrs. Mandell, if I may?" *If I may? Please?*

"Oy, I'm sick already. I thought, I thought we'd. What was I thinking? How can, a mistake, you're trapping me into."

"Ma, relax." Tamar puts her hand on my shoulder, shooting worried faces at everyone.

T-Jam, the reason for all these problems, pushes back his chair and stands, his hands pressed into the table. "May I speak?" Again he asks permission? Just say something already. Something I can live with. Something I can take to the—to the—

"Who's stopping you from talking?" I point at his chest, "Enough with these stories from a million years ago. Let's talk here and now. We have family in Israel. How do you feel about Israel?"

Finally he looks straight at me, like a real man. "I think Israel has made remarkable achievements with very few resources."

"What's he saying?" I ask Tamar. "What does he mean, remarkable achievements?" Back to T-Jam, "You think they should give back the land?"

T-Jam runs his fingers through his hair and says, "In 1948 the population in what became Israel was forcibly removed, creating a displaced people. Now Israel is a thriving reality, but a lot of people were unfairly treated. Some acknowledgement and compensation for that would be appropriate."

Already my blood pressure pumping to my head. "Displaced people? Acknowledgement and compensation? Unfair treatment? *Feh*. And again *feh*. Maxie told you, yes? Her grandfather and I," I point at myself, at them, at the whole room, my arms making big circles. "We were born in Europe. Both of us. We met here, in America. You know why we had to meet in America? You know what happened to us in Europe? You know the war where they rounded us up like—like sheep to slaughter—everything taken from us, stripped naked, gassed—" I'm losing my breath.

"Safta, please. Don't go there." Maxie says.

"You don't tell me where I should go."

T-Jam stands up. Maxie stands as well, taking T-Jam's hand. "We don't have to carry your history. It was horrible, but we don't have to relive it. T-J, Tawfiq-Jamal and I. We'll live our own lives."

A look passes between them. How tall she stands. How sure she is.

Now T-Jam talks like he's giving a lecture. "I don't have a plan for peace in the Middle East. I also don't think that's a reasonable expectation on which to base your approval of our relationship. But I assure you," that *chuztpadik* smile. "I *am* circumcised."

Okay, I guess maybe that piece of information, my fault. Still, good to know.

T-Jam turns to Tamar. "Maxie's lucky to have a mother, and a grandmother like you. With your heritage and history. Family, it's the most important thing." Finally! "Why do you think I'd ever want to diminish that? I'm not the enemy, just the 'other.'"

Other, shmother. Family. He says family is the most important thing. Proof. I need proof. Maxie squeezes his hand. She looks straight at me. T-Jam is still talking.

"To be grounded in identity? To hold onto tradition? I cherish that. My family suffered for who they are. When we moved, ran away, we couldn't get away from it fast enough. My father changed his name, to fit in. I get that. It was what he needed to do. And I always felt ashamed. Less than. But I, I want to feel rooted. I want a history. You've held onto yours, after unspeakable horrors. But not just hold on. You live it. Every day. You make a conscious decision every single day, to each other. To the bigger family."

Yes, yes. Almost. Almost he's there.

Maxie, I see now that she's all red. Like about to burst. Now she almost yells, "Safta. Enough!"

Enough? She says to me enough?

"It has to stop. Lines. We draw lines. We keep inside our lines. We always draw inside our lines." I never saw her like this, so angry. Even Tamar's eyes are big now. "Time to get rid of them, make one big blur. No lines. No black, no white, pink, or brown, or yellow. A mush. One big—" she spreads her arms apart then slaps them together hard. "They don't help anything." She looks at me and I can see she's thinking how to say this craziness. "With all the issues we're facing, the massive messed up state of everything wrong on this planet, tell me one good thing, one significant contribution that ever came out of all the divisions we hold onto? Religion, nationalism, racism. Homophobia. Any of it."

One word. Religion. Maybe I'm not the most religious, not like Mordy, but what's she saying? To throw it away?

Like the storm passed, Maxie's voice, more normal, suddenly. She looks like the girl I know. "Safta, I'm not saying to get rid of traditions, of learning. Or a way of life that I, I, love. But, the other stuff, the stuff that makes us insular and—mean."

Mean? She calls me mean? Not me, mean. They're mean. They, they. They killed us. Treated us like animals. Took away—I look at her face. At this boy's face. So young. They think they know everything. They know from nothing. They never.

No. Not true. Why he, his family, had to run away? He, they did something wrong? Just where and who and when he was born. Still, he came always in his suit, always he special went out of his way to bring for me that good coffee. He is who he is. People the same, under the outside covers. Inside, hearts, blood, what makes us laugh, cry, little babies? No differences.

My Sheyfe, she's perfect. But some people could disagree. They'd be wrong, of course. This boy, he has parents who must think the same. But, but—no. She's a *pisher,* what she's saying to throw everything away. Nothing left? "The traditions. The learning. The Torah, who we are, not just a big pot of soup of nothing."

T-Jam sounds very serious now. "No. Not nothing. Of course not, Mrs. Mandell. Each spice adds flavor; you need the different tastes. They make the soup what it is." He looks at Maxie now. Only at Maxie. "No matter what, any children Maxie and I have will be Jewish. In Judaism, lineage is passed through the mother. We'd add that. They'd carry that to the mix."

Children. Jewish. He said it, Mordy. He said it. Children. The grandchildren. Not nothing. Even if they're *shtupped* into this crazy mess, they'll be who they are. Who we are. Not afraid. Not running. Not fighting. Proud.

Children. A life. A forever.

"Safta? Safta?" From like far away I hear them. Maxie's hand on my shoulder. And I see, my ring on her hand. But no, it's where it always is. Where it's been all these years. But, also, I see it on her finger, those long strong fingers, like Mordy's, only for a girl. Capable hands. It looks bigger on her hand, the tiny diamond in the middle of the gold flower petals like its blooming again in the sun.

My story. In her hands now. Her story. *Be'shert.* Their whole lives ahead of them, to say, and do, and yet, like two old people already. Like there was no choice but for this to be. Who knows, even, one day, a baby girl. Maybe my name?

Well Mordy? A little give and take, what can it hurt? Better than to lose her altogether, no? Could it be? Her children, their children, to add their own flavor, our flavors, too. See her face. So happy. Our Sheyfe. And you know what else, I already called Rabbi Schwartz. Just to ask, and he confirmed. The mother's Jewish, all that counts.

This boy—he has some talent. Maybe he'll yet amount to something. He can open a studio. Photographs *and* paintings. Weddings, bar mitzvahs—those never go away. It's a living. They'll make a life.

CHAPTER SIXTY

Goldie

TAMAR, IN HER RUNNING OUTFIT like her daily uniform, looks at me from over her coffee mug. What looking? Like studying, more.

"What? I shouldn't give him a chance? Maybe even he saved my life? You leave that California Berkeley behind and everything you talked about all the years, the free love, the being equal, all that stuff, you forget?"

She rolls her eyes. "Must be the meds you're on. You know, it's the drugs in California that makes everyone so dopey."

Always she has to have the last word? "What day is it?" I ask. "When do I need to go back to the doctor?"

"The procedure is next week, Tuesday. They said it will knock you out for a while. So, is there anything you need to get done in the next few days? Anything you want me to set up for you?"

So soon?

I don't know what I look like, but she quick adds, "In and out, you won't even have to stay overnight. Really, you'll be fine."

"Fine? Nothing's fine. Tamar, listen, all I'm asking, I don't want, I want to be here, at the end, not in a hospital."

"Ma, I'm sorry. I didn't mean, when I said about the drugs—I'm an idiot."

I'm the sick one and she looks so much in pain.

"Tamar, listen. I want maybe you should help me with something else. That letter, from that lawyer. I have this account Harry, there's this money. A lot of money. I need to do something about it. I'm not gonna leave behind a mess for you to deal with." I shrug. "So, it's my headache. He's gone. He should rest in peace, and not like he knew he was going to go like that. So quickly."

I have to get this right, I don't have more chances.

Not really an idea, but in my head, the story from T-Jam, what he told me, his father, like Mordy's father. Like my mama. Like all those pictures all the time on the television, the stories of the bombed-out buildings, the children missing arms, legs, everyone walking, walking, with their *pecklach* on their backs. *Schlepping* the grandmothers like on stretchers because they can't walk. Wearing all those *shmatas,* maybe all they have? Like the Jews in the desert for forty years, nothing changes? Big progress, a hundred, a thousand years later—same thing.

Tamar is looking at me. Waiting. Yes, yes, I was telling her. My idea.

"So all these people, they're people, no?"

"Yeah?" Tamar like she doesn't know how to look at what I'm saying.

"Don't look so worried. I know what I'm saying, maybe I'm just not saying it so good." I look around the kitchen. How I love this house. "Why some people, they have *mazel* in their lives, and others, for no reason, such terrible things they have to go through?"

So hard to find the right words. "Everyone so caught up in their everyday, paying bills, trying to—" I see I'm losing the thread here. "All right, all I'm trying to say is, so I have this, I don't know what to call it, this windfall. And it's not like I can take it with me. And it's not like it's mine to give away either, to you. Or Maxie. Or Esti and hers. Daddy, he would know what to do, but he's not here. But I know, too.

"I want to make from this account, a scholarship. A real one." Never we talk about it, but all the anger she had, all the years. To give her a chance, I told myself. And I was right. But also, I was wrong. "To give to a refugee. An orphan what deserves it. Somebody who needs it. I don't care from which country, only maybe not the ones where they shout all the time death to the Jews. I don't know, though, if they're running away, then not their fault what the crazies say. Just they should know, maybe, that it's from a Jew? To stop the hating?" For sure, though, there will be interviews. Not just anybody. I'm not stupid. "You know how to do this, right? From your work?"

And Tamar, now she's crying.

"*Feh,*" I wave at her. "What are you crying about? You're sorry I'm not giving it to you?" But I don't look at her when I say this, I look instead at the wall behind her.

She wipes her nose and laughs. "Exactly. I was hoping for a new car at least."

CHAPTER SIXTY-ONE

Goldie

MAXIE ON ONE SIDE. T-Jam on the other. One step, one step. To get down the block from the house I used the walker. But once on the sand, I had to leave it behind. "Maybe we can find a stick, I can use like a cane?" Quick, I add, "Please."

T-Jam and Maxie look at each other over my head. Yeah. I know. Sounds a little stupid, but it hurts nothing to say it. When I remember.

"It'll sink in the sand, Safta. Just one step at a time, there's no rush."

Each of them has a hand around my back, waiting while I leave the walker on the pavement and step onto the sand. I can't believe it took so long, but here, finally, I'm on the beach. First thing I pick my head up and I look to where the sky and the ocean meet. The same. And the ocean makes its noises, and the air carries its smells, and the birds fly out over the waves, the tops of them turning white and light, still blue in the middle where they bend into the circle before they crash down and hit the sand. Just at that point, when they're curling is when you jump into them, right in the middle, and they carry you back to the shore.

It's late in the day now, so the sun's not burning hot, just soft, making sparkles, always I like those crystals on the water, and the beach is almost empty. Here and there a left-behind pail and shovel, a towel all twisted in the sand, a broken chair with the metal part rusted and plastic strips with the threads all coming apart, popsicle sticks and cardboard hotdog holders and soda and beer cans. Could be now, could be fifty years ago the same. I'm careful where I put my foot, not so much because of shells but from the holes and hills all the families make here and there when they park themselves for the day.

Finally, step after step and the sand under my feet feels harder, easier to stand on because we're reaching to the water. Behind us, the white lifeguard chair, tall, wide enough for two. Always our blanket next to it, the girls should know where to find us when they came out of the water. Who knows, when they were older, they knew where not to find us, probably. But always the beach, no matter what, our place.

My place. "I'm all right, you can let go," I tell the kids.

They stand close to me, but these two, they give me my space. First, I pull off the hat the doctor told me I had to wear, to get away from the sun. *Feh.* I take off the sweater also, underneath I'm in a sleeveless housedress. And under that, a bathing suit! Me, in a suit, but sure, I have drawers full of them. All this running away from light, from sun. Years I'll have to rot in the dark, all covered up. For now, I'm here, breathing it all in. Breathing that sea air and feeling the wet sand always stuck between my toes and all over my legs, and the black tar—never you would see it, but always a sticky black streak on your body, with such a thick dark and oily smell that would smear all over the place.

And also, and also, like no time passed, because here, time doesn't pass, the sea-soaked wood, and also the big wet stones covered in green slippery gunk and decaying shells and all those hot, hot days when my skin roasted under the sun, that smell too—all covered in Coppertone and baby oil, to be dark and shiny and pretty for Mordy at night. I'd put my hair, all stiff from the salt water shower, up in a ponytail on those nights when finally it got dark. Short breezy nights but still the air always wet with ocean spray, licking my still-hot skin. So much I was overflowing from all the sun and smells and heat from the whole day aching to come out into the cool dark where from not so far away that we couldn't hear it, but not too loud, like background music private-playing just for us, the ding-ding from the pinball arcades on the boardwalk.

The hollers and yells from the roller coasters, the gong when somebody won something big, and firecrackers all the time going off. This was our musical, all mixed up with hope. Still I can taste it, like it got under my sunburnt skin, always peeling more and more layers, knowing, just knowing that the future was all there for us, and how it would be wonderful and salty and so good.

"Safta, should we go into the water?" Maxie, quiet, squeezes my hand. My Maxie, my Sheyfe, that I almost let her go?

The waves, not too big, the sunset calm. "Yes, yes."

T-Jam on one side, Maxie on the other, but now only holding my hands. One step, another. Not like how I used to run, fast as I could, to dive, pushing forward my whole body into the first wave I reached. Now, the water cold, so cold, but only around my feet, my toes digging into the ground so I don't fall. The next wave comes, a little harder, nothing scary, but it goes up my legs higher, and I laugh. And shiver, excited, how it feels between my legs, icy and tingly. How it used to make me jump, my skin all electric, my whole body alive when it reached me in my most private spot, tickling me, exploring me, like only Mordy did.

Now the water makes a circle around my legs, pulling me in a bit, and I grab the kids' hands, maybe too tight. Then I breathe, I'm okay. I know this water. Another step. I can let go their hands, the water will hold me, but they're there. Next to me. Not letting me go. Another step. Another step. Now the water is over my knees.

Maxie and T-Jam, wet and smiling, are looking at each other. This strange man and my beautiful granddaughter. They can smell and feel everything here, too. *Vey is mir*, this thing between them, like the undertow, impossible to fight once it grabs you. But so young, so stupid, they'll dive in headfirst, churning and spinning and when the ocean spits them out, they'll laugh and jump right back into the waves.

How did I become this? One of the old ladies dipping, splashing their breasts, but really only standing at the edge, not getting really wet? "Come, come," I say to the children. "Help me sit down."

"Sit, in the sand?" Maxie sounds unconvinced, but T-Jam puts one big tattooed arm—*feh*—around my waist, and the other behind my legs, like he's making for me a chair.

"Relax," he tells me, "lean back."

Slowly slowly, he leads me down, until I'm sitting on the ocean floor, the water around my chest. I push myself with my hands, a little bit, a little bit, and keep my legs up, and I'm on the water, floating, and he's there, Mordy, and he's smiling, so handsome, such big shoulders and powerful arms just a little bit away. I splash a little with my hands and kick with my legs, pushing to reach him, and he swims to me, and he's close, so close almost he's going to hold me in the water. But no, it's not him, it's the waves that lift me and drop me, and overhead the birds are making their noises, and I rest there, comfortable. Another wave comes, gentle and slow, and I pull up my arm to wave goodbye to Mordy.

Not yet. Soon though. Soon enough. I'm carried, softly, softly, back to the shore.

"I'm ready," I call to the children. "Make your picture."

Enjoy more about

The Goldie Standard

Meet the Author

Check out author appearances

Explore special features

About the Author

Born and raised in Brooklyn, **Simi Monheit** calls Northern California home. Simi is a graduate of Stanford's Online Novel Writing Certificate program, has a Master's degree in Computer Science and an undergraduate degree in English. She started writing after a career in technology. Her work has appeared in JewishFiction.net, *The Forward, Moment, Chautauqua, HerStry, Pacifica Literary Review* and *Lilith Magazine*. Simi most recently was a Pushcart Prize nominee (2020), placed in the 2020 *Writer's Digest* literary fiction short story contest, and even won the 2022 Pacifica Literary Review bodice ripper contest.

Acknowledgements

It takes a lifetime of friends, family, teachers, advocates, and experiences to write a book.

Thanks to:

Sibylline Press, for believing in the power, brilliance, and relevance of "old lady" stories. Thank you, Vicki DeArmon and Julia Park Tracey for believing in Goldie, and for giving the rest of the world a chance to meet her too.

Gail Ansel, R. Cathey Daniels, Roy Dufrain, Tracy Hill, Megan McDonald: you're my rocks, my sounding board, you hold my feet to the fire and my fingers to the keyboard. Looking at you, Gail, and all those Thursday afternoons with Goldie!

GLOW: Enid Brock, Paula Mahoney, Sarah Savasky, Robin Somers, Becky Wecks, the Gloriously Glamorous Ladies of Writing: My friends and confidants whose weekly check-ins, catchups and essay writing keep my feet on the ground and my head in the stars.

Josh Mohr, Samantha Dunn, Matty Monheit: Teachers, cheerleaders, and advocates.

Laurel Cyrluk. Always there. Enough said.

And finally, Apo and Yayla, my most refreshingly different readers. The two of you: inspirations, bottomless sources of creativity, energy, and life. My breath, my heart, the loves of my life.

YIDDISH WORDS AND REFERENCES IN THE GOLDIE STANDARD:

A yur un a mitvach: A year and a Wednesday, like, a year and a day ... meaning forever.

Alte kackers: Alte is old. Kacker is a reference to incontinence, a generally disparaging (and considered accurate) label for older people. Sometimes abbreviated to AKs. Very commonly used, especially self referentially among Aks.

Alte-bubbie: Great grandmother

Am Yisrael Chai: Hebrew, The Nation of Israel lives. This is a common sentiment/statement expressed by Jewish people since the beginning of time, implying that against all odds, we're still here. And will be.

Balabusta: a good housekeeper. The similarity to Ball Buster is purely coincidental.

Be'shert: Destiny, fate. Usually used in a romantic context. The love of your life is your be'shertes.

Bereshet: בְּרֵאשִׁית In the beginning. The very first word in the Old Testament. (Yiddish and Hebrew)

Bet: The letter bet, which makes the B sound. The very first letter in the Old Testament. (Yiddish and Hebrew)

Bissel: a small amount. Just a bit.

Bitta: German. Please

Bracha: Blessing.

Bubbameiser: Old wives tale. A BS story.

Budinski: A nosy person who butts into everyone else's business.

Chutzpah: Does this really require an explanation? Me writing this book, that took chutzpah. Asking anyone to read it, massive chutzpah!

De ershata zaich is tezeyin an erhlicher yid: The first, most important thing is to be a righteous Jew. Implying being a mensch. (See mensch).

Du sprichst Deutsch?: You speak German? German

Etza: Advice, a piece of wisdom.

Fabissena: Embittered. Frequently used with Un'taam. Meaning flavorless. Someone can be described as an untaam and a fabissena. This is the person you hope to never encounter, but somehow always do, as a coworker, co-parent, co-anything! They're out there.

Fa'shlufana: from shluff, to sleep. Someone not quite with it, missing all the clues.

F'shvitzed: Sweaty. Shivtz is sweat.

Facackta or ferkakta or fakokta: messed up, sounds like F**ked up, doesn't it?

Feh: needs an explanation? A syllable conveying all manner of disgust, disparagement, impatience.

Frima Yid: A strictly observant Jew.

Gan Eden: The Garden of Eden. Heaven on earth.

Ganz Meshuga: Totally crazy. As in batshit crazy.

Ganz nakadik: completely naked

Geshrei: Hollering. An unpleasant yelling.

Goyim: Any people who aren't Jewish. Outsiders. Literal translation: nations.

Greena: Greenhorn. A freshly arrived immigrant. Not ripe yet.

Har Sinai: Mount Sinai

Ich habe in der Schule gelernt: I learned in school. German.

Ikh bin fayn, fayn, nor dem shofer: I'm fine, fine. It's just the driver. (Yiddish)

Ikh bin in di mashin, ikh vet zeyn bay di shpitol bay 10 iklokk: I'm in the car, I'll be at the hospital by 10:00 o'clock (Yiddish)

Ikh farshtey nisht. Vau zenen mir: I don't understand. Where are we? (Yiddish)

Ja, ikh bin aoyf meyn veg: Yes, I'm on my way.

Kishkes: Intestines, or guts. To feel something like a kick to your kishkes. It's also a type of delicacy – term used loosely – called stuffed derma - a beef or fowl intestine stuffed with a mixture, as of flour, fat, onion, and seasonings, and roasted.

Kvelled: to feel pride. Usually about something personal, like a child or grandchild's every accomplishment.

L'chaim: to life. Often used as a toast, you drink a l'chaim to celebrate an occasion.

Leibchen: German. Term of endearment for someone who is very dear to you.

Macher: A bigshot. Someone with influence, power and usually money. A mover and a shaker.

Mann Tracht, Un Gott Lacht: Man plans, and God laughs. (Yiddish expression) authors note: Ain't it the truth!

Mazel or mazal: Luck. As in Mazal Tov, which is literally Good Luck. Used like Congratulations. Life is good when you have mazal.

Mekhasheyfe: A witch. Not only is she fabisenna and an un'taam, she's also evil.

Mensch: An absolute decent person. The highest accolade.

Mien alta yerin: my old age

Minyan: a quorum of ten, traditionally men but more progressive groups accept variations, over the age of 13, required for traditional Jewish public worship.

Mish arayin: to mix in.

Mishegas: An absurdity

Nebbish: dweeb, loser, last person picked for a team.

Nisht ahein and nisht aheir: neither here nor there, absolutely nothing to get excited about.

Nisht fun anzerier: not one of us

Nisht mit aleyman: not all together there. Something significant is missing.

No chupa, no shtupa: A classic. Chupa is the canopy under which brides and grooms stand during wedding ceremonies. To Shtup means to stuff something into a tight space. No chupa no shtupa. Obvious now?

Parnassa: Income. Source of income. Wages.

Pecklach: Bags, big bags used for hauling large amounts of stuff

Pish: urinate.

Pisher: a derogatory term for someone young, inexperienced and full of themselves. It literally translates to someone urinating, the implication that this person is still in diapers yet has (unworthy) opinions.

Plaplen: yammer, gab, babble

Putz: little dick. As in he's a putz. like shmuck. Both mean penis, but a putz is more of a jerk, a shmuck is more of a very nasty person serving his own self interests.

Rebbe: spiritual leader, teacher, mentor

Royt leyts: red lights

Saba: Hebrew, Grandfather. Zayde in Yiddish. Saba and Safta, Bubbie and Zayde, Grandma and Grandpa.

Safta: can also be spelled savta. Grandmother, in Hebrew. Same as the Yiddish Bubbie.

Schlemiel: a klutz, someone who's clueless.

Schlepper: like nebbish, someone inept who just plods along.

Schoen: now, already

Seforim: Religious texts/books.

Shalom Bayis: Household peace.

Sheyfe, sheyfela: An endearment, typically bestowed on children, meaning little lamb.

Shiksas: Non-Jewish woman. Every Jewish boy's dream, every Jewish mother's nightmare. Typically imagined as leggy, blue-eyed blondes.

Shmatas: rags

Shmegegie: a very stupid, incompetent person

Shtupped: stuffed (see no chupa no shtupa)

Shuckle: shake, as in shake, rattle and roll.

Sitting Shiva: the seven day mourning period following a death. The bereaved stay at home, where they are visited and tended to for a full week by friends and family.

Tachlis: "getting down to business," As in, lets talk tachlis. No more beating around the bush.

Tchotchkes: knick knacks, junk.

Tefillin: phylacteries, are a set of small black leather boxes with leather straps containing scrolls of parchment inscribed with verses from the Torah. They are worn, traditionally by men only, however that is changing, during daily morning prayer.

The Forvertz: Oldest Yiddish newspaper, and still in print.

Tsemished: confused

Tsoros: sorrows, the weight of the world

Tuchos: Butt, ass, backside

Tzherbrochen toph: A broken pot lid. This is used when someone is a particularly bad singer. Implying that the sounds this person makes sound like noises escaping a boiling pot.

Varum: German, why

Vasser: water

Ven de schmekel shtait, de saychel geyt: When the penis stands, intelligence disappears. Author note: So much better in Yiddish, it rhymes! My closest attempt, in English: When the penis is erect, judgement is wrecked.

Vey is mir: woe onto me. A frequent expression.

WEVD: an NYC Yiddish speaking radio station, "The station that speaks your language"

Yalmalke: skullcap, a small head covering worn by observant Jewish men. (some women wear them as well). Also known as a kippah. Worn as a sign of respect and a reminder that there is always someone above you.

Yerusha: inheritance

Yichus: elevated status

Yiddisha Kint: A Jewish child

Yom Tov: holiday. Any Jewish holiday, (Chanuka, Passover, etc is a Yom Tov)

Zaidy: Grandfather, goes with Bubbie. Yiddish. The Hebrew equivalent is Saba, partnered with Safta.

Book Club Questions

The Goldie Standard by Simi Monheit

1. After Harry serenades Goldie with "DO YOU LOVE ME?" Goldie states, "In one lifetime, lots of different ways to love." What are some of the different ways to love that are depicted in this story?

2. Jewish Assimilation is regarded as one of the biggest threats to Judaism's endurance. In *The Vanishing American Jew; In Search of Jewish Identity for the Next Century* Alan Dershowitz writes, "we can overcome this new threat to the continuity of American Jewish life and emerge with a more positive Judaism for the twenty-first century--a Judaism that is less dependent on our enemies for its continuity, and that rests more securely on the considerable, but largely untapped, strengths of our own heritage." Are these notions reflected in Goldie's story? Do her views shift over time? Is Goldie a more modern woman by the end? Do you believe that Goldie is capable of accepting T-Jam Bin Naumann as a partner for her beloved Maxie? Why? Or why not?

3. As a child Goldie had no control over the events that shaped her life. As an adult, she does all she can to control her children (and grandchildren's) decisions. At the end of the book she muses "And I was right. But also, I was wrong." Was she right or wrong? Or both?

4. Goldie and Mordy shared an epic love. How does their relationship help provide a better understanding of Goldie's personality?

5. Does the author's use of voice and dialogue work? Did you find the sprinkling of Yiddishisms effective or distracting?

Sibylline
PRESS

Sibylline Press is proud to publish the brilliant work of women authors over 50. We are a woman-owned publishing company and, like our authors, represent women of a certain age.

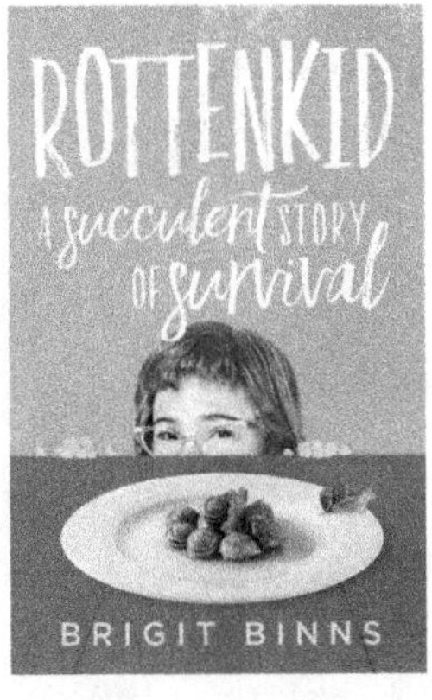

Rottenkid: A Succulent Story of Survival

BY BRIGIT BINNS

Pub Date: 3/5/24
ISBN: 9781960573995
Memoir, Trade paper, $19, 320 pages

Prolific cookbook author Brigit Binns' coming-of-age memoir—co-starring her alcoholic actor father Edward Binns and glamorous but viciously smart narcissistic mother—reveals how simultaneous privilege and profound neglect led Brigit to seek comfort in the kitchen, eventually allowing her to find some sense of self-worth. A memoir sauteed in Hollywood stories, world travel, and always, the need to belong.

1666: A Novel

BY LORA CHILTON

Pub Date: 4/2/24
ISBN: 9781960573957
Fiction, Trade paper, $17, 224 pages

The survival story of the Patawomeck Tribe of Virginia has been remembered within the tribe for generations, but the massacre of Patawomeck men and the enslavement of women and children by land hungry colonists in 1666 has been mostly unknown outside of the tribe until now. Author Lora Chilton, a member of the tribe through the lineage of her father, has created this powerful fictional retelling of the survival of the tribe through the lives of three women.

I Never Do This: A Novel

BY ANESA MILLER

Pub Date: 4/16/24
ISBN: 9781960573988
Fiction, Trade paper, $17, 216 pages

This gothic novel presents the unforgettable voice of a young woman, LaDene Faye Howell, who finds herself in police custody recounting her story after her paroled cousin Bobbie Frank appears and engages her in a crime spree in the small town of Devola, Ohio.

The Goldie Standard: A Novel

BY SIMI MONHEIT

Pub Date: 5/7/24
ISBN: 9781960573971
Fiction, Trade paper, $19, 328 pages

Hilarious and surprising, this unapologetically Jewish story delivers a present-day take on a highly creative grandmother in an old folks' home trying to find her Ph.D granddaughter a husband who is a doctor—with a yarmulke, of course.

Bitterroot: A Novel

BY SUZY VITELLO

Pub Date: 5/21/24
ISBN: 9781960573964
Fiction, Trade paper, 18, 296 pages

A forensic artist already reeling from the surprise death of her husband must confront the MAGA politics, racism and violence raging in her small town in the Bitterroot Mountains of Idaho when her gay brother is shot and she becomes a target herself.

Sibylline
PRESS

Printed in the USA
CPSIA information can be obtained
at www.ICGtesting.com
JSHW021112010424
60342JS00003B/3